In essence science fiction reduces the
entire continuum of human knowledge
to a sort of board game, and by
systematically changing the rules of the
game one or a few at a time investigates
the possibility of alternate societies . . .
Science fiction gives us a sort of
catalogue of possible worlds. From
the wish-book we can pick the ones
we want . . .
Some sf people are right-wingers and
some are left; some are deeply religious,
some not at all; some battle for
women's lib or black power or the
freedom of the drug scene and some are
firmly for the Establishment; and yet
all of them are able to join in the
game . . .
Perhaps the Method can spread.
Perhaps the world at large can learn
from sf. And perhaps then the ants won't
have to replace us after all.

FREDERIK POHL

Frederik Pohl

In The
Problem Pit

CORGI BOOKS
A DIVISION OF TRANSWORLD PUBLISHERS LTD

IN THE PROBLEM PIT

A CORGI BOOK 0 552 10334 9

First publication in Great Britain

PRINTING HISTORY
Corgi edition published 1976

Corgi Books are published by Transworld Publishers Ltd.,
Century House, 61–63 Uxbridge Road,
Ealing, London, W.5.
Made and printed in Great Britain by
Hunt Barnard Printing Ltd., Aylesbury, Bucks.

For Betsy,
far out and fine

Contents

In The
Problem Pit

Introduction: Science-Fiction Games

Choosing which stories to put in an anthology is a lot like being asked which two of my four children should go into a "best of the family" collection. Like most writers, I try to maintain a pose of public professionalism. Also like most writers, in fact I bleed and die with everything I write. The stories don't always turn out to be masterpieces. I will go farther than that: I have written some stories that by anybody's standards, including my own, are awful. (They comprise a thick wad of wastepaper in my file cabinet, or at least the ones that didn't get published anyway do.) But in no case is it the story's fault, it is only mine. And whatever I privately know, it gives me some kind of pain to admit to anyone that this child is in any way deficient, and almost as much pain to claim that this other child is better than the rest.

So I have used several sets of criteria in picking out the contents of this volume: some are personal favorites, some are new, and some are that special kind of sf I call "science-fiction games."

And to make it possible for you to know what I mean by a science-fiction game, I am also including an essay on the subject at the end of the book. It may not explain all of these particular stories, but I hope it will go some way toward explaining why I, and a lot of other people like me, have considered science fiction not a bad thing to devote our lives to.

FREDERIK POHL

Red Bank, New Jersey
November, 1974

In the Problem Pit

Sometimes people ask me where I get the idea for a science-fiction story, and I never know how to answer that. There is seldom a single idea involved, is one reason. When I wrote "In the Problem Pit," I had just come back from visiting the big radio telescope at Arecibo; not long before, I had spent a weekend with an encounter group in New Jersey; before that, I had taken part in a World Future Society discussion of group problem-solving methods in Washington . . . and all those things (plus a casual remark of my minister's wife about why she preferred female gynecologists, and a friendly conversation with a young Canadian metalworker) came together in my head . . . and "In the Problem Pit" came out.

David

Before I left the apartment to meet my draft call I had packed up the last of Lara. She had left herself all over our home: perfumes, books, eye shadow, Tampax, ivory animals she had forgotten to take and letters from him that she had probably meant for me to read. I didn't read them. I packed up the whole schmear and sent it off to her in Djakarta, with longing and hatred.

Since I was traveling at government expense, I took the hyperjet and then a STOL to the nearest city and a cab from there. I paid for the whole thing with travel vouchers, even the cab, which enormously annoyed the driver; I didn't tip him. He bounced off down the road muttering in Spanish, racing his motor and double-clutching on the switchbacks, and there I was in front of the pit facility, and I didn't want to go on in. I wasn't ready to talk to anybody about any problems, especially mine.

There was an explosion of horns and gunned motors from down the road. Somebody else was arriving, and the drivers were fighting about which of them would pull over to let the other pass. I made up my mind to slope off. So I looked for a cubbyhole to hide my pack and sleeping bag in and found it behind a rock, and I left the stuff there and was gone before the next cab arrived. I didn't know where I was going, exactly. I just wanted to walk up the trails around the mountains in the warm afternoon rain.

It was late afternoon, which meant it was, I calculated, oh, something like six in the morning in Djakarta. I could visualize Lara sound asleep in the heat, sprawled with the covers kicked off, making that little ladylike whistle that served her in place of a snore. (I could not visualize the other half of the bed.)

I was hurting. Lara and I had been married for six years, counting two separations. And the way trouble always does, it had screwed up my work. I'd had this commission from the library in St. Paul, a big, complicated piece for over the front foyer. Well, it hadn't gone well, being more Brancusi and interior-decorator art than me, but still it had been a lot of work and just about finished. And then when I had it in the vacuum chamber and was floating the aluminum plating onto it, I'd let the pressure go up, and air got in, and of course the whole thing burned.

So partly I was thinking about whether Lara would come back and partly whether there was any chance I could do a whole new sculpture and plate it and deliver it before the library purchasing commission got around to canceling my contract, and partly I wasn't thinking at all, just huffing and puffing up those trails in the muggy mist. I could see morning glories growing. I picked up a couple and put them in my pocket. The long muscles in my thighs were beginning to burn, and I was fighting my breathing. So I slowed down, spending my concentration on pacing my steps and my breathing so that I could keep my head away from where the real pain was. And then I found myself almost tripping over a rusted, bent old sign that said *Pericoloso* in one language and *Danger* in another.

The sign spoke truth.

In front of me was a cliff and a catwalk stretching out over what looked like a quarter of a mile of space.

I had blundered on to the old telescope. I could see the bowl way down below, all grown over with bushes and trees. And hanging in the air in front of me, suspended from three cables, was a thing like a rusty trolley car, with spikes sticking out of the lower part of it.

No one was around; I guess they don't use the telescope any more. I couldn't go any farther unless I wanted to go out on the catwalk, which I didn't, and so I sat down and breathed hard. As I began to get caught up on my oxygen debt, I began to think again; and since I didn't want to do that, I pulled the crushed morning glories out of my pocket and chewed on a few seeds.

Well, I had forgotten where I was. In Minneapolis you grow them in a window box. You have to pound them and crush them and soak them and squeeze them, hundreds of seeds at a time, before you get anything. But these had grown in a tropical climate.

I wasn't stoned or tripping, really. But I was—oh, I guess the word is "anesthetized." Nothing hurt any more. It wasn't just an absence of hurting, it was a positive *not* hurting, like when you've broken a tooth and you've finally got to the dentist's office and he's squirted in the novocaine and you can feel that not-hurting spread like a golden glow across your jaw, blotting up the ache as it goes.

I don't know how long I sat there, but by the time I remembered I was supposed to report in at the pit the shadows were getting long.

So I missed dinner, I missed signing in properly, I got there just in time for the VISTA guard to snap at me, "Why the hell can't you be on time, Charlie?" and I was the last one down the elevators and into the pit. Everybody else was gathered there already in a big room that looked like it had been chopped out of rock, which I guess it had, with foam cushions scattered around the floor and, I guess, 12 or 14 people scattered around on the cushions, all with their bodies pointed toward an old lady in black slacks and a black turtleneck, but their faces pointed toward me.

I flung down my sleeping bag and sat on it and said, "Sorry."

She said, rather nicely, "Actually, we were just beginning."

And everybody looked at me begrudgingly, as though they had no choice but to wait while I blew my nose or built myself a nest out of straws or whatever I was going to do to delay them all still further, but I just sat there, trying not to look stoned, and after a while she began to talk.

Tina's Talk

Hello. My name is Tina Wattridge, and I'm one of your resource people.

I'm not the leader of this group. There isn't any leader. If the group ever decides it has to have a leader, well, it can pick one. Or if you want to be a leader, you can pick yourself. See if anybody follows. But I'm not it, I'm only here to be available for answering questions or giving information.

First, I will tell you what you already know. The reason you are all here is to solve problems.

(She paused for a moment, scratching her nose and smiling, and then went on.)

Thank you. A lot of groups start complaining and making jokes right there, and you didn't. That's nice, because I didn't organize this group, and although I must say I think the groups work out well, it isn't my fault that you're here. And I appreciate your not blaming it on me.

Still, you are here, and we are expected to state some problems and solve them, and we will stay right here until we do that, or enough of it so that whoever's watching us is satisfied enough to let us go. That might be a couple of weeks. I had a group once that got out in 72 hours, but don't expect that. Anyway, you won't know how long it is. The reason we are in these caves is to minimize contact with the external world, including all sorts of times cues. And if any of you have managed to smuggle watches past the VISTA people, please give them to me now. They're not allowed here.

I saw some of you look interested when I talked about who is watching us, and so I ought to say right now I don't know how they watch or when, and I don't care. They do watch. But they don't interfere. The first word we will get from them is when the VISTA duty people unlock the elevator and come down and tell us we can go home.

Food. You can eat whenever you want to, on demand.

If you want to establish meal hours, any group of you can do so. If you want to eat singly, whenever you want to, fine. Either way you simply sign in in the dining room— "sign in" means you type your names on the monitor; they'll know who you are; just the last name will do—and order what you want to eat. Your choices are four: "Breakfast," "snack," "light meal" and "full meal." It doesn't matter what order you eat them in or when you want them. When you put in your order, they make them and put them in the dumbwaiter. Dirty dishes go back in the dumbwaiter except for the disposable ones, which go in the trash chute. You can ask for certain special dishes—the way you want your eggs, for instance—but in general you take what they give you. It's all explained on the menu.

Sleep. You sleep when you want to, where you want to. In these three rooms—this one, the problem pit and the eating room, as well as the pool and showers—the lights are permanently on. In the two small rooms out past the bathrooms and laundry the lights can be controlled, and whoever is in the room can turn them on or off any way you like. If you can't agree, you'll just have to work it out.

(She could see them building walls between themselves and her, and quickly she tried to reduce them.)

Listen, it's not as bad as it sounds. I always hate this part because it sounds like I'm giving you orders, but I'm not; those are just the ground rules and they bind me too. And, honestly, you won't all hate it, or not all of it. I've done this 15 times now, and I look forward to coming back!

All right, let's see. Showers, toilets and all are over there. Washer-dryers are next to them. I assume you all did what you were told and brought wash-and-wear clothes, as well as sleeping bags and so on; if you didn't, you'll have to figure out what to do about it yourselves. When you want to wash your clothes, put your stuff in one of the net bags and put it in the machine. If there's something already in the machine, just take it out and leave it on the table. The owner will pick it up when he wants it, no doubt. You can do three or four people's wash in a single cycle without any trouble. They're big machines. And there's plenty of water—you people who come from the Southwest and the Plains States don't have to worry. Incidentally, the sequenced water-supply system that you use there to conserve potable water was figured out right in this cave. The research and development people had to work it over hard, to get the fluidic controls responsive enough, but the basic idea came from here; so, you see, there's a point to all this.

(She lit a cigarette and looked cheerfully around at the group, pleased that they were not resisting, less pleased that they were passive. She was a tall and elderly red-headed woman, who usually managed to look cheerful without smiling.)

That brings me to computation facilities, for those of you who want to work on something that needs mathematical analysis or data access. I will do a certain amount of keyboarding for you, and I'll be there to help—that's basically my job, I guess. There are two terminals in the pit room. They are on-line, real-time, shared-time programs, and those of you who are familiar with ALGOL, COBOL, and so on can use them direct. If you can't write a program in computer language, you can either bring it to me—up to a point—or you can just type out what you want in clear. First, you type the words HELP ME; then you say what you want; then you type THAT'S ALL. The message will be relayed to a programmer, and he will help you if I can't, or if you don't want me to. You can blind-type your queries if you don't want me looking over your shoulder. And sign your last name to everything. And, as always, if more of you want to use the terminals than we have terminals, you'll have to work it out among you. I don't care how.

Incidentally, the problem pit is there because some groups like to sit face to face in formal surroundings. Sometimes it helps. Use it or not, as you like. You can solve problems anywhere in these chambers. Or outside, if you want to go outside. You can't leave through the elevator, of course, because that's locked now. Where you can go is into the rest of the cave system. But if you do that, it's entirely your own responsibility. These caves run for at least 80 miles and maybe more, right down under the sea. We're at least ten miles by the shortest route from the public ones where the tourists come. I doubt you could find your way there. They aren't lighted, and you can very easily get lost. And there are no, repeat no, communications facilities or food available there. Three people have got lost and died in the past year, although most people do manage to find their way back—or are found. But don't count on being found. No one will even start looking for you until we're all released, and then it can take a long time.

My personal advice—no, I'm sorry. I was going to say that my personal advice is to stay here with the rest of us, but it is, as I say, your decision to make, and if you want to go out you'll find two doors that are unlocked.

Now, there are two other resource people here. The rest of you are either draftees or volunteers. You all know which you are, and for any purposes I can think of it doesn't matter.

I'll introduce the two other pros. Jerry Fein is a doctor. Stand up, will you, Jerry? If any of you get into anything you can't handle, he'll help if he can.

And Marge Klapper over there is a physiotherapist. She's here to help, not to order you around, but—advice and personal opinion again, not a rule—I think you'll benefit from letting her help you. The rest of you can introduce yourselves when we get into our first session. Right now I'll turn you over to—what? Oh, thanks, Marge. Sorry.

The pool. It's available for any of you, any time, as many of you as want to use it. It's kept at 78 degrees, which is two degrees warmer than air temperature. It's a good place to have fun and get the knots out, but, again, you can use it for any purpose you like. Some groups have had active, formal problem-solving sessions in it, and that's all right too.

Now I think that's it, so I'll turn you over to Marge.

Marge Interacting

Marge Klapper was 24 years old, pretty, married but separated, slightly pregnant but not by her husband, and a veteran of eight problem-group marathons.

She would have challenged every part of the description of her, except the first and the last, on the grounds that each item defined her in terms of her relationship to men. She did not even like to be called "pretty." She wasn't in any doubt that she was sexually attractive, of course. She simply didn't accept the presumption that it was only her physical appearance that made her so. The men she found sexually attractive came in all shapes and sizes, one because he was so butchy, one because of his sense of humor, one because he wrote poems that turned into bars of music at the end. She didn't much like being called a physiotherapist, either; it was her job classification, true, but she was going for her master's in Gestalt psychology and was of half a mind to become an M.D. Or else to have the baby that was just beginning to grow inside her; she had not yet reached a decision about that.

"Let's get the blood flowing," she said to all of them, standing up and throwing off her shorty terry-cloth robe. Under it she wore a swimsuit with a narrow bikini bottom and a halter top. She would have preferred to be nude, but her breasts were too full for unsupported calisthenics. She thought the way they flopped around was unaesthetic, and at times it could be actively painful. Also, some of the group were likely to be shy about nudity, she knew from experience. She liked to let them come to it at their own pace.

Getting them moving was the hard part. She had got to the pit early and chatted with some of them ahead of time, learning some of the names, picking out the ones who would work right away, identifying the difficult ones. One of the difficult ones was the little dark Italian man who was "in construction," he had said, whatever that meant; she had sat down next to him on purpose, and now she pulled him up next to her and said:

"All right. Let's start nice and slow and get some of the fug out of our heads. This is easy: we'll just reach."

She lifted her arms over her head, up on tiptoe, fingers upstretched. "High as you can go," she said. "Look up. Let's close our eyes and feel for the roof."

But what Marge was feeling for was the tension and needs of the group. She could almost taste, almost smell, their feelings. What Ben Ittri, next to her, was feeling was embarrassment and fear. The shaggy man who had come in late: a sort of numb pain, so much pain that it had drowned out his receptors. The fat girl, Dolores: anger. Marge could identify with that anger; it was man-directed anger.

She put the group through some simple bending energetics, or at least did with those who would cooperate. She had already taken a census of her mind. Not counting the three professionals, there were five in the group who were really with the kinetics. She supposed they were the volunteers, and probably they had had experience of previous sessions. The other eight, the ones she assumed were draftees, were a spectrum of all the colors of disengagement. The fat girl simply did not seem physically able to stand on tiptoes, though her anger carried her through most of the bending and turning; it was like a sack of cement bending, Marge thought, but she could sense the bones moving under the fat. The bent old black man who sat obstinately on the floor, regarding the creases on his trousers, was a different kind of problem; Marge had not been able to see how to deal with him.

She began moving around the room, calling out instructions. "Now bend sidewise from the waist. You can do it with your hands up like this, or you might be more comfortable with your hands on your hips. But see how far you can go. Left. Right. Left—"

They were actually responding rather well, considering. She stopped in front of a slight black youth in a one-piece Che Guevara overall. "It's fun if we do it together," she said, reaching out for his hands. He flinched away, then apologetically allowed her to take his hands and bend with him. "It's like a dance," she said, smiling, but feeling the tension in his arms and upper torso as he allowed himself unwillingly to turn with her. Marge was not used to that sort of response from males, except from homosexuals, or occasionally the very old ones who had been brought up under the Protestant ethic. He didn't seem to be either of those. "You know my name," she said softly. "It's Marge."

"Rufous," he said, looking away from her. He was acutely uncomfortable; reluctantly she let him go and moved on. She felt an old annoyance that these sessions would not allow her to probe really deeply into the hangups she uncovered, but of course that was not their basic purpose; she could only do that if the people themselves elected to work on that problem.

The other black man, the one who was so obdurately sitting on the floor, had not moved; Marge confronted him and said, "Will you get up and do something with me?"

For a moment she thought he was going to refuse. But then, with dignity, he stood up, took her hands and bent with her, bending left, bending right. He was as light as a leaf but strong, wire rather than straw. "Thank you," she said, and dropped his hands, pleased. "Now," she said to the group, "we're going to be together for quite a while, so let's get to know each other, please. Let's make a circle and put our arms around each other. Right up close! Close as you can get! All of us. Please?"

It was working out nicely, and Marge was very satisfied. Even the old black man was now in the circle, his arms looped around the shoulders of the fat girl on one side and a middle-aged man who looked like an Irish tenor on the other. The group was so responsive, at least compared to most groups in the first hour of their existence as groups, that for a moment Marge considered going right into the pool, or non-verbal communication—but no, she thought, that's imposing my will on them; I won't push it.

"All right, that's wonderful," she said. "Thank you all."

Tina said, "From here on, it's all up to you. All of you. There's tea and coffee and munch over there if anyone wants anything. Marge, thank you; that was fun."

"Anytime," called Marge, stretching her legs against the wall. "I mean that. If any of you ever want to work out with me, just say. Or if you see me doing anything and want to join in, please do."

"Now," said Tina, "if anybody wants to start introducing himself or talking about a problem, I, for one, would like to listen."

Introductions

The hardest thing to learn to do was wait.

Tina Wattridge worked at doing it. She pushed a throw pillow over to the floor next to the corner of a couch and sat on it, cross-legged, her back against the couch. Tina's opinion of Marge Klapper was colored by the fact that she had a granddaughter only seven or eight years younger than Marge, which, Tina was aware, led her to think of the therapist as immature; nevertheless, there was something in the notion that the state of the body controlled the state of the mind, and Tina let her consciousness seep into her toes, the tendons on the soles of her feet, her ankles, her knees, all the way up her body, feeling what they felt and letting them relax. It was good in itself, and it kept her from saying anything. If she waited long enough, someone would speak . . .

"Well, does anybody mind if I go first?"

Tina recognized the voice, was surprised and looked up. It was Jerry Fein. It was not against the rules for one of the pros to start, because there were no rules, exactly. But it unusual. Tina looked at him doubtfully. She had never worked with him before. He was the plumpish kind of young man who looks older than he is; he looked about forty, and for some reason Tina was aware that she didn't like him.

"The thing is," said Dr. Fein, haunching himself backward on the floor so that he could see everyone in the group at once, "I do have a problem. It's a two-part problem. The first part isn't really a problem, except in personal terms, for me. I got a dose from a dear friend two months ago." He shrugged comically. "Like shoemaker's children that never have shoes, you know? I think we doctors get the idea somewhere in med school that when we get into practice we'll be exempt from diseases, they're only things that happen to patients. Well, anyway, it turned out to be syphilis, and so I had to get the shots and all. It's not too bad a thing, you know, but it isn't a lot of fun because there are these resistant strains of spiro-chetes around, and I had one of the toughest of them, Mary-Bet 13 it's called—so it didn't clear up overnight. But it is cleared up," he added reassuringly. "I mention this in case any of you should be worrying. I mean about maybe using the same drinking glass or something.

"But the part of the problem I want to throw in front of you is, why should anybody get syphilis in the first place? I mean, if there are any diseases in the world we could wipe out in thirty days from a standing start, syphilis and gonor-rhea are the ones. But we don't. And I've been thinking about it. The trouble is people won't report themselves. They won't report their contacts even more positively. And they never, *never* think of getting an examination until they're already pretty sure they've got a dose. So if any of you can help me with this public health problem that's on my mind, I'd like to hear."

It was like talking into a tape recorder in an empty room; the group soaked up the words, but nothing changed in their faces or attitudes. Tina closed her eyes, half hoping that someone would respond to the doctor, half that someone else would say something. But the silence grew. After a moment the doctor got up and poured himself a cup of coffee, and when he sat down again his face was as blank as the others.

The man next to Tina stirred and looked around. He was young and extremely good-looking, with the fair hair and sharp-featured face of a Hitler Youth. His name was Stanwyck. Tina had negative feelings toward him, too, for some reason she could not identify; one of the things she didn't like about Jerry Fein was his sloppiness—he was wearing two shirts, one over the other, like a Sicilian peasant. One of the things she didn't like about Stanwyck was his excessive neatness; like the old black man, Bob Sanger, he was wearing a pressed business suit.

But Stanwyck didn't speak.

The fat girl got up, fixed herself a cup of tea with sugar and milk, took a handful of raisins out of a bowl and went back to her place on the floor.

"I think I might as well talk," said somebody at last. (Tina exhaled, which made her realize she had been holding her breath.)

It was the elderly black man, Sanger. He was sitting, hugging his knees to himself, and he stayed that way all the time he was talking. He did not look up but addressed his words to his knees, but his voice was controlled and carrying. "I am a volunteer for this group," he said, "and I think you should know that I asked to join because I am desperate. I am seventy-one years old. For more than forty years I have been the owner and manager of a dental-supply manufacturing company, Sanger Hygiene Products, of Fresno, California. I do not have any response to make to what was said by the gentleman before me, nor am I very sympathetic to him. I am satisfied that God's Word is clear on the wages of sin. Those who transgress against His commandments must expect the consequences, and I have no desire to make their foulness less painful for them. But mine is, in a sense, also a public health problem; so perhaps it is not inappropriate for me to propose it to you now."

"Name?" Tina murmured.

He did not look up at her, but he said, "Yes, Mrs. Wattridge, of course. My name is Bob Sanger. My problem is that halidated sugar and tooth-bud transplants have effectively depleted the market for my products. As you all may be aware, there simply is not a great demand for dental therapy any more. What work is done is preventive and does not require the bridges and caps and plates we make in any great volume. So we are in difficulties such that, at the present projection, my company will have crossed the illiquidity level in at most

twelve months, more likely as little as four; and my problem
is to avoid bankruptcy."

He rubbed his nose reflectively against one knife-creased
knee and added, "More than three hundred people will be out
of work if I close the plant. If you would not care to help
me for my sake, perhaps you will for theirs."

"Oh, Bob, cut the crap," cried the fat girl, getting up for
more raisins. "You don't have to blackmail us!"

He did not look at her or respond in any way. She stood
by the coffee table with a handful of raisins for a moment,
looking around, and then grinned and said:

"You know, I have the feeling I just volunteered to go
next."

She waited for someone to contradict her, or even to agree
with her. No one did, but after a moment she went on. "Well,
why not? My name is Dolores Belli. That's bell-*eye*, not bell-
ee. I've already heard all the jokes and they're not too funny;
I know I'm fat, so what else is new? I'm not sensitive about
it," she explained. "But I *am* kind of tired of the subject.
Okay. Now about problems. I'll help any way I can, and I do
want to think about what both of you have said, Jerry and
Bob. Nothing occurs to me right now, but I'll see if I can
make something occur, and then I'll be back. I don't have any
particular problem of my own to offer, I'm afraid. In fact, I
wouldn't be here if I hadn't been drafted. Or truthfully," she
said, smiling, "I do have a problem. I missed dinner. I'd like
to see what the food is like here. Is that all right?"

When no one volunteered an answer, she said sharply,
"Tina? Is it all right?"

"It's up to you, Dolores," said Tina gently.

"Sure it is. Well, let's get our feet wet. Anybody want to
join me?"

A couple of the others got up, and then a third, all looking
somewhat belligerent about it. They paused at the door, and
one of them, a man with long hair and a Zapata mustache,
said, "I'll be back, but I really am starving. My name is David
Jaretski. I do have a problem on my mind. It's personal. I
don't seem to be able to keep my marriage together, although
maybe that's because I don't seem to be able to keep my life
together. I'll talk about it later." He thought of adding something else but decided against it; he was still feeling a little

stoned and not yet ready either to hear someone else's troubles
or trust the group with his own.

The man next to him was good-looking in the solid, self-
assured way of a middle-aged Irish tenor. He said, in a comfortable, carrying voice, "I'm Bill Murtagh. I ran for Congress
last year and got my tail whipped, and I guess that's what
I'll be hoping to talk to you folks about later on."

He did not seem disposed to add to that, and so the other
woman who had stood up spoke. Her blond schoolgirl hair
did not match the coffee-and-cream color of her skin or the
splayed shape of her nose, but she was strikingly attractive
in a short jacket and flared pants. "My name's Barbara Devereux," she said. "I'm a draftee. I haven't figured out a problem yet." She started to leave with the others, then turned
back. "I don't like this whole deal much," she said thoughtfully. "I'm not sure I'm coming back. I might prefer going
into the caves."

The Cast of Characters

In Terre Haute, Indiana, at the Headquarters of SAD, the
Social Affairs Department, in the building called the Heptagon, Group 95-114 had been put together with the usual care.
The total number was 16, of whom three were professional
resource people, five were volunteers and the remainder selectees. Nine were male, seven female. The youngest had just
turned 18; the oldest 71. Their homes were in eight of the 54
states; and they represented a permissible balance of religions,
national origins, educational backgrounds and declared political affiliations.

These were the people who made up the 114th group of
the year:

BELLI, Dolores. 19. White female, unmarried. Volunteer
(who regretted it and pretended she had been drafted; the
only one who knew this was untrue was Tina Wattridge, but
actually none of the others really cared). As a small child her
father had called her Dolly-Belly because she was so cutely
plump. She wanted very much to be loved. The men who appealed to her were all-American jocks, and none of them had
ever shown the slightest interest in her.

DEL LA GARZA, Caspar. 51. White male. Widower, no

surviving children. Draftee. In Harlingen, Texas, where he had lived most of his life, he was assistant manager of an A&P supermarket, a volunteer fireman and a member of the Methodist Church. He had few close friends, but everyone liked him.

DEVEREUX, Barbara. 31. Black female, unmarried. Draftee. Although she had been trained as an architect and had for a time been employed as a fashion artist, she was currently working for a life insurance agent in Elgin, Illinois, processing premiums. With any luck she would have had seven years of marriage and at least one child by now, but the man she loved had been killed serving with the National Guard during the pollution riots of the '80s.

FEIN, Gerald, M.D. 38. White male. Professional resource person, now in his third problem marathon. Jerry Fein was either separated or partially married, depending on how you looked at it; he and his wife had opted for an open marriage, but for more than a year they had not actually lived in the same house. Still, they had never discussed any formal change in the relationship. His wife, Aline, was also a doctor—they had met in medical school—and he often spoke complimentarily of her success, which was much more rapid and impressive than his own.

GALIFINIAKIS, Rose. 44. White female, married, no children. She had been into the Christ Reborn movement in her twenties, New Maoism in her thirties and excursions into commune living, Scientology and transcendental meditation since then, through all of which she had maintained a decorous home and conventional social life for her husband, who was an accountant in the income tax department of the state of New Mexico. She had volunteered for the problem marathon in the hope that it would be something productive and exciting to do.

ITTRI, Benjamin. 32. White male. Draftee. Ittri was a carpenter, but so was Jesus of Nazareth. He thought about that a lot on the job.

JARETSKI, David. 33. White male, listed as married but de facto wifeless, since Lara had run off with a man who traveled in information for the government. Draftee. David was a sculptor, computer programmer and former acid head.

JEFFERSON, Rufous, III. 18. Black male, unmarried. Draftee.

Rufous was studying for the priesthood in the Catholic Church in an old-rite seminary which retained the vows of celibacy and poverty and conducted its masses in Latin.

KLAPPER, Marjorie, B.A., Mem. Am. Guild Ther. 24. White female, separated. Professional resource person. Five weeks earlier, sailing after dark with a man she did not know well but really liked, Marge Klapper had decided not to bother with anything and see if she happened to get pregnant. She had, and was now faced with the problem of deciding what to do about it, including what to say to her husband, who thought they had agreed to avoid any relationship with anybody, including each other, until they worked things out.

LIM, Felice. 30. White female, married, one child. Technically a draftee, but she had waived exemption (on grounds of dependent child at home—her husband had vacation time coming and had offered to take care of the baby). Felice Lim had quite a nice natural soprano voice and had wanted to be an opera singer, but either she had a bad voice teacher or the voice simply would not develop. It was sweet and true, but she could not fill a hall, and so she got married.

MENCHEK, Philip. 48. White male, married, no children. Draftee. Menchek was an associate professor of English Literature in a girl's college in South Carolina and rather liked the idea of the problem marathon. If he hadn't been drafted, he might have volunteered, but this way there was less chance of a disagreement with his wife.

MURTAGH, William. 45. White male, married (third time), five children (aggregate of all marriages). Volunteer. Murtagh, when a young college dropout who called himself Wee Willie Wu, had been a section leader in the Marin County Cultural Revolution. It was the best time of his life. His original True Maoists had occupied a nine-bedroom mansion on the top of a mountain in Belvedere, overlooking the Bay, with a private swimming pool they used for struggling with political opponents and a squash court for mass meetings. But they were only able to stay on Golden Gate Avenue for a month. Then they were defeated and disbanded as counterrevolutionaries by the successful East Is Red Cooperative Mao Philosophical Commune, who had helicopters and armored cars. Expelled and homeless, Murtagh had dropped out of the revolutionary movement and back into school, got his degree at San Jose State and became an attorney.

SANGER, Robert, B.Sc., M.A. 71. Black male. Wife deceased, one child (male, also deceased), two grandchildren. Volunteer. Bob Sanger's father, a successful orthodontic dentist in Parsippany, New Jersey, celebrated his son's birth, which happened to occur on the day Calvin Coolidge was elected to his own full term as President, by buying a bottle of bootleg champagne. It was a cold day for November, and Dr. Sanger slipped on the ice. He dropped the bottle. It shattered. A week later the family learned that everyone drinking champagne out of that batch had gone blind, since it had been cooked up out of wood alcohol, ethylene glycol, Seven-Up and grape squeezings. They nicknamed the baby "Lucky Bob" to celebrate. Lucky Bob was, in fact, lucky. He got his master's degree just when the civil rights boom in opportunities for black executives was at its peak. He had accumulated seed capital just when President Nixon's Black Capitalism program was spewing out huge hunks of investment cash. He was used to being lucky, and the death of his industry, coming at the end of his own long life, threw him more than it might have otherwise.

STANWYCK, Devon. 26. White male, unmarried. Volunteer. Stanwyck was the third generation to manage the family real estate agency, a member of three country clubs and a leading social figure in Bucks County, Pennsylvania. When he met Ben Ittri, he said, "I didn't know carpenters would be at this marathon." His grandfather had brought his father up convinced that he could never do anything well enough to earn the old man's respect; and the father, skills sharpened by thirty years of pain, did the same to his son.

TEITLEBAUM, Khanya. 32. White female, divorced, no children. Draftee. Khanya Teitlebaum was a loving, big Malemute of a woman, six feet four inches tall and stronger than any man she had ever known. She was an assistant personnel manager for a General Motors auto-assembly plant in an industrial park near Baton Rouge, Louisiana, where she kept putting cards through the sorter, looking for a man who was six feet or more and unmarried.

WATTRIDGE, Albertina. 62. White female, married, one child, one grandchild. Professional resource person. A curious thing about Tina, who had achieved a career of more than thirty years as a group therapist and psychiatric counselor for undergraduates at several universities before joining the SAD problem-marathon staff, was that she had been 28 years old and married for almost four before she realized that every human being had a navel. Somehow, the subject had never come up in conversation, and she had always been shy of physical exposure. At first she had thought her belly button a unique and personal physical disfigurement. After marriage she had regarded it as a wondrous and fearful coincidence that her husband bore the same blemish. It was not until her daughter was born that she discovered what it was for.

David Again

It was weird never knowing what time it was. It didn't take long to lose all connection with night and day; I think it happened almost when I got off the elevator. Although that may have been because of the morning glory seeds.

It was sort of like a six-day bash, you know, between exams and when you get your grades, when no one bothers to go to classes but no one can afford to leave for home yet. I would be in the pool with the girls, maybe. We'd get out, and get something to eat, and talk for a while, and then Barbie would yawn, and look at the bare place on her wrist the way she did, and say, "Well, how about if we get a little sleep?" So we'd go into one of the sleeping rooms and straighten out our bags and get in. And just about then somebody else would sit up and stretch and yawn, and poke the person next to him. And they'd get up. And a couple of others would get up. And pretty soon you'd smell bacon and eggs coming down the dumbwaiter, and then they'd all be jumping and turning with Marge Klapper just as you were dropping off.

Barbie and Dolly-Belly and I stayed tight with each other for a long time. We hadn't picked each other out, it just happened that way. I felt very self-conscious that first night in the common room, still flying a little and expecting everybody could see what I was doing. It wasn't that they were so sexually alluring to me. There were other women in the group who, actually, were more my type, a girl from New Mexico who had that long-haired, folk-singer look, a lot like Lara. Even Tina. I couldn't figure her age very well. She might easily have been fifty or more. But she had a gorgeous teenage kind of figure and marvelous skin. But I wasn't motivated to go after them, and they didn't show any special interest in me.

Barbie was really very good-looking, but I'd never made it with a black girl. Some kind of leftover race prejudice, which may come from being born in Minnesota among all those fair-haired WASPs, I suppose. Whatever it was, I didn't think of her that way at first, and then after that there were the three of us together almost every minute. We kept our sleeping bags in the same corner, but we each stayed in our own.

And Dolly-Belly herself could have been quite pretty, in a way, if all that fat didn't turn you off. She easily weighed two hundred pounds. There was a funny thing about that. I had inside my head an unpleasant feeling about both fat women and black women, that they would smell different in a repulsive way. Well, it wasn't true. We could smell each other very well almost all the time, not only because our sleeping bags were so close together but holding each other, or doing non-verbal things, or just sitting back to back, me in the middle and one of the girls propped on each side of me, in group, and all I ever smelled from either of them was Tigress from Barbie and Aphrodisia from Dolly-Belly. And yet in my head I still had that feeling.

There was no time, and there was no place outside the group. Just the sixteen of us experiencing each other and ourselves. Every once in a while somebody would say something about the outside world. Willie Murtagh would wonder out loud what the Rams had done. Or Dev Stanwyck would come by with Tina and say, "What do you think about building underground condominium homes in abandoned strip mines, and then covering them over with landscaping?" We didn't see television; we didn't know if it was raining or hot or the world had come to an end. We hadn't heard if the manned Grand Tour fly-by had anything to say about the rings of Saturn, which it was about due to be approaching, or whether Donnie Osmond had announced his candidacy for the presidency. We, or at least the three of us, were living in and with each other, and about anything else we just didn't want to know.

Fortunately for the group, most of the others were more responsible than we were. Tina and Dev would almost always be in the problem pit, hashing over everybody's problems all the time. So would Bob Sanger, sitting by himself in one of the top rows, silent unless somebody spoke to him directly, or to his problem, or rarely when he had a constructive and well-thought-out comment to offer. So would Jerry Fein and that big hairy bird, Khanya. Almost everybody would be working hard a lot of the time, except for Willie Murtagh, who did God knows what by himself but was almost never in sight after the three of us decided we didn't like him much, that first night, and the young black kid, Rufous, who spent a lot of his time in what looked like meditation but I later found out was prayer. And the three of us.

I don't mean we copped out entirely. Sometimes we would look in on them. Almost any hour there would be four or five of them in the big pit, with the chairs arranged in concentric circles facing in so that no matter where you sat you were practically looking right in the face of everyone else. We even took part. Now and then we did. Sometimes we'd even offer problems. Barbie got the idea of making them up, like, "I'm worried," she said once, "that the Moon will fall on us. Could we build some kind of a big net and hang it between mountains, like?" That didn't go over a bit. Then Dolly tried a sort of complicated joke about how the CIA should react if Amazonia intervened in the Ecuadorian elections, with the USIS parachuting disc jockeys into the Brazilian bulge to drive them crazy with concentrated-rock music. I didn't like that a bit; the USIS part made me think of Lara's boy friend, which made me remember to hurt. I didn't want to hurt.

I guess that's why we all three of us stayed with made-up problems, and other people's problems: because we didn't want to hurt. But I didn't think of that at the time.

"Of course," Dolly-Belly said one time, when she and I were rocking Barbie in the pool, "we're not going to get out of here until Joe Good up there in the Heptagon marks our papers and says we pass."

I concentrated on sliding Barbie headward, slowing her down, sliding her back. The long blond hair streamed out behind her when she was going one way, wrapped itself around her face when she was going the other. She looked beautiful in the soft pool light, although it was clear, if it had needed to be clear, that she was a natural blond. "So?" I said.

Barbie caught the change in rhythm or something, opened her eyes, lifted one ear out of the water to hear what we were saying.

"So what's the smart thing for us to do, my David? Get down to work and get out faster? Or go on the way we're going?"

Barbie wriggled off our hands and stood up. "Why are we worrying? They'll let the whole group go at the same time anyway," she said.

Dolly-Belly said sadly, "You know, I think that's what's worrying me. I kind of like it here. Hey! Now you two swing me!"

Preliminary Reports

The one part of the job that Tina didn't like was filing interim reports with the control monitors up at the old radio-telescope computation center. It seemed to her sneaky. The whole thing about the group was that it built up trust within itself, and the trust made it possible for the people to speak without penalty. And every time Tina found the computer terminals unoccupied and dashed in to file a report she was violating that trust.

However, rules were rules. Still dripping from the pool, where nearly all the group were passing each other hand to hand down a chain, she sat before the console, pulled the hood over her fingers, set the machine for blind-typing and began to type. Nothing appeared on the paper before her, but the impulses went out to the above-ground monitors. Of course, with no one else nearby that much secrecy was not really essential, but Tina had trained herself to be a methodical person. She checked her watch, pinned inside her bra— another deceit—and logged in:

Day 4, hour 0352. WATTRIDGE reporting. INTERACTION good, CONSENUALITY satisfactory. No incapacitating illnesses or defections.

Seven individuals have stated problem areas of general interest, as follows:

DE LA GARZA. Early detection of home fires. Based on experience as a volunteer fireman (eight years), he believes damage could be reduced "anyway half" if the average time of reporting could be made ten minutes earlier. GROUP proposed training in fire detection and diagnosis for householders.

(That had been only a few hours before, when most of the group were lying around after a session with Marge's energetics. The little man had really come to life then. "See, most people, they think a fire is what happens to somebody else; so when they smell smoke, or the lights go out because wires have melted and a fuse blows, or whatever, they spend 20 minutes looking for cigarettes burning in the ashtrays, or putting new fuses in. And then half the time they run down to the kitchen and get a pan of water and try to put it out themselves. So by the time we get there it's got a good start, and there's three, four thousand dollars just in water damage getting it out, even if we can save the house.")

FEIN. National or world campaign to wipe out VD. States that failure to report disease and contacts is only barrier to complete control of syphilis and gonorrhea. GROUP proposal for free examinations every month, medallion in the form of bracelet or necklace charm to be issued to all persons disease-free or accepting treatment.

(That one had started as a joke. That big girl, Khanya, said, "What you really need is a sort of kosher stamp that everybody has to wear." And then the group had got interested, and the idea of issuing medallions had come out of it.)

LIM. Part-time professional assistance for amateur theater and music groups. States that there are many talented musicians who cannot compete for major engagements but would be useful as backup for school, community or other music productions. Could be financed by government salaries repaid from share of admissions.

MURTAGH. Failure of electorate to respond to real issues in voting. Statement of problem as yet unclear; no GROUP proposals have emerged.

SANGER. Loss of market for dental supplies. GROUP currently considering solutions.

STANWYCK. Better utilization of prime real estate by combining function. GROUP has proposed siting new homes underground, and/or building development homes with flat joined roofs with landscaping on top. Interaction continuing.

(Tina wanted to go on with Dev Stanwyck's problem, because she was becoming aware that she cared a great deal about solving problems for him, but her discipline was too good to let her impose her personal feelings in the report. And anyway, Tina did not believe that the problem Dev stated was anywhere near the real problems he felt.)

TEITLEBAUM. Stated problem as unsatisfactory existing solitaire games. (Note: There is a personality problem here presumably due to unsatisfactory relationships with other sex.) GROUP proposed telephone links to computer chess-, checker, or card-playing programs, perhaps to be furnished as a commercial service of phone company.

PERSONALITY PROBLEMS exhibited by nine group members, mostly marital, career or parental conflicts. Some resolution apparent.

TRANSMISSION ENDS.

No one had disturbed Tina, and she pushed the hood away from the keyboard and clicked off the machine without rising. She sat there for a moment, staring at the wall. The group was making real progress in solving problems, but it seemed to her strange that it also appeared to have generated one in herself. All therapists had blind spots about their own behavior. But even a blind person could see that Tina Wattridge was working herself in pretty deep with a boy not much too old to be her grandchild, Devon Stanwyck.

David Cathecting the Leader

One time when we were just getting ready to go to sleep, we went into the room we liked—not that there was much difference between them, but this one they had left the walls pretty natural, and there were nice, transparent, waterfally rock formations that looked good with the lights low—and Tina and Dev Stanwyck were sitting by themselves in a corner. It seemed as though Dev was crying. We didn't pay much attention, because a lot of people cried, now and then, and after a while they went out without saying anything, and we got to sleep. And then, later on, Barbie and I were eating some of the frozen steaks and sort of kidding Dolly-Belly about her fruit and salads, and we heard a noise in the shower, and I went in, and there were Tina and Dev again. Only this time it looked as though Tina was crying. When I came back I told the girls about it. It struck me as odd; Tina letting Devon cry was one thing, Devon holding Tina while she was crying was another.

"I think they're in love," said Dolly-Belly.

"She's twice as old as he is," I said.

"More than that, for God's sake. She's pushing sixty."

"And what has that got to do with it, you two Nosy Parkers? How does it hurt you?"

"Peace, Barbie," I said. "I only think it's trouble. You'd have to be blind not to see she's working herself in pretty deep."

"You've got something against being in love?" Barbie demanded, her brown eyes looking very black.

I got up and threw the rest of my "light meal, steak" away. I wasn't hungry any more. I said, "I just don't want them to get hurt."

After a while Dolly said, "David. Why do you assume being in love is the same as being hurt?"

"Oh, cut it out, Dolly-Belly! She's too old for him, that's all."

Barbie said, "Who wants to go in the pool?"

We had just come out of the pool.

Dolly said, "David, dear. What kind of a person was your wife?"

I sat down and said, "Has one of you got a cigarette?" Barbie did, and gave it to me. "Well," I said, "she looked kind of like Felice. A little younger. Blue eyes. We were married six years, and then she just didn't want to live with me any more."

I wasn't really listening to what I was saying, I was listening to myself, inside. Trying to diagnose what I was feeling. But I was having trouble. See, for a couple of weeks I'd always known what I felt about Lara, because I hurt. It was almost like an ache, as though somebody were squeezing me around the chest. It was a kind of wriggly feeling in my testicles, as though they were gathering themselves up out of harm's way, getting ready for a fight. It was as if I was five years old and somebody had stolen my tricycle. All of those things. And the thing was that I could feel them all, every one, but I suddenly realized I hadn't *been* feeling them. I had forgotten to hurt at all, a lot of the time.

I had not expected that would happen.

Along about that time, I do not know if there was a casual relationship, I became aware of the fact that I was feeling pretty chipper pretty much of the time, and I began to like it. Only sometimes when I was trying to get to sleep, or when I happened to think about going back to Minnesota and remembered there was nobody there to go back to, I hurt. But I could handle it because I knew it would go away again. The cure for Lara was Barbie and Dolly-Belly, even though I had not even kissed either of them, except in a friendly goodnight way.

Time wore on, we could only tell how much by guessing from things like the fact that we all ran out of cigarettes. Dolly's were the last to go. She shared with us, and then she complained that Barbie was smoking them twice as fast as she was, and I was hitting them harder than that; she'd smoke two or three cigarettes, and I'd have finished the pack. It was our mixed-up time sense, maybe? Then Rufous came and shared a meal with us once and heard us talking about it, and later he took me aside and offered to trade me a carton for a couple of bananas. I grabbed the offer, ordered bananas, picked them off the dumbwaiter, handed them to Rufous, took the cigarettes and was smoking one before it occurred to me that he could have ordered bananas for himself if he'd wanted them. Barbie said he knew that, he just wanted to give me something, but he didn't want me to feel obligated.

We were all running out of everything we'd brought in with us. There wasn't any dope. Dolly-Belly had brought in some grass, and I guess some of the others had too, but it was gone. Dolly smoked hers up all by herself the first night, or anyway the first time between when we decided we were sleepy and when we got to sleep finally, before we were really close enough to share.

We were all running out, except Willie the Weeper. He had cigarettes. I saw them. But he didn't smoke them. He also had a pocket flask that he kept nipping out of. And he kept ordering fruit off the dumbwaiter, which surprised me when I thought about it because I didn't see him eating any. "He's making cave drippings somewhere," Dolly told me.

"What's cave drippings?"

"It's like when you make homemade wine. Only you drink it as soon as it ferments. Any kind of fruit will do, they say."

"How do you know so much about it if you've never been here before?"

"Oh, screw you, David, are you calling me a liar?"

"No. Honestly not, Dolly-Belly. Get back to cave drippings."

"Well. It's kind of the stuff you made when you're in the Peace Corps in the jungle and you've run out of beer and hash. I bet you a thousand dollars Willie's got some stewing away somewhere. Only I don't smell it." And she splashed out of the pool and went sniffing around the connecting caves, still bare. There was a lot of Dolly-Belly to be bare, and quite a few of the people didn't care much for group nudity even then. But she didn't care.

Out of all the people in our group, 16 of us altogether, Willie was about the only one I didn't really care for. I mean, I didn't like him. He was one of those guys my father used to bring home for dinner when I was little. So very tolerant of kids, so very sure we'd change. So very different in what they did from the face they showed the world. Willie was always bragging about his revolutionary youth and his commitment to Goodness and Truth, one of those fake nine-percenters that, if you could see his income tax form, wasn't pledging a penny behind what he had to give. Even when he came in with us that first night and as much as asked us for help, you couldn't believe him. He wasn't asking what he did wrong, he was asking why the voters in his district were such perverse fools that they voted for his opponent.

Some of the others were strange, in their ways. But we got along. Little Rufous stayed to himself, praying mostly. That big broad Khanya would drive you crazy with how she had poltergeists in her house if you'd let her. Dev Stanwyck was a grade-A snob, but he was tight with Tina most of the time, and he couldn't have been all lousy, because she was all right. I guess the hardest to get along with was the old black millionaire, or ex-millionaire, or maybe-about-to-be-ex-millionaire, Bob Sanger. He didn't seem to like any part of us or the marathon. But he was always polite, and I never saw anybody ask him for anything that he didn't try to give. And so everybody tried to help him.

Some Solutions for Sanger

After several days, only Tina knew exactly how many, the group found itself united in a desire to deal with the problems of Bob Sanger, and so a marathon brainstorming took place in the problem pit. Every chair was occupied at one time or another. Some 61 proposals were written down by Rose Galifiniakis, who appointed herself recorder because she had a pencil.

The principal solutions proposed were the following:

1. Reconvert to the manufacture of medical and surgical equipment, specifically noble-metal joints for prostheses, spare parts for cyborgs, surgical instruments "of very high quality" and "self-warming jiggers that they stick in you when you have your Papp test, that are always so goddamn cold you scream and jump right out of the stirrups."

2. Take all the money out of the company treasury and spend it on advertising to get kids crazy about cotton candy.

3. Hire a promoter and start a national fad for the hobby of collecting false teeth, bridges, etc., "which you can then sell by mail and save all the dealers' commissions."

4. Reconvert to making microminiaturized parts for guided missiles "in case somebody invents a penetration device to get through everybody's antimissile screens."

5. Hire a lobbyist and get the government to stockpile dental supplies in case there is another Cultural Revolution with riots and consequently lots of broken teeth.

6. Start a saturation advertising campaign pitched to the sado-maso trade about "getting sexual jollies out of home dentistry."

7. Start a fashion for wearing different-colored teeth to match dresses for formal wear. "You could make caps, sort of, out of that plastic kind of stuff you used to make the pink parts of sets of false choppers out of."

8. Move the factory to the Greater Los Angeles area in order to qualify for government loans, subsidies, and tax exemptions under the Aid to Impoverished Areas bill.

9. Get into veterinarian dentistry, particularly for free clinics for the millions of cats roaming the streets of de-

populated cities "that some old lady might leave you a million dollars to take care of."

10. Revive the code duello, with fistfights instead of swords.

There were 51 others that were unanimously adjudged too dumb to be worth even writing down, and Rose obediently crossed them out. Bob Sanger did not say that. He listened patiently and aloofly to all of them, even the most stupid of them. The only effect he showed as the marathon wore on was that he went on looking thinner and blacker and smaller all the time.

Of the ten which survived the initial rounds, Numbers 2, 3, 6, 7, and 10 were ruled out for lack of time to develop their impact. Bob thanked the group for them, but pointed out that advertising campaigns took time, maybe years, and he had only weeks. "Especially when they involve basic changes in folkways," agreed Willie Murtagh. "Anyway, seriously. Those are pretty crazy to begin with. You need something real and tangible and immediate, like the idea I threw into the hopper about the Aid to Impoverished Areas funding."

"I do appreciate your helpfulness," said Bob. "It is a matter of capital and, again, time. I have not the funds to relocate the entire plant."

"Surely a government loan—"

"Oh, drop it, Willie," said Marge Klapper. "Time, remember? How fast are you going to get SAD to move? No, Bob, I understand what you're saying. What about the idea of the cats? I was in Newark once and there were like thousands of them."

"I regret to inform you that many of my competitors have anticipated you in this, at least insofar as the emphasis of veterinary dentistry in concerned," said Bob politely. "As to the notion of getting some wealthy person to establish a foundation, I know of no such person. Also the matter of stockpiling supplies has been anticipated. It is this that has kept us going since '92."

Rufous Jefferson looked up from his worry beads long enough to say, "I don't like that idea of making missiles, Mr. Sanger."

"It wouldn't work," said Willie the Weeper positively. "I

know. You couldn't switch over *and* get the government back in the missile business in time anyway."

"Besides," said Dolly-Belly, "everybody's got plenty of missiles put away already. No, forget it, fellows, we've bombed out except for one thing. It's your only chance, Bob. You've got to go for that surgical stuff. *And* that self-warming jigger. You don't know, Bob, you're not a woman, but I swear to God every time I go to my gynecologist I leap right up the wall when he touches me with that thing. Brrr!"

"Dumb," said Tina affectionately. "Dolores, dear, I bet you go to a man gynecologist."

"Well, sure," said Dolly defensively. "It's kind of a sex thing with me, I don't like to have women messing me around there."

"All right, but if you went to a woman doctor she'd know what it feels like. How could a man know? *He* never gets that kind of an examination."

Bob Sanger uncrossed his legs and recrossed them the other way. "Excuse me," he said with a certain amount of pain in his voice. "I am afraid I'm not quite following what you are saying."

Tina said with tact, "It's for vaginal examination, Bob. In order to make a proper examination they use a dilator, which is kept sterile, of course, so it has to be metal. And it's cold. *My* doctor keeps the sterile dilators in a little jar next to an electric light so they're warm . . . but she's a woman. She knows what it feels like. Long ago, when I was pregnant, I went to a male obstetrician, and it's just like they say, Bob. You jump. You really do. A self-warming dilator would make a million dollars."

Sanger averted his eyes. His face seemed darker than usual; perhaps he was blushing. "It is an interesting idea," he said, and then added reluctantly, "but I'm afraid there are some difficulties. I can't quite see a place for it in our product line. Self-warming, you say? That would make them quite expensive, and perhaps hard to sterilize, as well. Let me think. I can envision perhaps marketing some sort of little cup containing a sterile solution maintained at body temperature by a thermostat. But would doctors buy it? Assuming we were able to persuade them of the importance of it—and I accept your word, ladies," he added hastily. "Even so. Why wouldn't a doctor just keep them by an electric light, as Tina's does?"

"Come on, Bob. Don't you have a research department?" Willie demanded.

"I do, yes. What I don't have is time. Still it could have been a useful addition to our line, under other circumstances, I am sure," Bob said politely, once again addressing the crease in his trousers.

Then nobody said anything for a while until Tina took a deep breath, let go of Dev Stanwyck's hand and stood up. "Sorry, Bob," she said gently. "We'll try more later. Now how about the pool?"

And the group dispersed, some yelling and stripping off their clothes, and slapping and laughing as they headed for the pool chamber, one or two to eat, Bob Sanger remaining behind, tossing a dumbbell from hand to hand and looking angrily at his kneecap, left alone.

David Cathecting the Group

They keep the pool at blood temperature, just like one of Tina's thingamabobs. As, in spite of everything, the walls stay cold—I suppose because of the cold miles and miles of rock behind them—it stays all steamy and dewy in there. And the walls are unfinished, pretty much the way God left them when he poked the caves out of the Puerto Rican rock. Some places they look like dirty green mud, like the bottom of a creek. Some places they look like diamonds. There is one place that is like a frozen waterfall, and one like icicles melting off the roof; and when they built the pool and lighted it, they put colored lights behind the rocks in some places, and you can switch them to go on and off at random. We liked that a lot. We went racing in, and Dolly-Belly pushed me in right on top of Barbie and went to turn on the lights, and then she came leaping like a landslide into the pool almost on top of both of us. Half the water in the pool came surging out, it looked like. But it all drains right back and gets churned around some way to kill the bugs and fungi, and so we jumped and splashed most of it out again and yelled and dived and then settled down to just holding each other, half drowsing, until the pool got too crowded and we felt ourselves being pushed into a corner and decided to get out.

We put some clothes on and sort of stood in the corridor,

between the pool and the showers, trying to make up our minds what to do.

"Want to get some sleep?" Barbie asked, but not very urgently. Neither of us said yes.

"How about eating something?" I offered.

Dolly-Belly said politely, "No thanks. I'm not hungry now." I found one of Rufous the Third's cigarettes and we passed it around, trying to keep it dry although the girls' hair kept dripping on it, and then we noticed that we were in front of the door that opens into the empty caves. And we realized we had all been looking at it, and then at each other, and then at the door again.

So Dolly tried the knob, and it turned. I pushed on the door, and it opened. And Barbie stepped through, and we followed.

It closed behind us.

We were alone in the solid dark and cold of the caves. A little line of light ran around three sides of the door we had just come through; and if we listened closely, we could hear, very faintly, an occasional word or sound from the people behind it. That was all. Outside of that, nothing.

Barbie took one of my hands. I reached out and took Dolly's with the other.

We stood silently for a moment, waiting to see if our eyes would become dark-adapted, but it was no use. The darkness was too complete. Dolly-Belly was twisting around at the end of our extended arms' length, and after a moment she said, "I can feel along a wall here. There's a kind of a rope. Watch where you step."

Someone had put duckboards down sometime. Although we couldn't see a thing, we could feel what we were doing. I had socks on; the girls were barefoot. Since I had one hand in the hand of each of them, I couldn't guide myself by the rope or the wall, as Barbie and Dolly could, but we went very slowly.

We had done a sensitivity thing a while earlier, two sleeps and about 11 meals earlier, I think, blindfolding each of us in turn and letting ourselves be led around to smell and hear and feel things. It was like that. In the same way, none of us wanted to talk. We were extending our other senses, listening, and feeling, and smelling.

Then Dolly-Belly stopped and said, "End of the rope." She

disengaged her fingers and bent down. Barbie came up beside me, and I slipped my hand free of hers and around her waist.

Dolly said, "I think there are some steps going down. Be careful, hear? It's scary."

I let go of Barbie, passed myself in front of Dolly, felt with my toes, knelt down and explored with my fingertips. It was queasy, all right. I felt as though I were falling over forward, not being able to see where I might be falling. There were wooden steps there, all right. But how far down they went and what was at the end of them and how long they had been rotting away there and what shape they were in, I could not tell.

So we juggled ourselves around cautiously and sat on the top step, which was just wide enough for the three of us, even Dolly-Belly. We listened to the silence and looked at the emptiness, until Barbie said suddenly:

"I hear something."

And Dolly said, "I smell something. What do you hear?"

"What do you smell?"

"Sort of like vinegar."

"What I hear is sort of like somebody breathing."

And a light flared up at us from the bottom of the stairs, blinding us by its abruptness although it was only a tiny light, and the voice of Willie the Weeper said, "Great balls o' fahr, effen 'tain't the Revenooers come to bust up mah li'l ol' still!"

I flung my head away from the light and yelled, "Willie, for Christ's sake! What are you doing here?"

"Dumb question, my David," said Barbie beside me. "Don't you remember about cave drippings? Willie's got himself a supply of home brew out here."

"Right," said Willie benevolently. "Thought I recognized your voice, my two-toned sepia queen. Say, how are your roots doing?"

Barbie didn't say a word, and neither did any of the rest of us. After a moment Willie may have felt a little ashamed of himself, because he flicked off his light. "I've only got the one battery," he explained apologetically from the darkness. "Oh, wait a minute. Take a look." And he turned on the little penlight again, shined it at arm's length on himself, and then against the wall, where he had four fruit bowls covered by dinner plates and a bunch of paper cups. "I thought you might like to see my little popskull plant," he said pridefully, turning the light off again. "Care for a shot?"

"Why not?" said Barbie, and we all three eased ourselves down to the lower steps and accepted a paper cup of the stuff, sharing it among us.

"Straining it was the hard part," said Willie. "You may notice a certain indefinable piquancy to the bouquet. I had to use my underwear."

Barbie, just swallowing, coughed and giggled. "Not bad, Willie. Here, try it, David. It's a little bit like Dutch gin."

To me it tasted like the liquid that accumulates in the bottom of the vegetable bins in a refrigerator, and I said so.

"Right, that's what I mean. My compliments to the vintner, Willie. Do you come here a lot?"

"No. Oh, well, maybe, I guess so. I don't like being hassled around in there." I couldn't see his face in the darkness, but I could imagine it: angry and defensive. So, to make it worse, I said,

"I thought you volunteered for this."

"Hell! I didn't know it would be like this."

"What did you think it would be like, Willie?" Barbie asked. But her voice wasn't mocking.

He said, with pauses, "I suppose, in a way . . . I suppose I thought it would be kind of like the revolution. I don't suppose you remember. You're probably too young, and anyway it was mostly on the West Coast. But we were all together then, you know . . . I mean, even the ones we were fighting and struggling were part of it. Chaos, chaos, and out of it came some good things. We struggled with the chief of police of San Francisco in the middle of Market Street, and afterwards he was all bruised and bleeding, but he thanked me."

We didn't say anything. He was right, we were too young to have been involved except watching it on TV, where it seemed like another entertainment.

"And then," said Willie, "nothing ever went right." And he didn't say anything more for a long time, until Dolly-Belly said:

"Can I have another shot of drippings?"

And then we just sat for a while, thinking about Willie, and finally not thinking about anything much. I didn't feel blind any more, even with the light off. Just that bit from

Willie's flash had given me some sense of domain. I could remember the glimpse I had got: the flat, unreflective black wall off to my right, just past Dolly-Belly, the wooden steps down (there had been nine of them), the duckboards along the rough shelf above us, the faint occasional drip of water from the bumps in the cave roof over us, the emptiness off to the left past where the light from Willie's penlamp did any good, Willie's booze factory down below. With a girl on either side of me I didn't even feel cold, except for my feet, and after a while Willie put his hand on one of them. It felt warm and I liked it, but I heard myself saying, "You've got the wrong foot, Willie. Barbie's on my left, Dolly's on my right."

After a moment he said, "I knew it was yours. I'm already holding one of Dolly's." But he took it away.

Barbie said thoughtfully, "If you'd been a voter in your district, Willie, who would you have voted for?"

"Do you think I haven't asked myself that?" he demanded. "You're right. I would have voted for Tom Gdansk."

Dolly said, "It's time for a refill, Willie friend." And we all churned around getting our paper cups topped off and read-justing ourselves and when Willie prudently turned the pen-light off again, we were all sitting together against the wall, touching and drinking, and talking. Willie was doing most of the talking. I didn't say much. I wasn't holding back; it was just that I had had the perception that it was more important for Willie to talk than for me to respond. I let the talk wash over me. Time slowed and shuddered to a stop.

It came to me that we four were sitting there because it was meant from the beginning of time that we should be sitting there, and that sitting there was the thing and the only thing that we were ordained to do. My spattered statue for the library? It didn't matter. It was in a different part of reality. Not the part we four were in just then. Willie's wor-ries about being not-loved? It mattered that he was telling us about it (he was back to his third birthday, when his older brother's whooping cough had canceled Willie's party), but it didn't matter that it had happened. Dolly's fatness? *N'importe*. Barbie's fitful soft weeping, over she never said what? *De nada*. Lara leaving me for the USIS goon? *Machts nicht* . . . well, no. That did amount to something real and external. I could feel it working inside me.

But I was not prepared to let it interfere with the groupness of our group, which was a real and immanent thing in itself. After a while, Dolly began to hum to herself. She had a bad, reedy voice, but she wasn't pushing it, and it fitted in nicely behind Willie's talking and Barbie's weeping. We eased each other, all four of us. It must have been in some part Willie's terrible foul brew, but it could not have been all that; it was weak stuff and tasted so awful you could drink it only one round at a time. It was, in some ways, the finest time of my life.

"Time," I said wonderingly. "And time, and time, and all of the kinds of time." I don't suppose it meant anything, but it seemed to at that—yes. At that time. And for a time we talked timelessly about time, which, in my perception, had the quality of a mobile or a medallion or a coffee-table book, in that it was something one discussed for its pleasant virtues but not something that constrained one.

Except that there too there was some sort of inner activity, like stomach rumblings, going on all the time.

While we were there, what was happening in those external worlds we had left? In the world in the caves behind us? Had the group been judged and passed and discharged while we were gone? If it had, how would we ever know?

But Barbie said (and I had not known I had asked her, or spoken out loud) that that was unlikely because, as far as she could see, our group had done damn-all about solving any problems, especially its own, and if we were to be excused only after performance, we had all the performance yet to perform. Everybody knew the numbers. Most groups got out in some three weeks. But what was three weeks? Twenty-one sleeps? But we slept when we chose, and no two of us had exactly the same number. Sixty-three meals? Dolly had stopped eating almost entirely. How could you tell? Only by the solutions of problems, maybe. If you knew what standards were applied, and who the judges were. But I could see little of that happening, like Barbie, like all of us, I was still trapped in my own internal problems that, even there, came funneling in by some undetectable pipeline from that larger external world beyond the caves. And I had solved no part of them. Lara was still gone and would still be gone. Whatever time it was in Djakarta, she was there. Whatever was appropriate to that time, she was doing, with her USIS man and not with me, for I was not any part of her life and never would be again. She probably never thought of me, even. Or if she did, only with anger. "I feel bad about the anger," I said out loud, only then realizing I had been talking out loud for some time, "because I earned it richly and truly. I own it and acknowledge it as mine."

"So do you want to do anything about it?" asked somebody, Dolly I think, or maybe Willie.

I considered that for a timeless stretch. "Only to tell her about it," I said finally, "to tell her what's true, that I earned it."

"Do you want her back?" asked Willie. (Or Barbie.)

I considered that for a long time. I don't know whether I ever answered the question, or what I said. But I began to see what the answer was, at least. Really I didn't want her back. Not exactly. At least, I didn't want the familiar obligatory one-to-oneness with Lara, the getting up with Lara in the morning, the making the coffee for Lara, the sharing the toast with Lara, the following Lara to the bus twenty minutes after, the calling Lara at her office from my office, wondering who Lara was seeing for lunch, being home before Lara and waiting for Lara to come in, sharing a strained dinner with Lara, watching TV with Lara, fighting with Lara, swallowing resentments against Lara; I didn't even want going to bed with Lara or those few moments, so brief and in recollection so illusory, when Lara and I were peacefully at one or pleasuring each other with some discovery or joy. Drowsily I began to feel that I wanted nothing from Lara except the privilege of letting go of her without anger or pain; letting go of all pain, maybe, so that I did not have to have it eating at me.

But how much of this I said, or heard, I do not know, I only remember bits and tableaux. I remember Willie the Weeper actually weeping, softly and easingly like Barbie. I remember that there was a point when there was no more of the cave drippings left except some little bit that had just begun to work. I remember kissing Dolly, who was crying in quite a different and more painful way, and then I only remember waking up.

At first I was not sure where I was. For a moment I thought we had all got ourselves dead drunk and wandering, and perhaps had gone out into the cave and got ourselves

lost in some deadly, foolish way. It scared me. How could
we ever get back?

But it wasn't that way, as I perceived as soon as I saw that
we were huddled in a corner of one of the sleeping rooms.
I was not alone in my sleeping bag; Barbie was there with
me, her arms around me and her face beautiful and slack.
There was a weight across our feet which I thought was
Dolly.

But it wasn't. It was Willie Murtagh, wrapped in his own
bag, stretched flat and snoring, and Dolly was not anywhere
around.

Aspects of External Reality

Geology. About a hundred million years before the birth of
Christ, during the period called the Upper Cretaceous when
the Gulf of Mexico swelled to drown huge parts of the Southern United States, a series of volcanic eruptions racked the
sea that would become the Caribbean. The chains of islands
called the Greater and Lesser Antilles were born.

As the molten rock boiled forth and the pressure dropped,
great bubbles of trapped gas evolved, some bursting free into
the air, others remaining imprisoned as the cooling and
hardening of the lava raced against the steady upward crawl
of the gas. In time the rock cooled and became agelessly
hard. The rains drenched it, the seas tore at it, the winds
scoured it, and all of them brought donations: waveborne
insects, small animals floating on bits of vegetation or sturdily
swimming, air-borne dust, bird-borne seeds. After a time the
islands became densely overgrown with reeds and grasses,
orchids and morning-glories, bamboo, palm, cedar, ebony,
calabash, whitewood; it was a place of karst topography, so
wrinkled and seamed that it was like a continent's worth of
landscaping crammed into a single island, and overgrown
everywhere.

Under the rock the bubbles remained; and as the peaks
weathered, some of the bubbles thinned and balded at the
top, opened, and collapsed, leaving great, round, open valleys
like craters. When astronomers wanted to build the biggest
damned radio telescope the world had ever seen, they found
one of these opened-out bubbles. They trimmed it and

smoothed it and drained it and inlaid it with wire mesh to become the thousand-foot dish of the Arecibo Observatory. Countless other bubbles remained. Those that had been farther under the surface remained under the surface and were hidden until animals found them, then natives, then pirates, then geologists and spelunkers, who explored them and declared them to be perhaps the biggest chain of connected caverns ever found in the earth. Tourists gaped. Geologists plumbed. Astronomers peered, in their leisure hours. And then, when all radio telescopy was driven to the far side of the Moon by a thousand too many radio-dispatched taxicabs and a million too many radar ovens, the observatory no longer served a function and was abandoned.

But the caves remained.

Physical Description. After examining nearly all of the Puerto Rican cave system, a group of four linked caverns was selected and suitably modified. By blasting and hammering they were shaped and squared. Concrete flowed into the lower parts of the flooring to make them level. Wiring reached out to the generators of the old observatory, and then there were lighting, power, and communications facilities. In a separate cavern near the surface, almost burst through to the air, rack upon rack of salt crystals were stored; in the endless Puerto Rican sun the salt accepted heat, and when warmth was needed below, air was pumped through the salt. Decorators furnished and painted the chambers. Plumbers and masons installed fixtures and the pool. Water? There was endless water from the inexhaustible natural springs in the mountains. Drainage? The underground rivers that flowed off to the sea carried everything away. (When the astronomers came to build their telescope, they found that the valley had become a stagnant lake; its natural drain, through underground channels to the sea, had become blocked. Divers opened it, and the water swept sweetly away.) Two short elevator shafts, one for use and one for backup, completed the construction program. The result was an isolation pit exempt from the diurnal swing and the seasonal shift, without time or external stimuli, without distraction.

Support facilities. Maintenance, care and supervision of the problem pits is provided by a detachment of 50 VISTA volunteers, working out their substitute for military service. They tended the pumps, kept the machinery in repair, and did the housekeeping for the inmates. Their duties were quite light. The climate was humid but pleasant, especially in the northern hemisphere's winter months. Except for the long jackknifing drive to the city of Arecibo on the coast, for beer and company, the VISTA detachment was well pleased to be where they were. The principal everyday task was cooking, and that was no problem; it was all TV dinners, basically, prefabricated and prefrozen. All the duty chefs had to do was take the orders, pull them out of the freezers, pop them in the microwave ovens, and put them on the dumbwaiter. Plus, of course, something like scrambling eggs and buttering toast from time to time. There were seldom problems of any importance. The attempt of the United Brotherhood of Government Employees, in 1993, to organize the paramilitary services was the most traumatic event in the detachment's history. There had been a strike. Twenty-two persons, comprising the ongoing group of problem personnel, were temporarily marooned in the caves. For 18 days they were without food, light or communications, except for a few dumbwaiter loads of field rations smuggled down by one of the strikers. The inconvenience was considerable, but there were no deaths.

Monitoring and evaluation. Technical supervision is carried on by administratively separate personnel. There are two main areas of technical project control.

The first, employing sophisticated equipment originally designed for observatory use but substantially modified, is based near the old thousand-foot dish in the former administration and technical headquarters. Full information retrieval and communications capabilities exist, with on-line microwave links to the Heptagon, in Terre Haute, Indiana, via synchronous satellite. This is the top headquarters and decision-making station, and the work there is carried on by an autonomous division of SAD with full independent departmental status. The personnel of both technical supervision installations are interchangeable, and generally rotate duty from Indiana to Puerto Rico, six months or a year at a time.

The personnel of the technical project control centers are primarily professionals, including graduate students in social sciences and a large number of career civil service scientists in many disciplines. While stationed in Puerto Rico, most of these live along the coast with their families and commute to the observatory center by car or short-line STOL flight. They do not ordinarily associate with the VISTA crews, and only exceptionally have any firsthand contact with the members of the problem-solving groups, even the professional resource people included. This was not the original policy. At first the professionals actually participating in the groups were drawn by rota from the administrative personnel. It was found that the group identity was weakened by identification with the outside world, and so after the third year of operation the group-active personnel were kept separate, both administratively and physically. When off duty the group-active professionals are encourged to return to their own homes and engage in activities unrelated to the work of the problem pits.

The problem pits were originally sponsored by a consortium consisting of the Rand Corporation, the Hudson Institute, Cornell University, the New York Academy of Sciences, and the Puerto Rican Chamber of Commerce, under a matched-funds grant shared by SAD and the Rockefeller Foundation. In 1994 it was decided that they could and should be self-financing, and so a semipublic stock corporation similar to COMSAT and the fusion-power corporations was set up. All royalties and licensing fees are paid to the corporation, which by law distributes 35 percent of income as dividends to its stockholders, 11 percent to the State of Puerto Rico, and 4 percent to the federal government, reinvesting the balance in research-and-development exploitation.

Results to date. The present practice of consensual labor arbitration, the so-called "Nine Percent" income tax act, eight commercially developed board games, some 125 therapeutic personality measures, 51 distinct educational programs (including the technique of teaching elementary schoolchildren foreign languages through folksinging), and more than 1,800 other useful discoveries or systems have come directly from the problem-solving sessions in the Arecibo caves and elsewhere and from research along lines suggested by these sessions.

Here are two examples:

The Nine Percent Law. After the California riots, priority was assigned to social studies concerning "involvement," as the phrase of the day put it. Students, hereditarily unemployed aerospace workers, old people, and other disadvan-

taged groups who had united and overthrown civil government along most of the Pacific Coast for more than 18
months, were found to be suffering from the condition called
anomie, characterized by a feeling that they were not related
to the persons or institutions in their environment and had
no means of control or participation in the events of the
day. In a series of problem-pit sessions the plan was proposed which ultimately was adopted as the Kennedy-Moody
Act of 1993, sometimes called "The Nine Percent Law."
Under this act taxpayers are permitted to direct a proportion
of their income tax to a specific function of government, e.g.,
national defense, subsidization of scientific research, education, highways, etc. A premium of 1 percent of the total tax
payable is charged for each 10 percent which is allocated
in this way, up to a limit of 9 percent of the base tax (which
means allocating 90 percent of the tax payable). The consequences of this law are well known, particularly as to the
essential disbanding of the DoD.

The militia draft. After the 1991 suspension of Selective
Service had caused severe economic dislocation because of
the lack of employment for youths not serving under the
draft, a problem-pit session proposed resuming the draft
and using up to 60 percent of draftees, on a volunteer basis,
as adjuncts to local police forces all over the nation. It had
been observed that law enforcement typically attracted rigid
and often punitive psychological types, with consequent damage to the police-civilian relations, particularly with minority
groups. The original proposal was that all police forces cease
recruiting and that all vacancies be filled with national militia
draftees. However, the increasing professionalization of police
work made that impractical, and the present system of assign-
ing militia in equal numbers to every police force was
adopted. The success of the program may be judged from
the number of other nations which have since come to imitate
it.

In recent years some procedural changes have been made,
notably in giving preference to nongoal-oriented problem-
solving sessions, in which all participants are urged to generate
problems as well as solutions. A complex scoring system,
conducted in Terre Haute, gives credits for elapsed time, for
definition of problems, for intensity of application and for
(estimated) value of proposals made. As the group activity

inevitably impinges on personality problems, a separate score is given to useful or beneficial personality changes which occur among the participants. When the score reaches a given numerical value (the exact value of which has never been made public), the group is discharged and a new one convened.

The procedures used in the problem pits are formative, eclectic and heuristic. Among the standard procedures are sensitivity training, encounter, brainstorming, and head-cloning. More elaborate forms of problem-solving and deci-sion-making, such as Delphi, relevance-tree construction, and the calculus of statement, have been used experimentally from time to time. At present they are not considered to be of great value in the basic pit sessions, although each of them retains a place in the later R&D work carried on by pro-fessional teams, either in Terre Haute or, through subcon-tracting, in many research institutions around the country.

Selection procedures. Any citizen is eligible to volunteer and, upon passing a simple series of physical and psychologi-cal tests designed to determine fitness for the isolation ex-perience, may be called as openings occur. Nearly all volun-teers are accepted and actually participate in a pit session within 10 months to one year after application, although in periods when the number of volunteers is high, some propor-tion are used in sessions in other places than Arecibo, under slightly different ground rules.

In order to maintain a suitable ethnic, professional, reli-gious, sexual, and personality mix, and as part of a randomiz-ing procedure, about one half of all participants are selectees. These are chosen through Selective Service channels in the first instance, comprising all citizens who have not otherwise discharged their military obligation. Of course, the number thus provided is far in excess of need, and so a secondary lottery is then held. Those persons thus chosen are given the battery of tests required of volunteers, and those who pass remain subject to call for the remainder of their lives. As a matter of policy, many of the youngest age groups are given automatic deferments for a period of years, to provide a proper age mix for each working group.

Summary and future plans. The problem-pit sessions have proven so productive that there have been many attempts to expand them to larger formats, e.g., the so-called "Universal Town Meeting." These have achieved considerable success in special areas, but at the cost of limiting spontaneity and interpersonal interaction. Some studies have criticized the therapeutic aspects of pit sessions as distractive and irrelevant to their central purpose. Yet experimental sessions conducted on a purely problem-solving basis have been uniformly less productive, perhaps due to the emergence of a professionalist elite group who dominate such sessions; as their expertise is acquired through professional exposure over a period of time, their contributions are often too conventional and thus limited. The fresh, if uninformed, thoughts of nonexperts give the pit sessions their special qualities of innovation and daring. Most observers feel that the interpersonal quality of the sessions cannot be achieved on a mass scale except with the comcomitant danger of violence, personal danger and property destruction, as in the California Cultural Revolution. However, studies are still being pursued with the end in view of enlarging the scope and effectiveness of the sessions.

In conclusion, we can only agree with the oft-quoted extemporaneous rhyme offered by Sen. Moody at the ceremonies attendant on the tenth anniversary of the establishment of the problem pits:

> The pits are quirky,
> Perfection they're not.
> The best you can say's
> They're the best we've got.

The Statement of Tina's Problem

In Tina Wattridge's head lived a dozen people, all of whom were her and all of whom fought like tigers for sole ownership. Pit Leader Tina moved among the group, offering encouragement here, advice there, bringing one person to interact with another. Mother Tina remembered, after a third of a century, the costive agony of childbirth and the inexpressible love that drowned her when they first laid her daughter in her arms. Tina the Spy eavesdropped and snooped, and furtively slipped into the communications room to type out her reports on group progress. Homemaker Tina loathed the cockroach yellow paint on the walls of the main social room and composed unsent demands to the control authorities for new mats for the pool chamber, where the dank and the hard use had eaten them into disgraceful tatters. And all the Tinas were Tina Wattridge, and when they battled among themselves for her, she felt fragmented and paralyzed. When she felt worst was when one of the long-silent Tina's came arrogantly to the fore and drove her in a direction she had long forgotten. It was happening now. She knew what a spectacle she must seem to everyone present, most of all to the other parts of herself, but she could not help herself; she was in love; could not possibly be in love; was.

And while she was numb to everything but the external love and the interior pain of reproach, her group was exploding in a dozen directions. She couldn't cope; somehow she did cope, moment by moment, but always at the cost of feeling that there she had spent the last erg of energy, the last moiety of will and had nothing left—until another demand came. And they came every minute, it seemed. Bob Sanger shouting and trembling, demanding that the group be terminated and he be let to get back to his collapsing business. David Jaretski and Barbara Devereux screaming that their friend Dolores had blundered off into the caves to die. Marge Klapper (who should have known better!) whispering that she wanted to get out now, right now, to have the other man's baby pumped out of her so she could go back to the man she was married to. And back and forth to the teletypes, sneaking in reports; and worrying about every person there; and most of the time, all of the time, with her mind full of Dev Stanwyck and their utterly preposterous, utterly overpowering love.

She could not sleep. She would lie down exhausted, more often than not with Dev beside her, and sometimes there would be sex, fast and total, and sometimes there would be his passionate attempt to explain and justify all of his life. Sometimes nothing but exhaustion alone; she would feel herself falling away into sleep and hear Dev's breathing deepen beside her. And then some voice from the other room, or some memory, or some discomfort from the fold of the sleeping bag would come. Not much. Enough. Enough to pull her back from sleep, fighting angrily against it, and in a minute she would be wide awake with her mind furiously circling into a kind of panic.

Then she would get up, trying not to disturb Dev, trying to avoid the rest of the group, and head for the only place in the caves where she could have privacy, the toilets. And with the door locked, in the end stall, she would reach behind the flush tank and slide one piece of molding over another and take out the rough copies of her reports, trying to force her mind back onto her job.

Day 1, hour 2300. WATTRIDGE reporting. FEIN introduced VD epidemiology problem; no group uptake. SANGER states problem of approaching bankruptcy in dental findings industry; n.g.u. JEFFERSON made no overt statement but indicates sexual inadequacy problem. JARETSKI marital situation; wife has left him. ITTRI despondent career status; attributes lack of education. MURTAGH states criticism of Congressional election procedure; n.g.u. GROUP interaction in weak normal range.

They had all been strangers then. Dev Stanwyck's name did not even appear in that first report!

Day 4, hour 2220. WATTRIDGE reporting. KLAPPER and BELLI hostility; fought with bats without resolution. GROUP effective in bioenergetics and immersion therapy. Some preliminary diagnoses: DEVEREUX passive-aggressive, deep frustration feelings. BELLI compulsive and anal-retentive. STANWYCK latent homosexual father-dominated. (Note: I have personal feelings toward STANWYCK. I think of him as a son.)

She flipped hastily through the pages of the notebook, trying to ignore the fact that somebody was silently moving around outside the toilet door, apparently listening. Then she found the page she was looking for:

Day 13, hour 2330. WATTRIDGE reporting. Clique formation: BELLI-DEVEREUX-JARETSKI: semisexual triad, some boding to rest of group. STANWYCK-ITTRI, bivalent pairing, sociopersonal conflict vs. joint hostility to rest of group, little interaction. FEIN-KLAPPER-SANGER, weak professional communality of interest in medical areas; unstable bond, with individual links to other group members. No overt sexual interaction observed. Problem-solving: SANGER received full group brainstorm but did not consider any proposal satisfactory; forwarded for analysis. FEIN received approximately 30 minutes intensive discussion, no formal proposals but interaction taking place. ITTRI: Has become able to perceive own failure to make use of adult-education and other resources, accepts suggestions for courses and new career orientation. (Note: BELLI noticed in the pool that I was wearing my watch. I tried to persuade her that it was only an ornament and did not keep time. However, she told some of the others. STANWYCK in particular has been observing me closely, making these transmissions difficult even with blind-typing.)

And there it was, an absolute fraud! It hadn't happened that way at all. It had been Dev Stanwyck who had noticed it first, Dolly Belli only a day later; and Tina remembered cringingly with what anger and passion she had blown up at Dolly's half-joking question. It had stopped the questioning, all right; Dolly climbed out of the pool without another word, and her friends followed her. What else had it stopped: How close had Dolly been to opening up to the group at large?

And where had the anger come from? It was only when Tina had realized that the anger was all out of proportion to the stimulus that she had plumbed in her mind for another source and found it transferred from her own feelings about Dev Stanwyck.

Slowly she turned to a blank page and began her latest report:

Day 17, hour 2300. WATTRIDGE reporting. BELLI still missing. Tensions peaking. GROUP interaction maintaining plateau in high normal range. Sexual pairing marked: JARETSKI-DEVEREUX, KLAPPER-FEIN (temporary and apparently discontinued), ITTRI-TEITLEBAUM. Also WATTRIDGE-STANWYCK. (Note: I find this professionally disconcerting and am attempting to disengage. I am too old for him!)

She put down the pencil and wrinkled her eyes; repentance oft I swore, yes, but was I sober when I swore? How could she disengage herself from someone a third her age who found that she turned him on? And how could she not?

The breathing outside stopped for a moment, and then Dev's voice said, "Tina, is that you in there?"

She could not answer; some maiden shyness kept her from speaking while sitting on a toilet, or else she simply did not know what to say to Dev.

"I think you better come out," he went on. "Something's happening."

Hassling Willie

In the main social room Marge Klapper was facing Willie Murtagh across a mat. Both were tense and angry, which troubled Marge more than Willie because she did not like to be professionally inept. The one-night stand with Jerry Fein had left her upset, especially as Jerry didn't want to let it stay a one-night stand; she was angry; she wanted to get out to get rid of her souvenir of one other one-night stand; she wanted to go back to her husband and find out if the marriage could be made to work; and, most difficult of all, she wanted to do all those things while retaining her self-image as a competent professional intact. So she reached out for Willie:

"Do you want to fight?"

He stood angrily mute and shook his head.

She dropped the soft, inflated plastic bats and put a professional smile on her face. "Shall we push? Would you like to go in the pool?"

"No." He wasn't helping at all. He was uptight and souring the whole group with his tensions and giving her nothing to work on—nothing, she realized, except that intensity with which he was looking at her, as though hoping the next word out of her mouth would be what he wanted. So she tried again. She stepped up on the edge of the mat and said sweetly to Willie, "Would you like to try something with me? Let's jump."

Willie said, "Oh, Christ."

"Go on," Jerry Fein put in helpfully. "Shake the tensions out."

"Stay out of this, Jerry!" Marge snapped. And then forced herself to relax. "Like this, Willie," she said, jumping, coming down, jumping again. "Try it."

He glowered, looked around the room and gave a half-hearted hop.

"Great!" cried Marge. "Higher!"

He shrugged and jumped a mighty leap, twice as high as hers. Then another. "Beautiful, Willie," said Marge breathlessly. "Keep it up!" It was like an invisible seesaw, first Marge in the air, then Willie, Marge again; he began to move his feet like a Russian dancer, coming down with one knee half bent, then the other, turning his body from side to side. "Make a noise, Willie!" Marge yelled triumphantly, and demonstrated: "Yow! Whee! Hoooo!"

The whole group was joining in—anyway, that part of it that was in the room, all yelling with Willie. Marge felt triumphant and fulfilled; and then Tina had to come in and spoil it all.

"Sorry, Marge," she called from the doorway. "Listen, everybody. Does anybody know where Barbie and David are?"

"In the pool?" somebody guessed helpfully.

"No. I looked everywhere."

Marge panted angrily, "Tina, do you have to take attendance right now?"

"I'm sorry, Marge. But I'm afraid they've gone into the caves after Dolly. Is anyone else missing?"

The group looked around at itself. "Rufous!" cried Jerry Fein. "Where's he?"

Dev Stanwyck, as always tagging along after Tina, said in his superior way, "We've already checked the sleeping rooms. Rufous is there. Anybody else?"

No answer for a moment, and then three or four people at once: "Bob Sanger!"

Tina looked around, then nodded grimly. "Thanks." And she disappeared, Stanwyck hurrying after.

Nevertheless, the interruption had wrecked Marge's mood. And hadn't done any good for Willie, either; he was collapsed on the floor, staring into space.

"Well," said Marge heartily, "want to get back to it, Willie?"

He looked up and said, "I know where they are. It's kind of my fault." He straightened up and said, "Hell, it's *exactly* my fault. I was trying to get with that colored girl, and I said something I shouldn't have. Dolly took it the wrong

way and split for the caves, and I—well, I told David it was
his fault, so he went after her. I didn't actually think he'd
take Barbie with him."

"Or Sanger," said someone.

"I don't know anything about Sanger. But I know where
they are. They're wandering."

Tina said from the entrance, "No, not in the caves, they
aren't." All at once she looked every year of her age. "They're
outside," she said. "I just heard from the VISTA crew; they
identified four persons leaving the caves about a quarter of
a mile from here, one alone, then three more about an hour
ago."

"At least they're outside," said Willie thankfully.

"Oh, yes," said Tina, "they're outside. In the dark. Wandering around. Did you look at the terrain when you came in,
Willie?" She absentmindedly pressed her hands against her
face. It smeared her make-up, but she was no longer aware
she had it on. "One other thing," she said. "You can all go
home now. The word just came down over the teletype; our
group is discharged with thanks and, how did they say it?—
oh, yes. 'Tell them it was a good job well done,'" she said.

Running Home

I didn't really believe Willie even when it was clearly to
his advantage to tell the truth, but it was the way he said:
follow the piece of string he had laid out, exploring the caves
to keep from exploring his own head, and you came to a rock
slope, very steep but with places where somebody had once
cut handholds into it, and at the end of the handholds you
found yourself out in the fresh air. When we got out we
were all beat. Bob Sanger was the worst off of us, which
was easy to figure when you considered he was a pretty old
guy who hadn't done anything athletic for about as long as
Barbie and I had been alive. But he was right with us. "I'll
leave you now," he said. "I do appreciate your help."

"Cut it out, Bob," wheezed Barbie. "Where do you think
you're going?"

It had turned out to be night, and a very dark night with
a feeble tepid rain coming down, too—perhaps they had no
other kinds around there. I couldn't see his face, but I could
imagine his expression, very remote and contented with

whatever interior decisions he had reached. "I'll make my own way, thank you," he said politely. "It is only a matter of finding a road, and then following it downhill, I imagine."

"Then what?" I demanded. "We're AWOL, you know."

"That's why I have attorneys, Mr. Jaretski," he said cheerfully.

"Sitting on the bottom of the hill waiting for you?"

"Of course not. Really, you should not worry about me. I took the precaution of retaining my money belt when we checked our valuables. U.S. currency will get me to Ponce, and from there there are plenty of flights to the mainland. I'll be in California in no more than eight or nine hours, I should think."

"Listen, Bob!" I exploded—but stopped; Barbie squeezed my shoulder.

"Bob," she said, in a tone quite different from mine, "it isn't just that we're worried about you. We're worried about Dolly. Please help us find her."

Silence. I wished I could have seen his face. Then he said, "Please believe me, I am not ungrateful. But consider these facts. First, as I explained to all of you when we started this affair, it is of considerable importance to me to keep my company solvent. I believe that I have reasoned out a way to do so, and *I have no spare time*. I have no idea how much time we've wasted, and it may already be too late. Second, this is a big island. It is quite hopeless to search it for one girl with a long start, with no lights and no idea of where she has gone. I would help you if I could. I can't."

I said, trying to crawl down from my anger, "We don't have any other way to do it, Bob. I think I know where she is; anyway, that's where I want to look. But three of us can look fifty percent better than two."

"Call the VISTA crew," he said.

"I don't know where they are."

"Anyway, you're assuming she may be in some kind of danger. She is quite capable of taking care of herself."

"Capable, yes. Motivated, no. She's jealous and angry, Bob. Barbie and I were shacked up and it—" I hesitated; I didn't know exactly how to say it. "It spoiled things for her," I said. "I think she might do something crazy."

Sanger spluttered, "Your f-fornications are your own business, Mr. Jaretski! I must go. I—"

He hesitated and became, for him, confidential. "I believe that the discussion of my problem has in fact borne fruit. The, ah, gynecological instruments are an area in which I had little knowledge."

"You've invented a warmer for the thingy?" Barbie asked, interestedly.

"For the speculum, yes. A warmer, no. It isn't necessary. Metal conducts heat so rapidly that if it isn't warm it feels cold. Plastic such as our K-14A is as strong as metal, as poreless and thus readily sterilized as metal and has a very low thermal conductivity. I think—well. The remainder of what I think is properly my own business, Miss Devereux, and I want to get back to my own business to implement it before it is too late."

"Jesus, Bob," I said, really angry, "don't you feel anything at all? You got something good out of the group. Don't you want to help?"

I could hear him walking away. "Not in the least," he said.

"Won't you at least come over to the radio mirror with us to look? There's a road there . . ."

But he didn't even answer.

And we had wasted enough time, more than enough time. I took Barbie's hand, and we started off to where the faint sky glow suggested there were buildings. There was nothing much else in these hills; it had to be either the administration buildings around the radio dish or the cave entrance, and either way I could find my way from there. Of course, Dolly might not have gone to the dish. But where else would she go? Down the hill to civilization, maybe, but in that case she would be all right. But if she had gone to the dish, if she had been listening when I told her about the slippery catwalk and the five-hundred-foot drop—no, there was not much more time to waste.

There was no road near the outcropping with the crevice through which we had come. People had been there before. There was a sort of bruised part of the undergrowth that might have been a kind of path. It didn't help much. We bulldozed our way through the brush, with wet branches slapping at us and wet vines and bushes wrapping themselves around our legs; a little of that was plenty, on the up-and-down hillsides, but after half an hour or so we did hit a road. Something like a road, anyway; two parallel ruts that presumably were used from time to time, because the vegetation had not quite obliterated it. It circled a hill, and from the far side of it I could see not one but two glowing spots in the cloud. The nearer and brighter one looked like the entrance to the pit. Ergo, the other was where we wanted to go.

I think it took us a couple of hours to get there, and we didn't have the breath for much talking. We were lower down than I had been before. The suspended thing that looked like an old trolley car slung from wires was now higher up than we were; the rain had stopped, and the clouds were beginning to lighten with dawn coming. I stopped, gasping, and Barbie leaned against me, and the two of us stared around the great round bowl.

"I don't see her," Barbie said.

I didn't see her either. That was not all bad. The good part was that I didn't see her body spread out over the rusting wire mesh at the bottom of the bowl. "Maybe she didn't come here after all," I said.

"Where else would she go?"

"She could have got lost." Or she could have blundered down the mountains looking for a road. Or she could have found another cliff to jump off.

But I didn't think so, and then Barbie said, very softly, "Oh, look up there, my David. What's that that's moving?"

I looked. It was still gray and I could not be sure; but, yes, there was something moving.

It was actually in the big metal instrument cage, whatever it was.

I said, "I don't know, Barb. Let's go find out."

It was easy to say that, hard to do; the catwalk started out from the side of a hill but unfortunately not the hill we were on; we had to skirt one and circle around another before we reached the end of the catwalk. That was twenty minutes or so, I guess; and by then the day was brighter. And that was not all good. The bad part was that I could see the catwalk very clearly. It had not been used much for, I would guess, ten or fifteen years. Maybe more. It had a plank floor with spaces between the planks and spaces where planks seemed to have rotted out and fallen off. It had a wire-net side-barrier: rusty. The cables themselves, the over-

head ones from which it was slung and the smaller ones that
bound it to them, looked sturdy enough, but what good
would that do us if the boards split under us and we fell
through?

There were, however, only two alternatives, and neither of
them was any good. The tangible alternative was a sort of
bucket car that rose from the administration buildings to the
machine cage, but to get to that meant going halfway around
the bowl, and who could know if it would be working? The
intangible alternative was to turn away. So in effect we had
no alternatives, and I took Barbie's hand and led her out
onto the catwalk. By the time we were ten yards along it,
we became aware of wind (we had not felt it before) and
the rain (which slammed into us from the side). And we
became aware that the whole suspended walk was swaying,
and making creaking, testy, failing sounds as it swayed. We
walked as lightly as we could . . .

I was almost surprised when we discovered that we were
at the machine cage. Down between our feet was a whole
lot of emptiness, with the wire mesh and the greenery poking
through at the end. Over us was the machinery. And I didn't
know what to do next.

Barbie did; she called, "Dolly dear, are you up there?"

There was no answer.

I tried: "Dolly, please come down! We want you."

No answer, except what might have been the wind blowing, and might have been a sob.

Barbie looked at me. "Do you want to go up and look
around?"

I shook my head. There was a metal ladder, but it went
into a hatch and the hatch was shut. I really didn't like the
idea of climbing those few extra feet, but most of all I didn't
like the idea of driving Dolly farther and farther away, until
I drove her maybe out of some window. I yelled, "Dolly,
we didn't come all this way just to say good-bye. We want
you with us, Dolly!" I hadn't asked Barbie if that was true;
it didn't matter.

Silence that prolonged itself, and then there was a grating
sound and the hatch opened. Dolly peered down at us, looking cross but otherwise not unusual. "Crap," she said. "Okay,
you've soothed your consciences. Now go back to bed."

Barbie, holding on to the ladder—the whole structure was vibrating now—looked up at her and said, "Dolly, are you mad because David and I went to bed?"

With dignity Dolly said, "I have nothing to be angry about. Not to mention I'm used to it."

"Because it wasn't that big a deal, Dolly," Barbie went on. "It just happened that way. It could have been you and David, and I wouldn't have been mad."

"You're not me," said Dolly, and added, very carefully and precisely, "you're not a girl that's always been fifty pounds too fat, that everybody laughs at, that buys the kind of clothes you wear all the time and tries them on in front of a mirror, and then throws them out and cries herself to sleep."

She stopped there. Neither Barbie nor I said anything for a moment. Then I started, "Dolly dear—" But Barbie put her hand on my shoulder and stopped me.

She gathered her thoughts and then said, "Dolly, that's right, I'm not you. I'm me, but maybe you don't know what it's like to be me, either. Would you like me to tell you who I am? I'm a girl who really looked forward to this group, which took all the guts I had, because it meant letting myself hope for something, and then ran out of courage and never asked anybody for the help I wanted. I'm a black girl, Dolly, and that may not seem like much of a bad thing to you, but I happen to be a black girl who's going to die of it. Or to put it another way, Dolly dear, you're a girl who can make plans for Christmas, and I'm a girl who won't be here then."

You hear words like that, and for a minute you don't know what it is you've heard. I stood there, one hand holding on to the ladder, looking at Barbie with the expression of polite interest you give someone who is telling you a complicated story of which you have not yet seen the point. I couldn't make that expression go off my face. I couldn't find the right expression to replace it with.

Dolly said, "What the hell are you talking about?" And her voice was suddenly shrill.

"What I say," said Barbie. "It's what they call sickle-cell anemia. You white folks don't get it much, but us black folks, we get it. You know. All God's chillun got hemoglobin, but where your hemoglobin has something they call glutamic acid, my hemoglobin has something they call valine. Sounds like nothing much? Yeah, Dolly, but we die of it. Used to be we died before we grew up, most of the time, but they do things better now. I'm thirty-one, and they say I've got, oh, easily another five or six months."

Dolly's face pulled back out of the hatch, and her voice, muffled, yelled, "Wait a minute," and Dolly's legs and bottom appeared as she lowered herself down the ladder. When she got there, all she said was Barbie's name, and put her arms around both of us.

I don't know how long we stayed like that, but it was a long time. And might have been longer if we hadn't heard voices and looked up and saw people coming toward us along the catwalk. A hell of a lot of people, a dozen or so, and we looked again, and it was Bob Sanger leading all the rest.

"Why, son of a bitch," said Barbie in deep surprise. "You know what he did? He went and got the group to see if we needed help."

And Dolly said, "And you know what? We do. We all do." And then she said, "Dear Barbie. We could all be dead before Christmas. If David will have us, let's stick together a while. I mean—a while. As long as we want to." And before Barbie could say anything, she went on. "You know, I volunteered for this group. I didn't exactly ever say what I wanted, but I can tell you two. I guess I could tell all of them, and maybe I will." She took a deep breath. "What I wanted," she said, "was to find out how to be loved."

And I said, "You are."

The Wrap-Up

Tina Wattridge Final Report. Attached are the analysis sheets, work-ups, recommendations, and SR-4 situation cards.

There is one omission. I left out Jerry Fein's solution to his own problem. If you refer to D6H2140, you will find the problem stated (epidemiological control measures for VD). He ultimately provided his own solution, quote his words from my notes: "Suppose we make a monthly check for VD for the whole population. Everybody who shows up and is clear on the tests gets a little button to wear, like in the shape of a heart, with a date. You know, like the inspection sticker in a car. It could be like a charm bracelet for girls, maybe love beads for men. And if you don't pass the test that month, or start treatment if you fail, you don't get to wear the emblem." The reason I did not forward it was not that I thought it a bad idea; actually, I thought it kind of cute, and with the proper promotion it might work. What I did think, in fact what I was sure of, was that it was a setup. Jerry planted the problem and had the solution in his head when he came in, I guess to get brownie points. Maybe he wants my job. Maybe he just wanted to end the session sooner. Anyway he was playing games, and the reason I'm passing it on now is that I've come to the conclusion that I don't really care if he was playing games. It's still not a bad idea and is forwarded for R&D consideration.

One final personal note: Dev Stanwyck kissed me sweetly and weepily good-bye and took off for Louisiana with the Teiflebaum girl. I hated it, but there it is, and anyway— Well, I don't mind his being young enough to be my youngest son, but I was beginning to kind of mind being his mother. When I was a little girl, I saw an old George Arliss movie on TV; he played an Indian rajah who had tried to abduct an English girl for his harem, and after his plot was foiled, at the end of the picture, he said something that I identify with right now. He looked into the camera and lit a cigarette and said, "Ah, well. She would have been a damn nuisance anyhow."

All in all, it was a good group. I'm taking two weeks accumulated leave effective tomorrow. Then I'll be ready for the next one.

Let the Ants Try

In the late 1940s I worked in the advertising business for some years, largely at Popular Science Publishing Company, under a wonderful, tall, grave, intelligent man named George R. Spoerer. We lived about four blocks from each other in Greenwich Village and we both liked to walk, so when the weather was halfway decent we would walk home, and over three years I spent a lot of time with George in 45-minute strolling conversations.

One night he said, "Over the weekend I thought up a science-fiction story," and proceeded to tell me the story as we walked. "Good story," I said. "Why don't you write it?" "No," he said, "I want you to write it." After about six such exchanges I said I would, and I went home and that evening I did—and this is it.

Gordy survived the Three-Hour War, even though Detroit didn't; he was on his way to Washington, with his blueprints and models in his bag, when the bombs struck.

He had left his wife behind in the city, and not even a trace of her body was ever found. The children, of course, weren't as lucky as that. Their summer camp was less than 20 miles away, and unfortunately in the direction of the prevailing wind. But they were not in any pain until the last few days of the month they had left to live. Gordy managed to fight his way back through the snarled, frantic airline controls to them. Even though he knew they would certainly die of radiation sickness, and they suspected it, there was still a whole blessed week of companionship before the pain got too bad.

That was about all the companionship Gordy had for the whole year of 1960.

He came back to Detroit, as soon as the radioactivity had died down; he had nowhere else to go. He found a house on the outskirts of the city, and tried to locate someone to buy it from. But the Emergency Administration laughed at him. "Move in, if you're crazy enough to stay."

When Gordy thought about it all, it occurred to him that he was in a sort of state of shock. His fine, trained mind almost stopped functioning. He ate and slept, and when it grew cold he shivered and built fires, and that was all. The War Department wrote him two or three times, and finally a government man came around to ask what had happened to the things that Gordy had promised to bring to Washington. But he looked queerly at the pink, hairless mice that fed unmolested in the filthy kitchen, and he stood a careful distance away from Gordy's hairy face and torn clothes.

He said, "The Secretary sent me here, Mr. Gordy. He takes a personal interest in your discovery."

Gordy shook his head. "The Secretary is dead," he said. "They were all killed when Washington went."

"There's a new Secretary," the man explained. He puffed on his cigarette and tossed it into the patch Gordy was scrabbling into a truck garden. "Arnold Cavanagh. He knows a great deal about you, and he told me, 'If Salva Gordy has a weapon, we must have it. Our strength has been shattered. Tell Gordy we need his help.'"

Gordy crossed his hands like a lean Buddha.

"I haven't got a weapon," he said.

"You have something that can be used as a weapon. You wrote to Washington, before the war came, and said—"

"The war is over," said Salva Gordy. The government man sighed, and tried again, but in the end he went away. He never came back. The thing, Gordy thought, was undoubtedly written off as a crackpot idea after the man made his report; it was exactly that kind of a discovery, anyhow.

It was May when John de Terry appeared. Gordy was spading his garden. "Give me something to eat," said the voice behind Gordy's back.

Salva Gordy turned around and saw the small, dirty man

who spoke. He rubbed his mouth with the back of his hand.
"You'll have to work for it," he said.

"All right." The newcomer set down his pack. "My name is
John de Terry. I used to live here in Detroit."

Salva Gordy said, "So did I."

Gordy fed the man, and accepted a cigarette from him
after they had eaten. The first puffs made him light-headed
—it had been that long since he'd smoked—and through the
smoke he looked at John de Terry amiably enough. Company
would be all right, he thought. The pink mice had been company, of a sort; but it turned out that the mutation that made
them hairless had also given them an appetite for meat. And
after the morning when he had awakened to find tiny tooth-
marks in his leg, he'd had to destroy them. And there had
been no other animal since, nothing but the ants.

"Are you going to stay?" Gordy asked.

De Terry said, "If I can. What's your name?" When Gordy
told him, some of the animal look went out of his eyes, and
wonder took its place. "*Doctor* Salva Gordy?" he asked.
"Mathematics and physics in Pasadena?"

"Yes, I used to teach at Pasadena."

"And I studied there." John de Terry rubbed absently
at his ruined clothes. "That was a long time ago. You didn't
know me; I majored in biology. But I knew you."

Gordy stood up and carefully put out the stub of his cigarette. "It was too long ago," he said. "I hardly remember.
Shall we work in the garden now?"

Together they sweated in the spring sunlight that afternoon, and Gordy discovered that what had been hard work
for one man went quickly enough for two. They worked clear
to the edge of the plot before the sun reached the horizon.
John de Terry stopped and leaned on his spade, panting.

He gestured to the rank growth beyond Gordy's patch.
"We can make a bigger garden," he said. "Clear out that
truck, and plant more food. We might even—" He stopped.
Gordy was shaking his head.

"You can't clear it out," said Gordy. "It's rank stuff, a sort
of crabgrass with a particularly tough root. I can't even cut it.
It's all around here, and it's spreading."

De Terry grimaced. "Mutation?"

"I think so. And look." Gordy beckoned to the other man

and led him to the very edge of the cleared area. He bent down, picked up something red and wriggling between his thumb and forefinger.

De Terry took it from his hand. "Another mutation?" He brought the thing close to his eyes. "It's almost like an ant," he said. "Except—well, the thorax is all wrong. And it's soft-bodied." He fell silent, examining the thing.

He said something under his breath, and threw the insect from him. "You wouldn't have a microscope, I suppose? No—and yet, that thing is hard to believe. It's an ant, but it doesn't seem to have a tracheal breathing system at all. It's something different."

"Everything's different," Gordy said. He pointed to a couple of abandoned rows. "I had carrots there. At least, I thought they were carrots; when I tried to eat them they made me sick." He sighed heavily. "Humanity has had its chance, John," he said. "The atomic bomb wasn't enough; we had to turn everything into a weapon. Even I, I made a weapon out of something that had nothing to do with war. And our weapons have blown up in our faces."

De Terry grinned. "Maybe the ants will do better. It's their turn now."

"I wish it were." Gordy stirred earth over the boiling entrance to an anthole and watched the insects in their consternation. "They're too small, I'm afraid."

"Why, no. These ants are different, Dr. Gordy. Insects have always been small because their breathing system is so poor. But these are mutated. I think—I think they actually have lungs. They could grow, Dr. Gordy. And if ants were the size of men . . . they'd rule the world."

"Lunged ants!" Gordy's eyes gleamed. "Perhaps they will rule the world, John. Perhaps when the human race finally blows itself up once and for all . . ."

De Terry shook his head, and looked down again at his tattered, filthy clothes. "The next blow-up is the last blow-up," he said. "The ants come too late, by millions and millions of years."

He picked up his spade. "I'm hungry again, Dr. Gordy," he said.

They went back to the house and, without conversation, they ate. Gordy was preoccupied, and de Terry was too new in the household to force him to talk.

It was sundown when they had finished, and Gordy moved slowly to light a lamp. Then he stopped.

"It's your first night, John," he said. "Come down-cellar. We'll start the generator and have real electric lights in your honor."

De Terry followed the older man down a flight of stairs, groping in the dark. By candlelight they worked over a gasoline generator; it was stiff from disuse, but once it started it ran cleanly. "I salvaged it from my own," Gordy explained. "The generator—and that."

He swept an arm toward a corner of the basement. "I told you I invented a weapon," he added. "That's it."

De Terry looked. It was as much like a cage as anything, he thought—the height of a man and almost cubical. "What does it do?" he asked.

For the first time in months, Salva Gordy smiled. "I can't tell you in English," he said. "And I doubt that you speak mathematics. The closest I can come is to say that it displaces temporal coordinates. Is that gibberish?"

"It is," said de Terry. "What does it do?"

"Well, the War Department had a name for it—a name they borrowed from H. G. Wells. They called it a Time Machine." He met de Terry's shocked, bewildered stare calmly. "A time machine," he repeated. "You see, John, we can give the ants a chance after all, if you like."

Fourteen hours later they stepped into the cage, its batteries charged again and its strange motor whining . . .

And, forty million years earlier, they stepped out onto quaking, humid soil.

Gordy felt himself trembling, and with an effort managed to stop. "No dinosaurs or saber-toothed tigers in sight," he reported.

"Not for a long time yet," de Terry agreed. Then, "My Lord!"

He looked around him with his mouth open wide. There was no wind, and the air was warm and wet. Large trees were clustered quite thickly around them—or what looked like trees; de Terry decided they were rather some sort of soft-stemmed ferns or fungi. Overhead was deep cloud.

Gordy shivered. "Give me the ants," he ordered.

Silently de Terry handed them over. Gordy poked a hole

in the soft earth with his finger and carefully tilted the flask, dropped one of the ant queens he had unearthed in the back yard. From her belly hung a slimy mass of eggs. A few yards away—it should have been farther, he thought, but he was afraid to get too far from de Terry and the machine—he made another hole and repeated the process.

There were eight queens. When the eighth was buried he flung the bottle away and came back to de Terry.

"That's it," he said.

De Terry exhaled. His solemn face cracked in a sudden, embarrassed smile. "I—I guess I feel like God," he said. "Good Lord, Dr. Gordy! Talk about your great moments in history—this is all of them! I've been thinking about it, and the only event I can remember that measures up is the Flood. Not even that. We've created a race!"

"If they survive, we have." Gordy wiped a drop of condensed moisture off the side of his time machine and puffed. "I wonder how they'll get along with mankind," he said.

They were silent for a moment, considering. From somewhere in the fern jungle came a raucous animal cry. Both men looked up in quick apprehension, but moments passed and the animal did not appear.

Finally de Terry said, "Maybe we'd better go back."

"All right." Stiffly they climbed into the closet-sized interior of the time machine.

Gordy stood with his hand on the control wheel, thinking about the ants. Assuming that they survived—assuming that in 40,000,000 years they grew larger and developed brains —what would happen? Would men be able to live in peace with them? Would it—might it not make men brothers, joined against an alien race?

Might this thing prevent human war, and—his thoughts took an insane leap—could it have prevented the war that destroyed Gordy's family!

Beside him, de Terry stirred restlessly. Gordy jumped, and turned the wheel, and was in the dark mathematical vortex which might have been a fourth dimension.

They stopped the machine in the middle of a city, but the city was not Detroit. It was not a human city at all.

The machine was at rest in a narrow street, half blocking it. Around them towered conical metal structures, some of them a hundred feet high. There were vehicles moving in the street, one coming toward them and stopping.

"Dr. Gordy!" de Terry whispered. "Do you see them?"

Salva Gordy swallowed. "I see them," he said.

He stepped out of the time machine and stood waiting to greet the race to which he had given life.

For these were the children of ants in the three-wheeled vehicle. Behind a transparent windshield he could see them clearly.

De Terry was standing close behind him now, and Gordy could feel the younger man's body shaking. "They're ugly things," Gordy said mildly.

"Ugly! They're filthy!"

The antlike creatures were as big as a man, but hard-looking and as obnoxious as black beetles. Their eyes, Gordy saw with surprise, had mutated more than their bodies. For, instead of faceted insect eyes, they possessed iris, cornea and pupil—not round, or vertical like a cat's eyes, or horizontal like a horse's eyes, but irregular and blotchy. But they seemed like vertebrate's eyes, and they were strange and unnatural in the parchment blackness of an ant's bulged head.

Gordy stepped forward, and simultaneously the ants came out of their vehicle. For a moment they faced each other, the humans and the ants, silently.

"What do I do now?" Gordy asked de Terry over his shoulder.

De Terry laughed—or gasped. Gordy wasn't sure. "Talk to them," he said. "What else is there to do?"

Gordy swallowed. He resolutely did not attempt to speak in English to these creatures, knowing as surely as he knew his name that English—and probably any other language involving sound—would be incomprehensible to them. But he found himself smiling pacifically to them, and that was of course as bad . . . the things had no expressions of their own, that he could see, and certainly they would have no precedent to help interpret a human smile.

Gordy raised his hand in the semantically sound gesture of peace, and waited to see what the insects would do.

They did nothing.

Gordy bit his lip and, feeling idiotic, bowed stiffly to the ants.

The ants did nothing. De Terry said from behind, "Try talking to them, Dr. Gordy."

"That's silly," Gordy said. "They can't hear." But it was no sillier than anything else. Irritably, but making the words very clear, he said, "We . . . are . . . friends."

The ants did nothing. They just stood there, with the unwinking pupiled eyes fixed on Gordy. They didn't shift from foot to foot as a human might, or scratch themselves, or even show the small movement of human breathing. They just stood there.

"Oh, for heaven's sake," said de Terry. "Here, let me try."

He stepped in front of Gordy and faced the ant-things. He pointed to himself. "I am human," he said. "Mammalian." He pointed to the ants. "You are insects. That—" He pointed to the time machine—"took us to the past, where we made it possible for you to exist." He waited for reaction, but there wasn't any. De Terry clicked his tongue and began again. He pointed to the tapering metal structures. "This is your city," he said.

Gordy, listening to him, felt the hopelessness of the effort. Something disturbed the thin hairs at the back of his skull, and he reached absently to smooth them down. His hand encountered something hard and inanimate—not cold, but, like spongy wood, without temperature at all. He turned around. Behind them were half a dozen larger ants. Drones, he thought—or did ants have drones? "John," he said softly . . . and the inefficient, fragile-looking pincer that had touched him clamped his shoulder. There was no strength to it, he thought at once. Until he moved, instinctively, to get away, and then a thousand sharp serrations slipped through the cloth of his coat and into the skin. It was like catching oneself on a cluster of tiny fishhooks. He shouted, "John! Watch out!"

De Terry, bending low for the purpose of pointing at the caterpillar treads of the ant vehicle, straightened up, startled. He turned to run, and was caught in a step. Gordy heard him yell, but Gordy had troubles of his own and could spare no further attention for de Terry.

When two of the ants had him, Gordy stopped struggling. He felt warm blood roll down his arm, and the pain was like being flayed. From where he hung between the ants, he could see the first two, still standing before their vehicle, still motionless.

There was a sour reek in his nostrils, and he traced it to the ants that held him, and wondered if he smelled as bad to them. The two smaller ants abruptly stirred and moved forward rapidly on eight thin legs to the time machine. Gordy's captors turned and followed them, and for the first time since the scuffle he saw de Terry. The younger man was hanging limp from the lifted forelegs of a single ant, with two more standing guard beside. There was pulsing blood from a wound on de Terry's neck. Unconscious, Gordy thought mechanically, and turned his head to watch the ants at the machine.

It was a disappointing sight. They merely stood there, and no one moved. Then Gordy heard de Terry grunt and swear weakly. "How are you, John?" he called.

De Terry grimaced. "Not very good. What happened?"

Gordy shook his head, and sought for words to answer. But the two ants turned in unison from the time machine and glided toward de Terry, and Gordy's words died in his throat. Delicately one of them extended a foreleg to touch de Terry's chest.

Gordy saw it coming. "John!" he shrieked—and then it was all over, and de Terry's scream was harsh in his ear and he turned his head away. Dimly from the corner of his eye he could see the sawlike claws moving up and down, but there was no life left in de Terry to protest.

Salva Gordy sat against a wall and looked at the ants who were looking at him. If it hadn't been for that which was done to de Terry, he thought, there would really be nothing to complain about.

It was true that the ants had given him none of the comforts that humanity lavishes on even its criminals . . . but they had fed him, and allowed him to sleep—when it suited their convenience, of course—and there were small signs that they were interested in his comfort, in their fashion. When the pulpy mush they first offered him came up 30 minutes later, his multilegged hosts brought him a variety of foods, of which he was able to swallow some fairly palatable fruits. He was housed in a warm room, and, if it had neither chairs nor windows, Gordy thought, that was only because ants had no use for these themselves. And he couldn't ask for them.

That was the big drawback, he thought. That . . . and the memory of John de Terry.

He squirmed on the hard floor until his shoulderblades found a new spot to prop themselves against, and stared again at the committee of ants who had come to see him.

They were working an angular thing that looked like a camera—at least, it had a glittering something that might be a lens. Gordy stared into it sullenly. The sour reek was in his nostrils again . . .

Gordy admitted to himself that things hadn't worked out just as he had planned. Deep under the surface of his mind —just now beginning to come out where he could see it— there had been a furtive hope. He had hoped that the rise of the ants, with the help he had given them, would aid and speed the rise of mankind. For hatred, Gordy knew, started in the recoil from things that were different. A man's first enemy is his family—for he sees them first—but he sides with them against the families across the way. And still his neighbors are allies against the ghettos and Harlems of his town— and his town to him is the heart of the nation—and his nation commands life and death in war.

For Gordy, there had been a buried hope that a separate race would make a whipping-boy for the passions of humanity. And that, if there were struggle, it would not be between man and man, but between the humans . . . and the ants.

There had been this buried hope, but the hope was denied. For the ants simply had not allowed man to rise.

The ants put up their camera-like machine, and Gordy looked up in expectation. Half a dozen of them left, and two stayed on. One was the smallish creature with a bangle on the foreleg which seemed to be his personal jailer; the other a stranger to Gordy, as far as he could tell.

The two ants stood motionless for a period of time that Gordy found tedious. He changed his position, and lay on the floor, and thought of sleeping. But sleep would not come. There was no evading the knowledge that he had wiped out his own race—annihilated them by preventing them from birth, forty million years before his own time. He was like no other murderer since Cain, Gordy thought, and wondered that he felt no blood on his hands.

There was a signal that he could not perceive, and his guardian ant came forward to him, nudged him outward from the wall. He moved as he was directed—out the low exit-hole (he had to navigate it on hands and knees) and down a corridor to the bright day outside.

The light set Gordy blinking. Half blind, he followed the bangled ant across a square to a conical shed. More ants were waiting there, circled around a litter of metal parts. Gordy recognized them at once. It was his time machine, stripped piece by piece.

After a moment the ant nudged him again, impatiently, and Gordy understood what they wanted. They had taken the machine apart for study, and they wanted it put together again.

Pleased with the prospect of something to do with his fingers and his brain, Gordy grinned and reached for the curious ant-made tools . . .

He ate four times, and slept once, never moving from the neighborhood of the cone-shaped shed. And then he was finished.

Gordy stepped back. "It's all yours," he said proudly. "It'll take you anywhere. A present from humanity to you."

The ants were very silent. Gordy looked at them and saw drone-ants in the group, all still as statues.

"Hey!" he said in startlement, unthinking. And then the needle-jawed ant claw took him from behind.

Gordy had a moment of nausea—and then terror and hatred swept it away.

Heedless of the needles that laced his skin, he struggled and kicked against the creatures that held him. One arm came free, leaving gobbets of flesh behind, and his heavy-shod foot plunged into a pulpy eye. The ant made a whistling, gasping sound and stood erect on four hairy legs.

Gordy felt himself jerked a dozen feet into the air, then flung free in the wild, silent agony of the ant. He crashed into the ground, cowering away from the staggering monster. Sobbing, he pushed himself to his feet; the machine was behind him; he turned and blundered into it a step ahead of the other ants, and spun the wheel.

A hollow insect leg, detached from the ant that had been closest to him, was flopping about on the floor of the machine; it had been that close.

Gordy stopped the machine where it had started, on the same quivering, primordial bog, and lay crouched over the controls for a long time before he moved.

He had made a mistake, he and de Terry; there weren't any doubts left at all. And there was . . . there *might* be a way to right it.

He looked out at the Coal Measure forest. The fern trees were not the fern trees he had seen before; the machine had been moved in space. But the time, he knew, was identically the same; trust the machine for that. He thought: I gave the world to the ants, right here. I can take it back. I can find the ants I buried and crush them underfoot . . . or intercept myself before I bury them . . .

He got out of the machine, suddenly panicky. Urgency squinted his eyes as he peered around him.

Death had been very close in the ant city; the reaction still left Gordy limp. And was he safe here? He remembered the violent animal scream he had heard before, and shuddered at the thought of furnishing a casual meal to some dinosaur . . . while the ant queens lived safely to produce their horrid young.

A gleam of metal through the fern trees made his heart leap. Burnished metal here could mean but one thing—the machine!

Around a clump of fern trees, their bases covered with thick club mosses, he ran, and saw the machine ahead. He raced toward it—then came to a sudden stop, slipping on the damp ground. For there were *two* machines in sight.

The farther machine was his own, and through the screening mosses he could see two figures standing in it, his own and de Terry's.

But the nearer was a larger machine, and a strange design.

And from it came a hastening mob—not a mob of men, but of black insect shapes racing toward him.

Of course, thought Gordy, as he turned hopelessly to run—of course, the ants had infinite time to work in. Time enough to build a machine after the pattern of his own—and time to realize what they had to do to him, to insure their own race safety.

Gordy stumbled, and the first of the black things was upon him.

As his panicky lungs filled with air for the last time, Gordy knew what animal had screamed in the depths of the Coal Measure forest.

To See Another Mountain

When I wrote "To See Another Mountain," I had just got a new record player and some new records, including my first LP of the Mendelssohn Violin Concerto. (Actually his second, though only a few of us true-blue aficionados ever listen to his rather immature first.) My whole memory of writing the story is permeated with that lovely violin. That particular concerto happens to be my favorite, probably because one of the first real live concerts I ever attended featured it, played by Fritz Kreisler, fresh out of the hospital after being almost killed in a car accident and making his comeback. What an evening that was, with old Fritz staring out over packed Carnegie Hall and sawing away like a Vienna Woods carpenter, with a half smile on his face and the most beautiful sounds I had ever heard washing over us . . . So I had the concerto, I think it was Oistrakh's version, on the record player, and every time I came to a pause in the story I would get up and start it over again. I have always thought of it as the Mendelssohn story; and what astonishes me, reading it over now, is how little the concerto has to do with the story.

Trucks were coming up the side of the mountain again. The electric motors were quiet enough, but these were heavy-duty trucks and the reduction gears could be heard a mile off. A mile by air; that was 18 miles by the blacktop road that snaked up the side of the mountain, all hairpin curves with banks that fell away to sheer cliffs.

The old man didn't mind the noise. The trucks woke him up when he was dozing, as he so often was these days.

"You didn't drink your orange juice, Doctor."

The old man wheeled himself around in his chair. He liked the nurse. There were three who took care of him, on shifts, but Maureen Wrather was his personal favorite. She always seemed to be around when he needed her. He protested: "I drank most of it." The nurse waited. "All right." He drank it, noting that the flavor had changed again. What was it this time? Stimulants, tranquilizers, sedatives, euphoriants. They played him up and down like a yo-yo. "Do I get coffee this morning, Maureen?"

"Cocoa." She put the mug and a plate with two arrowroot cookies down on the table, avoiding the central space where he laid out his endless hands of solitaire; that was one of the things the old man liked about her. "I have to get you dressed in half an hour," she announced, "because you've got company coming."

"Company? Who would be coming to see me?" But he could see from the look in her light, cheerful eyes, even before she spoke, that it was a surprise. Well, thought the old man with dutiful pleasure, that was progress; only a few weeks ago they wouldn't have permitted him any surprises at all. Weeks? He frowned. Maybe months. All the days were like all the other days. He could count one, yesterday; two, the day before; three, last week—he could count a few simple intervals with confidence, but the ancient era of a month ago was a wash of gray confusion. He sighed. That was the price you paid for being crazy, he thought with amusement. They made it that way on purpose, to help him "get well." But it had all been gray and bland enough anyhow. Back *very* far ago there had been a time of terror, but then it was bland for a long, long time.

"Drink your cocoa, young fellow," the nurse winked, cheerfully flirting. "Do you want any music?"

That was a good game. "I want a lot of music," he said immediately. "Stravinsky—that *Sac* thing, I think. And Alban Berg. And—I know. Do you have that old one, 'The Three Itta Fishes?'" He had been very pleased with the completeness of the tape library in the house on the Hill, until he found out that there was something in that orange juice too. Every request of his was carefully noted and analyzed. Like the tiny microphones taped to throat and heart at night, his tastes in music were data in building up a picture of his condition. Well, that took some of the joy out of it, so the old man had added some other joy of his own.

The nurse turned solemnly to the tape player. There was a pause, a faint marking *beep* and then the quick running opening bars of the wonderful Mendelssohn concerto, which he had always loved. He looked at the nurse. "You shouldn't tease us, Doctor," she said lightly as she left.

Dr. Noah Sidorenko had changed the world. His Hypothesis of Congruent Values, later expanded to his Theory of General Congruences, was the basis for a technology fully as complex and even more important than the nucleonics that had come from Einstein's energy-mass equation. This morning the brain that had enunciated the principle of congruence was occupied in a harder problem: What were the noises from the courtyard?

He was going to have his picture taken, he guessed, taking his evidence from the white soft shirt the nurse had laid out for him, the gray jacket and, above all, from the tie. He almost never wore a tie. (The nurse seldom gave him one. He didn't like to speculate about the reasons for this.) While he was dressing, the trucks ground into the courtyard and stopped, and men's voices came clearly.

"I don't know who they are," he said aloud, abandoning the attempt to figure it out.

"They're the television crew," said the nurse from the next room. "Hush. Don't spoil your surprise."

He dressed quickly then, with excitement; why, it was a *big* surprise. There had never been a television crew on the mountain before. When he came out of the dressing room the nurse frowned and reached for his tie. "Sloppy! Why can't you large-domes learn how to do a simple knot?" She was a very sweet girl, the old man thought, lifting his chin to help. She could have been his daughter—even his granddaughter. She was hardly 25; yes, that would have been about right. His granddaughter would have been about that now—

The old man frowned and turned his head away. That was very wrong. He didn't have a grandchild. He had had one son, no more, and the boy had died, so they had told the old man, in the implosion of the Haaroldsen Free Trawl in the Mindanao Deep. The boy had been 19 years old, and

certainly without children; and there had been something
about his death, something that the old man didn't like to
remember. He squinted. Worse than that, he thought, something he *couldn't* remember any more.

The nurse said: "Doctor, this is for you. It isn't much, but
Happy Birthday."

She took a small pink-ribboned box out of the pocket of
her uniform and handed it to him. He was touched. He saw
his fingers trembling as he unwrapped the little package. That
distracted him for a moment but then he dismissed it. It was
honest emotion, that was all—well, and age too, of course.
He was 95. But it wasn't the worrying intention tremor that
had disfigured the few episodes he could remember clearly,
in his first days here on the Hill. It was only gratitude and
sentiment.

And that was what the box held for him, sentiment. "Thank
you, Maureen. You're good to an old man." His eyes stung. It
was only a little plastic picture-globe, with Maureen's young
face captured smiling inside it, but it was for him.

She patted his shoulder and said firmly: "You're a good
man. And a beautiful one, too, so come on and let's show
you off to your company."

She helped him into the wheelchair. It had its motors, but
he liked to have her push him and she humored him. They
went out the door, down the long sunlit corridors that di-
vided the guest rooms in the front of the building from the
broad high terrace behind. Sam Krabbe, Ernest Atkinson, and
a couple of the others from the Group came to the doors of
their rooms to nod, and to wish the old man a happy birthday.
Sidorenko nodded back, tired and pleased. He listened critically to the thumping of his heart—excitement was a risk, he
knew—and then grinned. He was getting as bad as the doctors.

Maureen wheeled the old man onto the little open elevator
platform. They dropped, quickly and smoothly on magnetic
cushions, to the lower floor. The old man leaned far over the
side of his chair, studying what he could see of the elevator,
because he had a direct and personal interest in it. Somebody had told him that the application of magnetic fields to
nonferrous substances was a trick that had been learned from
his General Congruences. Well, there was this much to it:
Congruence showed that all fields were related and inter-

changeable, and there was, of course, no reason why what was possible should not be made what is *so*. But the old man laughed silently inside himself. He was thinking of Albert Einstein confronted with a photo of *Enola Gay*. Or himself trying to build the communications equipment that Congruence had made possible.

The nurse wheeled him out into the garden.

And there before him was the explanation of the morning's trucks.

A whole mobile television unit had trundled up those terrible roads. And a fleet of cars and, yes, that other noise was explained, too; there was a helicopter perched on the tennis court, its vanes twisting like blown leaves in the breeze that came up the mountain. The helicopter had a definite meaning, the old man knew. Someone very important must have come up in it. The air space over the institute was closed off, by government order.

And reasoning the thing through, there was a logical conclusion; government orders can be set aside only by government executives, and—yes. There was the answer.

"Are you sure you're warm enough?" the nurse whispered. But Sidorenko hardly heard. He recognized the stocky blue-eyed man who stood chatting with one of the television crew. Sidorenko's contacts with the world around him were censored and small, but everyone would recognize *that* man. His name was Shawn O'Connor; he was the President of the United States.

The President was shaking his hand.

"Dear man," said President O'Connor warmly, "I can't tell you how great a pleasure this is for me. Oh, no. You wouldn't remember me. But I sat in on two of your Roose lectures. Ninety-eight, it must have been. And after the second I went up and got your autograph."

The old man shook hands and let go. 1998? Good lord, that was close to 50 years ago. True, he thought, cudgeling his memory, not very many persons had ever asked for the autograph of a mathematical physicist, but that was an endless time past. He had no recollection whatever of the event. Still, he remembered the lectures well enough. "Oh, of course," he said. "In Leeds Hall. Well, Mr. President, I'm not certain but—"

"Dear man," the President said cheerfully, "don't pretend. Whatever later honors I have attained, as an engineering sophomore I was an utterly forgettable boy. You must have met a thousand like me. But," he said, standing straighter, "you, Dr. Sidorenko, are another matter entirely. Oh, yes. You are probably the greatest man our country has produced in this century, and it is only the smallest measure of the esteem in which we hold you that I have come here today. However," he added briskly, "we don't want to spoil things for the cameramen, who will undoubtedly want to get all this on tape. So come over here, like a good fellow."

The old man blinked and allowed the cameramen to bully the President and himself into the best camera angles. One of them was whistling through his teeth, one was flirting with the nurse, but they were very efficient. The old man was trembling. All right, I'm 95, I'm entitled to a little senility, he thought; but was it that? Something was worrying him, nagging at his mind.

"Go ahead, Mr. President," called the director at last, and tailored men a blue and silver ribbon.

The camera purred faintly, adjusting itself to light and distance, and the President began to speak. "Dr. Sidorenko, Shawn O'Connor took from the hand of one of his alert, well-today's investiture is one of the most joyous occasions that has been my fortune—" Talk, talk, thought the old man, trying to listen, to identify the tune the cameraman had been whistling and to track down the thing that was bothering him all at once. He caught the President's merry blue eyes, now shadowed slightly as they looked at him, and realized he was trembling visibly.

Well, he couldn't *help* it, he thought resentfully. The body was shaking; the conscious mind had no control over it. He was ashamed and embarrassed, but even shame was a luxury he could only doubtfully afford. Something worse was very close and threatening to drown out mere shame, a touch of the crawling fear he had hoped never to feel again and had prayed not even to remember. He assumed a stiff smile.

"—of America's great men, who have received the honors due them. For this reason the Congress, by unanimous resolution of both Houses, has authorized me—"

The old man, chilled and shaking, remembered the name of the tune at last.

The bear went over the mountain,
The bear went over the mountain.
The bear went over the mountain—
And what do you think he saw?

It worried him, though he could not say why.

"—not only your scientific achievements which are honored, Dr. Sidorenko, great though these are. The truths you have discovered have brought us close to the very heart of the universe. The great inventions of our day rest in large part on the brilliant insight you have given our scientific workers. But more than that—"

Oh, stop, whispered the old man silently to himself, and he could feel his body vibrating uncontrollably. The President faltered, smiled, shrugged and began again: "More than that, your humanitarian love for all mankind is a priceless—"

Stop, whispered the old man again, and realized with horror that he was not whispering at all. He was screaming. "*Stop!*" he bawled, and found himself trying with withered muscles to stand erect on his useless feet. "*Stop!*" The cameras deserted the President and swung in to stare, with three great glassy eyes, at the old man; and for old Sidorenko terror struck in and fastened on him. Something erupted. Something exploding and bursting, like a crash of automobiles in flame; someone shouted near him with a voice that made him cringe. He saw the nurse run in with a hypodermic, and he felt its bite.

Endless hours later (though it took less than 60 seconds for the blood to pump the drug to his brain) he felt the falling, spiralling falling that he remembered from other needles at other times, and there was the one moment of clearness before sleep. Maureen was staring down at him, the needle still in her hand. "I'm sorry I spoiled the party, dear," he whispered, his eyes closing, and then he was firmly asleep.

It really wasn't worth the trouble. Why should they want to waste so much effort on curing him?

The nurse fussed: "There's nothing to worry about, Doctor. A fine, big man like you. Sure you had a bad spell. What's that? Do you think the President himself has never had a bad spell?"

"Why don't they leave me alone, Maureen?" he whispered.

"Leave you alone, is it! And you with twenty good years inside of you."

"You're a good girl, Maureen," he said faintly, hoarding his strength. It was really more than they had a right to expect of him, he thought drowsily. He couldn't afford many blow-ups like this morning's, and it seemed they were always happening. Still, it was nice of the President.

He was a little more alert now, the effects of the needle, and its later measured, balancing antidotes, beginning to wear off. This was Wednesday, he remembered. "Do I have to go in with the Group?" he whined.

"Doctor's orders, Doctor," she said firmly, "and doctor as you may be, you're not doctor enough to argue with doctor's orders." It was an old joke, limp to begin with, but he owed her a smile for it. He paid her, faintly.

After lunch she wheeled him into the Group meeting room. They were the last to arrive.

Sam Krabbe, said, surly as always in the Group though he was pleasant enough in social contacts, outside: "You take a lot of hostility out on us, Sidorenko. Why don't you try being on time?"

"Sam forgets," said the Reynolds woman to the air. "It isn't up to Sidorenko, as long as he and Maureen act out that master-slave thing of having her push his chair. If she doesn't want to pay us the courtesy of promptness, Sidorenko can't help it." Marla Reynolds had murdered her husband and four teenaged children; she had told the Group so at least 50 times. Sidorenko thought of her as the only legitimate lunatic the Group owned—except himself, of course; the old man kept an open mind about himself.

He struggled to hold his head up and his eyes open. You didn't get any benefit out of the Group's sessions unless you *participated*. The way to *participate* started with keeping the appearance of alertness and proceeded through talking (when you didn't really want to talk at all), to discharging emotion (when you were almost certain you had no emotion left to discharge). This he knew. Dr. Shugart had told him, in private analysis and again before the entire Group.

The old man sighed internally. Sam Krabbe could be relied on to interpret everyone's motives for them; he was doing it now. Short, squat, middle-aged . . . well, "middle-aged" by the standards of Dr. Sidorenko. Actually Sam Krabbe was

close to 70. Sidorenko glanced up at the attentive, involved
face of his nurse and let the conversation wash over him.

Sam: "What about that, Maureen? Do you have to focalize
your aggressions on us? I'm getting damned sick and tired of
it, for one."

Nelson Amster took over (35 years old, a bachelor, his life
a chain of false steps and embarrassments because he saw his
mother in every other female he met): "It's a stinking female
attention-getting device, Sam. Ignore it."

Marla Reynolds: "That's fine talk from a pantywaist like
you!"

Eddie Atkinson (glancing first at the bland face of Dr.
Shugart for a cue): "Come on, you old harpies. Give the girl
a break. What do you say, Dr. Shugart? Aren't they just dis-
placing their own hostilities onto Maureen and the doctor?"

Dr. Shugart, after a moment's pause: "Mmm. Maureen, do
you have a reaction to all this?"

Maureen, her eyes lively but her voice serious: "Oh, I'm
sorry if I've made trouble. I didn't think we were late. Honestly. If there was any displacement it was certainly on the
subconscious level. I *love* you all. I think you're the finest,
friendliest Group I ever—and—well, there just isn't any am-
bivalence at all. Honestly."

Dr. Shugart, nodding: "Mmm."

The old man turned restlessly in his chair. Pretty soon, he
thought with a familiar and tolerable ache, they would all
start looking at him and prodding him to *participate*. All but
Dr. Shugart, anyway; the psychiatrist didn't believe in prodding, except in a minor emergency as a device to pass along
the burden of talk from himself to one of the Group. (Though
he always said he was part of the Group, not its master: "The
analyst is only the senior patient. I learn much from our sessions.") But the others would prod, they had no such professional hesitations, and Sidorenko didn't like that. He was still
turning over inside himself the morning's fiasco; true, he
should voice it, that was what the Group was for; but the
old man had learned in nearly a century to live his life his
own certain way, and he wanted to think it out for himself
first. The best way to keep the Group off him was to volunteer
a small remark from time to time. He said at the first opportunity: "I'm sorry, ladies and gentlemen. I didn't mean to
upset you."

Everyone looked at him.

Ernie Atkinson scolded: "We're not here to apologize, Sidorenko. We only want you to know your *motives*."

Marla Reynolds: "One wonders if all of us know just why we *are* here? One wonders how the rest of us are to get proper attention, if some of us get first crack at the doctor's thought because they are more *important*."

Sidorenko said weakly: "Oh, Mrs. Reynolds—Marla—I'm sure there's nothing like that. Is there, Dr. Shugart?"

Dr. Shugart, pausing: "Mmm. Well, why *are* we here? Does anyone want to say?"

The old man opened his mouth and then closed it. Some evenings he joined with these youngsters in the Group, as demanding and competitive as any of them, but this was not one of the nights. Energy simply did not flow. Sidorenko was glad when Sam Krabbe took over the answer.

"We're here," said Sam pompously, "because we have problems which we haven't been able to solve alone. By Group sessions we help each other discharge our basic emotions where it is safe to do so, thus helping each other to reduce our problems to dimensions we can handle." He waited for agreement.

"Parrot!" smirked Ernie Atkinson.

"The doctor doesn't like our using pseudo-psychiatric double-talk," Marla Reynolds accused the air.

"All right, let's see you do better!" Sam flared.

"Gladly! Easily!" cried Atkinson. He hooked a thumb in his lapel and draped a leg over the arm of the chair. "The institution is a place where very special and very concentrated help can be given to a very few." ("Snob," Nelson Amster hissed.) "I'm not a snob! It's the plain truth. We get broad-spectrum therapy here, everything from hormones to hypnosynthesis. And the reason we get it is that we *deserve* it. Everybody knows Dr. Sidorenko. Amster created a whole new industry with mergers and stock manipulations. Marla Reynolds is one of the greatest composers—well, the greatest *woman* composers—of the century." ("Damn some people!" grated Marla). "And I myself—well, I need not go on. We are worth treating, all of us. At any cost. That's why the government put us here, in this very expensive, very thorough place."

"Mmm," said Dr. Shugart, and considered for a moment. "I wonder," he said.

Ernie Atkinson suddenly shrank a good two sizes. His dark little face turned sallow. The leg slid off the arm of the chair. "What's that, Doc?" he asked dismally.

Dr. Shugart said: "I wonder if that's a *personal* motivation."

"Oh, I see," cried Atkinson, "it's what *each* of us is here for that's important, eh? Well, what about it? How about your motivations, Sidorenko?"

The old man coughed.

It always came to this, reliably. He would put out the weak decoy remarks but it would do no good, one of the Group would pounce past the decoys to reach his flesh. Well, there was no fighting it.

"I—" he began, and stopped, and passed a hand over his face. Maureen was close beside him, her eyes warm and intent. "I know I shouldn't apologize," he apologized, "but it has been a bad day. You know about it. The thing is, I'm an old man, and even Dr. Shugart tells me that the old cells aren't in quite the shape they used to be. There was," he said mildly, as though he were reading off a dossier from a statistical sample, "a stroke a few years ago. Fortunately it limited itself; they're not operable, you know, when you get to a certain age. The blood vessels turn into a kind of rotten canvas and, although you can clamp off the hemorrhage, it only makes it pop again on the other side of the clamp, and —I'm wandering. I apologize," he finished wryly.

"Mmm," Dr. Shugart said. "There's no such thing as totally undirected speech."

"Of course. All right. But that's why I apologize, because I'm not getting around very rapidly to an answer.

"I had my—trouble—a few years ago. I don't remember much about it, except that I gather I was delusional. Thought I was God, was the way it was expressed to me once. Well, if I had been a younger man I suppose I could have been treated more easily. I don't know. I'm not. Time was, I know, when most doctors wouldn't bother with a man of ninety-five, even if he did happen to be," he said wryly, "celebrated not only for his scientific attainments but for his broad love for mankind. I mean, there's a point of obsolescence. Might as well let the old fool die."

He choked and coughed raspingly for a second. The nurse reached for him, but he waved her off.

"Mmm," said Dr. Shugart.

And the nurse whispered in a hard bright voice: "I love you, Noah Sidorenko."

He sat up straight, suddenly struck to the heart.

"I love you," she said stubbornly, "and I'll *make* you get well. It can't hurt you if I tell you I love you. I'm not asking for anything. It's a free gift."

The old man swallowed.

"Don't argue with me, old sport," she said tenderly, and patted his creased cheek. "Now, how about some psychodrama? Let's do the big one! The slum you lived in, Doctor —remember? The night you were so scared. The accident. Stretch out," she ordered, wheeling him to a couch and helping him onto it. He went along, dazed. She scolded: "No, curl up more. You're four years old, remember? Marla, pull that chair over and be the mother. Ernie, Sam. Let's go out in the hall. We'll be cars speeding along the elevated highway outside the window. And let's make some noise! Honk, honk! Aooga!"

But it hadn't been like that at all, he told himself a few hours later, trying to go to sleep. It had been a big frightening experience in his childhood. Very possibly it was the thing that had caused his later troubles (though he couldn't remember the troubles well enough to be sure). But it was not what they were portraying in psychodrama. They were showing a frightened child, and the old man was stubbornly certain there was more to it than that. But very likely it was lost forever.

It was only natural that at the age of 95 a great many experiences should be lost forever. (Such as meeting a sophomore who asked for an autograph, when you could have had no idea that the sophomore would grow up to be President.)

He thought of the white man, wondered who the white man was, and shifted restlessly in the bed. He could feel his old muscles tensing up.

Curse the fool thing, the old man said to himself, referring to his own body; it has lost the knack of living. But it wasn't the body that was at fault, really. It was the brain. The body was only crepe and brittle sticks, true, but the heart still beat, blood flowed, stomach acids leached the building-blocks they needed from the food he ate. The body worked. But the brain worked against it; it was brain, not body, that tautened his muscles and shortened his breath.

That fantastic girl, the old man thought ruefully, she had said: *I love you.* Well. Let's interpret what she *meant*, he commanded, it could only have been an expression of the natural affection a nurse has for a patient. Still, it was ridiculous, the old man told himself, striving to catch a free and comfortable breath.

That was the worst thing about the tension. You couldn't breathe. With much effort Noah Sidorenko wedged his elbows under him and raised his chest cage a trifle, not quite off the mattress, but resting lightly on it, relieving some of the pressure his shriveled body exerted. It helped, but it didn't help enough. He thought wistfully of free-fall. Rocket jockies, he dreamed, floated endlessly with no pressure at all; how *deeply* they must be able to breathe! But, of course, he couldn't live to get there, not through rocket acceleration.

He was wandering, when he wanted most particularly to think clearly.

He turned on one side and pressed the tip of his nose lightly with a finger. Sometimes opening the nostrils wide helped to get a breath. He thought of what the microphones taped to rib and throat must be recording, and grinned faintly. Funny, though, he thought, that Maureen hadn't come in to check on him. The purpose of the microphones was to warn the nurse when he needed attention. Surely he needed attention now.

He listened critically to his thumping heart. Ka-*bump*, ka-*bump*, ka-*bump*. It made a little tune:

The *bear went over* the *moun*-tain

The song was very disturbing to him, though he did not even now know why. Somehow it was connected with that scene in his youth, the crashing cars and the white man. The old man sighed. He had come very close to remembering all of it once. They had put him in silence. "Silence" was an acoustically dead chamber, 20 feet cubed, hung with muffling fabric and strung with spiderwebs of the felt; there was no echo and no sound from outside could come in. It was a conventional tool of study for mental disorders; strapped in a canvas cot, hung in the center of the cube, eyes closed, hearing deadened, a subject began very quickly to seek within himself. Fantasies came, delusions came. And ultimately knowledge came, if the subject could stand it; but three out of five reached hysteria before they reached any worthwhile insight, and the old man was one of the three. He had nearly died . . .

He paused to count the times he had nearly died under therapy of one kind or another, but it was too hard. And besides, he was beginning to think that he was nearly dying again. He pushed himself back on his elbows and fought once more for breath.

This one was very bad.

He slumped back on the bed and reached out for the intercom button. "Maureen," he whispered.

She slept in the room next to him, and though he seldom woke in the night—there was something in the evening cocoa to make sure of that—when it happened that he did, if he called, she was there promptly, sometimes in a pink wrapper, once or twice in lounging pajamas. But not tonight. "Maureen," he whispered to the intercom again, but there was no answer.

The old man, with an effort, rolled onto his side. The movement dislodged one of the taped microphones. He felt it tear his skin and, simultaneously, heard the sharp alarm *ping* in Maureen's room. But the alarm didn't bring her.

The old man opened his eyes wide and stared at the intercom. "I have to get up," he told it reasonably, "because if I lie here I think I will die."

It was impossible, of course. But what could he lose by trying? He pushed himself to the edge of the bed. The chair was within reach, but very remote to Noah Sidorenko, who had not stood on his own feet in years . . .

And then he was in the chair. Somehow he had made it! He sat erect and gasping, for a moment. The pain was bad, but it was better sitting up. Then his hand found the buttons of the little electric motors.

He spun slowly, navigated the straits between the nurse's desk and the corner of the bed, went out the door, as it opened quietly before him.

Maureen's room was empty. The outer door opened, too.

That was good, he thought; he hadn't been sure it would open; it was never very clear to him whether he was a prisoner or not. It was, after all, a sort of madhouse he was in . . . But it opened.

The hall was empty and silent. He listened for the familiar *grunch, grunch* of Ernie Atkinson grinding his teeth in his sleep, but even that was stilled tonight. He rolled on. The lift rose silently to meet him.

He let it carry him gently down, and turned inward. The lower hall was blindingly bright. He made his way to Dr. Shugart's office.

He paused. There were voices.

No wonder he hadn't heard Ernie Atkinson's grinding teeth! Here was Atkinson, his voice coming plain as day: "I don't care what you say, we weren't getting through to him. No. The Group and psychodrama aren't working."

And Dr. Shugart's voice: "They *have* to work." Yes, the old man thought dazedly, it was Shugart's voice all right. But where was the hesitation, the carefully balanced, noncommittal air? It cracked sharp as a whip!

And Maureen's voice: "Do I have to go on building up this emotional involvement with him?"

Shugart crackled: "Is it so distasteful?"

"Oh, no!" (The old man sighed. He found he had stopped breathing until she answered.) "He's an old dear, and I *do* love him. But I'd like to give him little presents because I want to, not because it's part of his therapy."

Shugart rasped: "It's for his own good. This is one of the finest brains in the world, and it's falling apart. We've tried everything. Radical procedures—silence, psychosurgery, chemotherapy—are too much for him to take. Remember what happened when Dr. Reynolds tried electroshock? So we've got to work with what we've got."

The old man stirred.

Old as he might be, and insane if they liked, but he wasn't going to linger out here and listen. A quarter after one in the morning, and the whole Institute was gathered here in Shugart's office, plotting the recovery of himself.

"All right," he gasped, rolling in, "what *is* this?"

They gaped at him.

"All of you!" he said strongly. "What are you doing to me? Is it a hoax?"

Shugart moved restlessly. Marla Reynolds reached up to pat her hair, avoiding his eyes.

"You, *Doctor* Reynolds? Want to explain? I mean—I mean," he said in a changed tone, no longer gasping, "there seems to be only one explanation. There's a conspiracy of some sort, and I'm the target."

Maureen got up and walked toward him. "Come in, Doctor," she said, in a voice of resignation tinged with pleasure. "Maybe it's better this way. We're not going to get very far continuing to lie to you, are we? So I guess we'll have to tell you the truth."

The tune rocked crazily through his head. The old man spun his chair and turned pleadingly to Maureen. "Of course, Doctor," she said, understanding without words, and fetched him a fizzy drink. "Only a little stimulant," she coaxed.

The old man glanced at Dr. Shugart. Shugart laughed. "Who do you think has been prescribing for you? There isn't a human being in the Institute without a first-rate degree. Maureen's our internist—*with*, of course, a thorough grounding in psychology."

The old man drank reproachfully, looking at Maureen. She said, clouding: "I know. It isn't fair, but we had to get you well."

"*Why?*"

Maureen said somberly: "A brain like yours doesn't come along too often. I'm not a physicist, but as I understand it Congruence comes close to doing what Einstein tried with the unified field theory. You were on the point of doing something more when you—when you—"

"When I went crazy," the old man said crudely. She shook her head. "All right, I used a bad word. But that's it, isn't it?" The girl nodded. "I see."

But the stimulant wasn't doing much good. Ninety-five years, he thought confused, and perhaps I won't see that other mountain. It was hard to accept, hard to believe he had been hoaxed, hard to believe that it wasn't working, that the delusions would not be cured. "I'm flattered," he whispered hoarsely, and tried to hand the glass back to Maureen. It clattered to the floor and bounced without breaking. Marla with her schizoid detachment, Ernie with his worries, Sam Krabbe and his surly anger—doctors acting parts? The room swooped around Sidorenko; he was cut off from his reference points. And they were all afraid; he could see it, it was a gamble they had taken, that he would never find out, and now they didn't know what would happen. And he—

He didn't know either.

"I'm sorry to be so much trouble," he gasped.

"You mustn't feel personal guilt," Dr. Shugart said anxiously. "These personality disorders—personality *traits*—go with greatness. Sir Oliver Lodge swore he believed in levitation. Think of Newton, sleepless and paranoid. Think of Einstein. Religious mania is very common," the doctor assured him, "and you were spared that, at least. Well, almost—of course, certain aspects of your—"

"Shut up!" cried Maureen, and reached for the old man's wrist. He stared up at her, touched by the worry in her face, trying to find words to tell her there was nothing to worry about, nothing to fear. He felt his heart lunging against his ribs and his breathing seemed, oddly, to have stopped. He made a convulsive effort and drew an enormous, loud breath. Why, that was almost—what did they call it?—a death rattle. He did it again.

"Doctor!" moaned the nurse, but he found the strength to shake his wrist free of her. This was interesting. He was beginning to remember something, or to imagine something—

They were all coming toward him.

"Leave me alone," he croaked. He held them off while he practiced breathing again; it wasn't hard; he could do it. He closed his eyes. He heard Maureen catch her breath and opened them to glare at her, then closed them again.

Noah Sidorenko's brain was perfectly lucid.

He saw—or remembered? But it was as though he were seeing it with an internal eye—all of his previous life, the childhood, the government office where he had received the first scholarship, the four professors quizzing him for his doctor's, even the cloudy days of therapy and breakdown.

The old man thought: It all began 90 years ago, I was all right until then . . . and he had to laugh, though laughing choked him, because 90 years ago he had been all of five years old. But up until then there had been nothing to worry about.

Was it the crash? Yes. And fire. The white man. The song about the bear. The terrible auto smash, just outside his window—for his window had looked out on an elevated automobile highway in Brooklyn, the Gowanus Parkway, where cars raced bumper to bumper, 50 miles an hour, within five yards of the bed he slept in. *Whoosh. Whoosh.* All day long and all night. At night the strokes were slow, a lagging wire-brush riff; in the mornings and evenings they were faster, *whooshwhooshwhoosh,* a quick rataplan. He listened to them and dreamed tunes around them. And there was the night he had gone to sleep and wakened screaming, screaming.

His mother rushed in—poor woman, she was already widowed. (Though she was only 25, the old man thought with amazement. Twenty-five! Maureen was that.) She rushed in, and though the boy Noah was terrified he could see through the shadow of his own terror of hers. "Momma, Momma, the white man!" She caught him in her arms. "Please, my God, what's the matter?" But he couldn't answer, except with sobs and incoherent words about the white man; it was a code, and she was not skilled to read it. And time passed, ten minutes or so. He was not comforted—he was still crying and afraid—but his mother was warm and she soothed him. She bounced him on her knee, ka-*bump,* ka-*bump,* ka-*bump,* and even though he was crying he remembered the song with that beat, *He SAW anOTHer MOUNTain, he SAW anOTHer MOUNTain,* and the cars whooshed by and in the next room the little TV set murmured and laughed. "You're missing your program, Momma," he said; "Go to sleep, dear," she answered; he was almost relaxed. *Crash.* Outside the window two cars collided violently. A taxicab was bound for New York with a boy in a satin jacket at the wheel and four others crammed in the back; the boy at the wheel was high on marijuana and he hit the divider. The cab leaped crazily across into the Long Island-bound lane. There was not much traffic that night, but there was one car too many. In it a 30-year-old advertising salesman rushed to meet his wife and baby at Idlewild. He never met them. The cars struck. The stolen taxicab was hurled back into its own lane, its gas tank split, its doors flung open. Four boys in the jackets of the Gerritsen Tigers died at once and the fifth was thrown against the retaining wall—not dead; but not with enough life left to him to matter. He stood up and tried to run, and the burning gasoline made him a white-hot phantom, auraed and terrible. He lurched clear across the roadway to just outside Noah's window and died there, flaming, hanging over the wall, 15 feet above the wreck of the space salesman's convertible.

"The white man!" screamed someone in Noah's room, but it was not the boy but his mother. She looked from the white-flamed man outside to her son, with eyes of fear and horror; and from then on it was never the same for him.

"From the time I was five," the old man said aloud, wondering, "it was never the same. She thought I was—I don't know. A devil. She thought I had the power of second sight, because I'd been scared by the accident before it happened."

He looked around the room. "And my son!" he cried. "I knew when he died—telepathy, at a distance of a good eight thousand miles. And—" he stopped, thinking. "There were other things," he mumbled . . .

Dr. Shugart fussed kindly: "Impossible, don't you see? It's all part of your delusion. Surely a scientist should know that this—*witchcraft* can't be true! If only you hadn't come down here tonight, when you were so close to a cure . . ."

Noah Sidorenko said terribly: "Do you want to cure me again?"

"Doctor!"

The old man shouted: "You've done it a hundred times, and a hundred times, with pain and fear, I've had to undo the cure—not because I want to! My *God*, no. But because I can't help myself. And now you want me to go through it again. I won't let you cure me!" He pushed the electric buttons; the chair began to spin but too slowly, too slowly. The old man fought his way to his feet, shouting at them. "Don't you see? I don't want to do this, but it does itself; it's like a baby that's getting born, I can't stop it now. It's *difficult* to have a baby. A woman in labor," he cried, seeing the worry in their eyes, knowing he must seem insane, "a woman in labor is having a fit, she struggles and screams—and what can a doctor do for her? Kill the pain? Yes, and perhaps kill the baby with it. That happened, over and over, until the doctors learned how, and—and you don't know how . . .

"*You mustn't kill it this time!* Let me suffer. Don't cure me!"

And they stood there looking at him. No one spoke at all.

The room was utterly silent; the old man asked himself, Can I have convinced them? But that was so improbable. His words were such poor substitutes for the thoughts that raced about his thumping head. But—the thoughts, yes, they were clear now; maybe for the first time. He understood. Psionic power, telepathy, precognition, all the other hard-to-handle gifts that filled the gap between metaphysics and muscle . . . they lay next door to madness. Worse! By definition, they *were* "madness", as a diamond can be "dirt" if it clogs the jet of a rocket. They were mad, since they didn't fit self-defining "sane" science.

But how many times he had come so close, all the same! And how often, how helpfully, he had been "cured." The delusional pattern had been so clear to "sane" science; and with insulin shock and hypnosynthesis, with electrodes in his shaved scalp and psychodrama, with Group therapy and the silence—with every pill and incantation of the sciences of the mind they had, time after time, rooted out the devils. Precognition had been frightened out of him by his mother's panic. Telepathy had been electroshocked out of him in the Winford Retreat. But they returned and returned.

Handle them? No, the old man admitted, he couldn't handle them, not yet. But if God was good and gave him more time, an hour or two perhaps . . . or maybe some years; if the doctor was improperly kind and allowed him his "delusion"—why, he might learn to handle them after all. He might, for example, be able to peer into minds at will and not only when some randomly chosen mind, half-shattered itself, created such a clamorous beacon of noise that then the (telepathically) nearly deaf might hear it. He might be able to stare into the future at will, instead of having his attention chance-caught by the flicker of some catastrophic terror projecting its shadow ahead. And this ancient and useless hulk that was his body, for example. He might yet force it to live, to move, to walk about, to stand—

To stand?

The old man stood perfectly motionless beside his chair. To stand? And then, rather late, he followed the direction of the staring eyes of Maureen and Shugart and the others.

He *was* standing.

But not as he had visioned it, in wretched bedridden hours. He was standing tall and straight; but between the felt soles of his slippers and the rubber tiles of the office floor there were eight inches of untroubled air.

No. They wouldn't cure him again, not ever. And with luck, he realized slowly, he might now proceed to infect the world.

The Deadly Mission of Phineas Snodgrass

When I was still in my teens, L. Sprague de Camp published a wonderful novel called Lest Darkness Fall, *which had to do with a man who was thrust back through time into the years just before Rome fell to the barbarians, and through skill and sagacity averted that fall and, thus, the Dark Ages. This is both a sort of belated rejoinder to de Camp and a snap at the heels of the pronatalists and other sweet, dangerous people who believe that there is some way of dealing with the world's ills that does not include population limitation.*

This is the story of Phineas Snodgrass, inventor. He built a time machine.

He built a time machine and in it he went back some two thousand years, to about the time of the birth of Christ. He made himself known to the Emperor Augustus, his lady Livia and other rich and powerful Romans of the day and, quickly making friends, secured their cooperation in bringing about a rapid transformation of Year One living habits. (He stole the idea from a science-fiction novel by L. Sprague de Camp, called *Lest Darkness Fall*.)

His time machine wasn't very big, but his heart was, so Snodgrass selected his cargo with the plan of providing the maximum immediate help for the world's people. The principal features of ancient Rome were dirt and disease, pain and death. Snodgrass decided to make the Roman world healthy and to keep its people alive through twentieth-century medicine. Everything else could take care of itself, once the human race was free of its terrible plagues and early deaths.

Snodgrass introduced penicillin and aureomycin and painless dentistry. He ground lenses for spectacles and explained the surgical techniques for removing cataracts. He taught anesthesia and the germ theory of disease, and showed how to purify drinking water. He built Kleenex factories and taught the Romans to cover their mouths when they coughed. He demanded, and got, covers for the open Roman sewers, and he pioneered the practice of the balanced diet.

Snodgrass brought health to the ancient world, and kept his own health, too. He lived to more than a hundred years. He died, in fact, in the year A.D. 100, a very contented man.

When Snodgrass arrived in Augustus's great palace on the Palatine Hill, there were some 250,000,000 human beings alive in the world. He persuaded the principate to share his blessings with all the world, benefiting not only the hundred million subjects of the Empire, but the other one hundred millions in Asia and the tens of millions in Africa, the Western Hemisphere and all the Pacific islands.

Everybody got healthy.

Infant mortality dropped at once, from 90 deaths in a hundred to fewer than two. Life expectancies doubled immediately. Everyone was well, and demonstrated their health by having more children, who grew in health to maturity and had more.

It is a feeble population that cannot double itself every generation if it tries.

These Romans, Goths, and Mongols were tough. Every 30 years the population of the world increased by a factor of two. In the year A.D. 30, the world population was a half billion. In A.D. 60, it was a full billion. By the time Snodgrass passed away, a happy man, it was as large as it is today.

It is too bad that Snodgrass did not have room in his time machine for the blueprints of cargo ships, the texts on metallurgy to build the tools that would make the reapers that would harvest the fields—for the triple-expansion steam turbines that would generate the electricity that would power the machines that would run the cities—for all the technology that 2,000 subsequent years had brought about.

But he didn't.

Consequently, by the time of his death conditions were no longer quite perfect. A great many were badly housed.

On the whole, Snodgrass was pleased, for all these things could surely take care of themselves. With a healthy world population, the increase of numbers would be a mere spur to research. Boundless nature, once its ways were studied, would surely provide for any number of human beings.

Indeed it did. Steam engines on the Newcomen design were lifting water to irrigate fields to grow food long before his death. The Nile was dammed at Aswan in the year 55. Battery-powered streetcars replaced oxcarts in Rome and Alexandria before A.D. 75, and the galley slaves were freed by huge, clumsy diesel outboards that drove the food ships across the Mediterranean a few years later.

In the year A.D. 200 the world had now something over twenty billion souls, and technology was running neck-and-neck with expansion. Nuclear-driven ploughs had cleared the Teutoburg Wald, where Varus's bones were still mouldering, and fertilizer made from ion-exchange mining of the sea produced fantastic crops of hybrid grains. In A.D. 300 the world population stood at a quarter of a trillion. Hydrogen fusion produced fabulous quantities of energy from the sea; atomic transmutation converted any matter into food. This was necessary, because there was no longer any room for farms. The Earth was getting crowded. By the middle of the sixth century the 60,000,000 square miles of land surface on the Earth was so well covered that no human being standing anywhere on dry land could stretch out his arms in any direction without touching another human being standing beside him.

But everyone was healthy, and science marched on. The seas were drained, which immediately tripled the available land area. (In 50 years the sea bottoms were also full.) Energy which had come from the fusion of marine hydrogen now came by the tapping of the full energy output of the Sun, through gigantic "mirrors" composed of pure force. The other planets froze, of course; but this no longer mattered, since in the decades that followed they were disintegrated for the sake of the energy at their cores. So was the Sun. Maintaining life on Earth on such artificial standards was prodigal of energy consumption; in time every star in the Galaxy was transmitting its total power output to the Earth, and plans were afoot to tap Andromeda, which would care for all necessary expansion for—30 years.

At this point a calculation was made.

Taking the weight of the average man at about a hundred and thirty pounds—in round numbers, 6×10^4 grammes—and allowing for a continued doubling of population every 30 years (although there was no such thing as a "year" anymore, since the Sun had been disintegrated; now a lonely Earth floated aimlessly towards Vega), it was discovered that by the year 1970 the total mass of human flesh, bone, and blood would be 6×10^{27} grammes.

This presented a problem. The total mass of the Earth itself was only 5.98×10^{27} grammes. Already humanity lived in burrows penetrating crust and basalt and quarrying into the congealed nickel-iron core; by 1970 all the core itself would have been transmuted into living men and women, and their galleries would have to be tunnelled through masses of their own bodies, a writhing, squeezed ball of living corpses drifting through space.

Moreover, simple arithmetic showed that this was not the end. In finite time the mass of human beings would equal the total mass of the Galaxy; and in some further time it would equal and exceed the total mass of *all* galaxies everywhere.

This state of affairs could no longer be tolerated, and so a project was launched.

With some difficulty resources were diverted to permit the construction of a small but important device. It was a time machine. With one volunteer aboard (selected from the 900 trillion who applied) it went back to the year 1. Its cargo was only a hunting rifle with one cartridge, and with that cartridge the volunteer assassinated Snodgrass as he trudged up the Palatine.

To the great (if only potential) joy of some quintillions of never-to-be-born persons, Darkness blessedly fell.

Golden Ages Gone Away

This is a sort of reminiscence of what the world of science fiction has been like over the last 30 or 40 years —or at least, that part of it that I inhabited. We are all being encouraged to write our autobiographies these days —it is part of the "age of respectability"—and some of us are proving very easy to persuade. By publishing this short sketch here, I hope to postpone my own succumbing by at least, oh, umm, maybe a month.

When the Apollo 15 astronauts landed on the moon they named craters after characters and scenes in stories by Ray Bradbury, Arthur Clarke, Heinlein, Verne, Frank Herbert, and E. E. Smith. University libraries beg the privilege of collecting the papers of science-fiction writers. Routinely we get called on to keynote a scientific gathering or advise large corporations on how to run their affairs. We are very Establishment, these days. So much so that when I teach my college course in science fiction and divide the history of sf into four eras, the name I use for the present stage is the Age of Respectability.

It was not always thus. Time was when science fiction was one pulp category out of a dozen, no more respectable than sports or horror, nowhere near as financially successful as the detectives and the westerns. The magazines typically had names like *Thrilling Wonder Stories* or *Super Science Stories*. The covers matched the titles. A typical scene would be a fire-eyed monster covered with green scales, crashing through the window of a spaceship intent on the rape of a terror-stricken blonde in a stainless-steel bra.

How did we get from *there* to *here*?

It was not a straight line. It was a couple of quantum jumps that really didn't seem like much at the time to us who lived through them (is a germ in an astronaut's bloodstream aware that he has gone to the moon and back?), but have come since to be looked on as golden ages in science fiction. For the world in general these golden ages were gritty, troublesome times; one coincided with the buildup and first disastrous years of the second World War, the other with the sullen McCarthy period in the United States; there was little joy in either, for most people. But for science fiction they were yeasty times . . .

As far as I am concerned, the first golden age began around 1937. Probably the dating is personal to me; it happens that 1937 was when I first made a professional appearance, with a poem in *Amazing Stories*. But that's close enough, and all the dates are a little fuzzy. (Even that date, because as it happens I wrote the poem in 1935, and it was accepted in 1936, and published in 1937—and paid for in 1938, because that was how things went in those days.) It was around that time, at any rate, that John Campbell took over *Astounding Stories* from F. Orlin Tremaine; the Thrilling Group's editorial collective of Leo Margulies, Mort Weisinger, and others had replaced father figure Hugo Gernsback himself on *Wonder Stories;* Raymond A. Palmer was about to acquire *Amazing Stories* from white-bearded T. O'Conor Sloane, Ph.D. And then or in the next couple of years, writers like Theodore Sturgeon, Robert A. Heinlein, Isaac Asimov, Ray Bradbury, and a dozen others, better known or less, were about to make their debuts.

It wasn't only in the titles and the covers of the magazines that science fiction was a different breed of cat then. The craftsmanship was poorer. Thematically, it was limited. Large areas of discussion common in today's science fiction simply did not then exist: race, for one. If a black man appeared in a 1937 sf story he was likely to be either a villain or a shambling Stepin Fetchit figure of low comedy—or if neither of those, he was certain to come from Mars. Sex was a dirty word. It existed on the covers, but inside the magazines it was important mostly for its consequences: usually a state of mind which caused the principal boy to invent space travel so that he could win the principal girl. What he did with her after he won her was not described.

These were areas of science fiction which were not explored because they were off limits. There were other areas, and more important ones, which writers did not investigate because they didn't know they were there. In sf as in any other creative effort, today's practitioners stand on the shoulders of their predecessors. None of the kinds of sf that we write today fell as a gift from heaven. Each was given to us by some single writer somewhere in the world who woke up one morning and proceeded to invent a new kind of sf story, and some of them were just doing the inventing at that time. Their insights and innovations provided capital on which all of us have since drawn.

For instance, there was A. E. Van Vogt, a young Canadian who had been reading science fiction for some time and, at the age of 27, decided he could do as well as the published writers. He was right. His first stories included "Black Destroyer" and "Discord in Scarlet," and with them he was an immediate success. The impact of "Discord in Scarlet" was perhaps helped along by the otherwise irrelevant fact that at the time the advertising department of *Astounding* was playing with two-color printing on a few pages, as a ploy to lure in advertisers, and so some of the pictures for "Scarlet" were scarlet—we will see again how front-office decisions have had large effects on science fiction—but they would have been hits anyway. Van Vogt had enlarged the canvas for everyone with his alien protagonists. Other writers had invented aliens —Wells made them real in *The War of the Worlds*, Weinbaum made them personalities in *A Martian Odyssey*—but Van Vogt's aliens carried the whole story; we saw events through their eyes and discovered that to them Earthmen were aliens.

Then there was that former bulldozer artist, hotel clerk, and would-be trapeze artist (he gave it up after six years' training, figuring that if he hadn't caught on by then he must be in the wrong line of work), Theodore Sturgeon. He started slow with a smart-alecky little joke piece called "Ether Breather," but before long he found a line of country all his own, with stories like "Killdozer" and "Microcosmic God" and dozens more. Sturgeon once said that all of his stories were about a single subject and that subject was love. What most writers have to say about their own work is interesting only to psychologists, but there is truth to this statement; he did indeed bring into science fiction a sort of tenderness and compassion which was very much his own—but which, too, has become a part of the repertoire for a hundred writers since.

Then there were L. Sprague de Camp and Robert A. Heinlein. I link them together because in their early work at least they were rather alike, and quite different from anybody else. Their heroes were not aliens or supermen. They were not even heroes. They were the kind of fellow who pumped your gas at any crossroads filling station. What was special about de Camp and Heinlein was the engineering exactitude with which they fleshed out their imaginings. Their cities were complete with toilets and tax collectors; they were not stage sets but habitats, and though they might be filled with thousand-year-hence machines, one felt they were real and could be built and made to work. Heinlein and de Camp taught the rest of us to imagine in detail, warts and all.

One could go on forever cataloguing writers from this time. It is hard to omit the likes of L. Ron Hubbard, that dominating, picaresque creature who learned how to make his fantasies come true with Dianetics and Scientology, or a dozen writers hardly remembered now, but new and innovative then, like Ross Rocklynne and Malcolm Jameson. But the most interesting thing about these writers is not only what they are in themselves, but the organizing fact about them all. What gave them a home in science fiction was a single editor, with a single magazine. The magazine was *Astounding Stories* (now rechristened *Analog* as part of the general process of dignifying what we do), and the editor was, right up until his death the other day, John W. Campbell.

That particular golden age is usually called the Golden Age of Campbell's *Astounding,* and it was all that. There were other writers, good ones. There were other magazines, with merits of their own. But Campbell was the one who picked up everything and put it down again in a different and better form. As one who has labored long in that same vineyard, I cannot conceal my admiration for his feat. In a period of no more than a few years he single-handedly wrote off a whole generation of science-fiction writers and bred a new one to his own new standards.

That statement is so true that it is partly true even where it is false. There were writers—Clifford D. Simak, Jack Williamson, Murray Leinster—who were ornaments to Campbell's

Golden Age, and who had been ornaments to other magazines while Campbell was still an undergraduate at M.I.T. What he did with them was almost more remarkable. He made them new writers. From purveyors of space opera and gimmick adventure, Campbell retooled them into writers who competed on equal terms with the best of his new breed.

How did he do it? I'm not sure I know. Perhaps Campbell never knew himself; perhaps no one can tell how much was due to his own wit and wisdom, and how much to the power of an idea whose time has come. Certainly the '30s and '40s were years of technological ferment. The fission of the uranium atom was discovered in 1938, and Campbell recognized its importance and had his writers using it in stories in a matter of months. It was a time of marvels. It seemed that every day there was a faster plane, or a bigger ocean liner, or a taller building. It was a time for looking ahead, and one of Campbell's great innovations was the systematic process of describing possible futures that the think tanks have called morphological mapping.

Of course, after a while other people began to see what he had done. Some of his writers were won away from him by the blandishments of other editors. New writers came along, and new things happened in science fiction, to which John Campbell and *Astounding* contributed only a minor part. But those few years of growth and change are a landmark forever, and they are all John Campbell's.

It was a golden age for me, too, although I really had no role in those Campbell years of *Astounding*, I did manage to appear once or twice, in pseudonymous or collaborative stories of no great importance, and I even managed to be one of the competitors wooing his discoveries away from him when, at the age of 19, I became editor of two sf magazines of my own, *Astonishing Stories* and *Super Science Stories*.

But I came at science fiction in a different way. I was a writer and editor pretty early, but long before that I was a fan.

That was the other revolution that took place in science fiction around the beginning of our golden age: The development of fandom, as an auxiliary force and seedbed for science-fiction writers.

The beginnings of fandom are lost in antiquity; it may be

as far back as 1930 when the first trufans appeared: here and there around the world, mostly in the big cities of the United States, addict met addict and started a club. They weren't big, and they didn't last, but around 1932 *Wonder Stories* tried to type its circulation by starting a big mail-order club called the Science Fiction League. It did nothing for *Wonder Stories*, but it was the making of fandom. While *Wonder* was slipping steadily down the drain, the SFL was signing up members, chartering local clubs, bringing fanpower into contact with itself. Chapter Number One was in Brooklyn, and by mid-1933 it was having monthly meetings at which 15 or 20 of us teenagers (plus an occasional old man of 20 or 25) solemnly debated whether A. Hyatt Verrill or John Taine was the best writer in science fiction and bragged about our collections. Live chapters sprang up in Chicago, Los Angeles, and Philadelphia (the latter two are still in existence, though they've changed names and membership lists over the years). A few split off from the SFL, and new clubs were born.

Along about 1937 (remember that landmark date!) a group of us formed a club of our own called the Futurian Society of New York. The founders and general big men were Don Wollheim, Robert W. Lowndes (editor of various science-fiction and fantasy magazines over the years) and myself; the troops included people like my late collaborator C. M. Kornbluth, Richard Wilson, and Isaac Asimov; and a little later on, Damon Knight, Judith Merril, Hannes Bok, and others joined up. We were all pretty young. Don Wollheim was probably our senior citizen, for he had been old enough to vote in 1936, and he was senior in an even more important respect: he had actually sold a story or two to *Wonder Stories*.

That proved it could be done, and so the rest of us started out to win our share of the gold and glory.

We worked hard. Probably we worked hard because it didn't really seem like work to write science-fiction stories. (In all truth, it hardly seems like work now. In my downest moments I find to say for our world at least that it has managed to pay me a lifelong living for doing things I would have been perfectly happy to do for nothing.) Not all of our work was aimed at the paying markets, for all of us had our own little fan magazines—mimeographed or hectographed, published in editions of a dozen or a hundred copies—for which we wrote invariably rotten amateur stories and sometimes quite good scathing attacks on everybody else. But our sights were aimed higher, and by and by most of us began to sell to the newsstand magazines. Not easily. Not often. But all the same, somehow, we began to break in. Asimov got the new editor of *Amazing* to buy a story called "Marooned Off Vesta," which for some reason he does not usually include in his book collections these days. Wollheim and John B. Michel together managed to get a story into *Astounding*. Bob Lowndes sold a poem to *Unknown*. In permutations and combinations beyond counting we collaborated: Wollheim with Michel, Kornbluth with myself, Lowndes with somebody, Dirk Wylie with Dick Wilson . . . sometimes three of us would join forces on a single story, sometimes even more. The all-time record may have been six Futurians collaborating on a single 2,500-word story, which sold somewhere for a fraction of a cent a word, bringing each of them a dollar and change for their efforts. After a while, in 1939, I somehow got it into my head that I could edit a science-fiction magazine.

I had no particular reason for believing this, but it didn't look particularly hard. So I went to see an editor named Robert O. Erisman, whom I had come to know in the course of having a dozen or two stories rejected by him, and explained to him that as it seemed too difficult to make a living out of writing stories I would be delighted to become his assistant, please. He was marvelously kind. He didn't throw me out of his office. He didn't give me a job, either, but he suggested that I go to see another editor who was in charge of a large chain of pulps that did not include an sf magazine and see if I could talk him into giving me a shot at it. And so I went to see Rogers Terrill at Popular Publications, and Rog surprised all of us by giving me a desk and a budget and a printing schedule and orders to create a couple of sf magazines.

The budget was tiny, to be sure. My salary was even tinier. But there I was, buying stories and hiring artists and having a hell of a time. It was so much fun that the rest of the Futurian Society wanted to play that game too, and so Bob Lowndes persuaded a publisher named Louis Silberkleit to put him in charge of a magazine called *Future*, and Don Wolheim convinced a father-and-son team named Albert that what they needed was an sf magazine called *Cosmic Stories* with him as editor (they went along, but only up to a point:

the sticking point was that they refused to pay for the stories, so Don had the problem of getting his writers to donate their stories). And all of a sudden, we Futurians were no longer on the outside looking in, we were the inside. We were being allowed to act out our fantasies in the real world. The inmates had taken charge of the institution.

Camelot never lasts; a war came along and blew us all away. Some of us went into the service. Others stayed out, but the magazines died in the wartime paper shortages. And that interlude passed into history.

But a few years later, a little older and hopefully a shade wiser, we were all back for more.

The war ended in 1945. Three or four years later the publishing industry had got back to its normal state of rosy optimism shaded by bankruptcies, and science fiction began to move again. Honorable hardcover houses (Random House was the biggest) brought out sf collections from the magazines; four or five fans around the country took their savings out of the bank and set up as semipro book publishers specializing in sf and fantasy, and there was talk of new magazines.

In the years just around 1950 occurred another of those editorial revolutions like John Campbell's; the difference was that this new golden age appeared on two fronts at once.

We mentioned earlier that business-office decisions have had major effects on the history of science fiction. Two of the quirkier ones occurred here. The publishers of *Ellery Queen's Mystery Magazine* decided that for corporate strength it ought to add a couple of titles. And an Italian publisher of gamy comics was making so much money that he decided to break into the American publishing world.

What the *Ellery Queen* people did was talk to their contributor Anthony Boucher, then mostly known as a mystery writer with a few sf stories and fantasies to his credit. Tony proposed what they called *The Magazine of Fantasy* (the title later broadened to include *and Science Fiction,* or *F&SF* for short). They thought it worth trying out. Tentatively. They brought it out as a one-shot, and were pleased enough with the sales to try it again as a quarterly, as a bi-monthly, and ultimately as a monthly.

What the Italian publisher did was to open a New York

office and then go looking for magazines to publish. I will not list the magazines because it is too painful; but somehow someone put "science fiction" on the list, and their editor, Vera Cerutti, was appointed to make it happen. Vera didn't know that much about sf, but she knew that she didn't, and more than that she knew somehow who did. His name was Horace Gold.

The Golden Age of Gold sounds like either a misfired attempted joke or a Shostakovich ballet, but it was very real. Around 1950, Horace Gold was a prematurely bald man in his mid-30s, somewhat the worse for a World War II disability but well able to cope with the world. Where the coping was difficult it was the world that had to change, not Horace. He had written God's own quantity of material of all kinds, and among the comic scenarios and the radio scripts and the true detectives there were a few sf stories—not bad, but not great—and a couple of outstanding fantasies: "Trouble with Water," and above all a fine, tingly novel called *None but Lucifer* (which, for reasons which cannot possibly be any good, has never appeared in book form, to everyone's loss).

All this was commendable, but was there anything in that record which qualified Horace Gold to make sf over in a new and better form? If so, it is hard to identify the diagnostic symptom; yet that's what he did. He wasn't scientifically trained. His own writing was best where it had least to do with science fiction. But he had two traits that served him well. For one, he had a mind that retained everything; for another, he had persistence that moved mountains. Horace Gold's chosen weapon was the telephone. There are few writers active in sf in the decade of the '50s who do not remember the phone ringing at any hour, at all hours, and Horace's voice picking up a month-old conversation about writing a story or revising one without missing a beat.

His new magazine was called *Galaxy*. It began with a burst of bombastic promises about a new kind of science fiction. The funny thing was that it made them good. In its first years it published any number of wise and witty and wonderful stories—by Alfred Bester, Fritz Leiber, William Tenn, Robert Sheckley, Robert A. Heinlein (wooed away from *Astounding*), Clifford D. Simak (coaxed out of semiretirement), and countless others. Very few of those writers set out to write for

Galaxy. Even fewer intended to write the stories they ultimately published. Mountie-like, Horace Gold tracked them down wherever they hid and made them stand and deliver. I mean no denigration of him when I say that he himself suggested relatively few stories to his writers. (There are exceptions, including one of the most successful of my own.) But Horace's talent was not tutorial. It was obstetrical. When he came at you with those forceps, the story got born. Nearly every one of those early stories has appeared in the best sf anthologies, some of them a dozen times and more; a publisher offered a not-so-small fortune, not long ago, for the privilege of reprinting all those issues verbatim; and that's what Horace Gold did, all by himself.

And uptown at the offices of *The Magazine of Fantasy*, Tony Boucher and his sidekick, J. Francis McComas, were doing something rather similar with a quite different list of writers. Their notion was that it was possible to merge the two previously disparate streams of science fiction: the literary-humanist tradition (the novels of Wells, Olaf Stapledon, S. Fowler Wright, and others) and the gimmicky, high-flying, innovative, adventurous sf of the pulps. They made it happen. They broadened the universe of discourse for sf writers to include everything there is. Nothing was off limits. No concept could not be explored.

If this seems like a small thing, consider what the world was like in those days of the early '50s. It was the Joe McCarthy era in the United States. Dissent was penalized. Careers were being blasted. In those years, when senators and Presidents headed for the storm cellar, when journalists and statesmen guarded their tongues, science fiction was the home of free speech—almost the only public forum there was, for some people, in some ways. One still meets graying ministers and scientists who remember those 1950s issues of *Galaxy* and *F&SF* with eternal gratitude, for letting them think about the unthinkable when it was costly to speak out loud.

But that Camelot ended, too, with a whimper. All golden ages come to an end. Pericles met the Peloponnesian War; the Caesars lost out to Alaric and the barbarians. What defeated that golden age of science fiction was a stock manipulation.

It was one of those front-office things we have seen before, but on a heroic and catastrophic scale. Magazine publishers do not deliver their publications to your local newsstand themselves. They employ intricate chains of distributors and wholesalers to do the job. Until the mid-1950s there were two major channels for national distribution: the collective resources of a dozen independents and their wholesalers on the one hand, and on the other the massive, ancient American News Company with its countless subsidiaries.

In the mid-1950s a stock investor looked upon the American News balance sheet and found it good. Over the decades it had acquired vast equities in restaurants and warehouses and real estate, and all of those assets had been bought when the world was young and prices were low. You could buy up the stock, he mused, and sell off all the assets, and close up the company, and come out with a ruddy fortune. And so he did. ANC was liquidated, and dealt the magazine business in general a blow from which it has never recovered —as anyone can see who has tried to buy a copy of *Look* or *Collier's* lately.

So science-fiction magazines were done in, most of them. There were 37 titles at the peak of the boom in the 1950s; at last count, there were perhaps half a dozen struggling to stay alive. There's still plenty of science fiction—in books. But the magazines are only a shadow . . .

It *could* be different. A new publisher to take a chance. Another Campbell, or a latter-day Gold. Some bright new ideas, and some bright new writers to make them real . . . But that's another story, and a different Golden Age!

Rafferty's Reasons

I wrote this story twice—once when I was in my early 20s, when it went the rounds of the magazines without connecting, and again 10 or 15 years later, when I came across the yellowed sheets and decided I knew what I had done wrong the first time, and could do it right the second. When I finished it I was quite pleased with it. It happened that that same day I finished another story with which I was not very pleased at all. I sent both of them to my favorite editor, with a note saying, "You'll like one of these, I'm sure, but the other I have doubts about and I won't be disappointed if you reject it." By return mail came a manuscript, a check and a letter saying, "Boy, were you right!" Only he bought the wrong one.

It was the year of the projects, and nearly Election time. *Vote for Mudgins!* screamed the posters. *He put us back to work!*

Even Rafferty was back at work, taken off the technological dole, and he sat there in his boss's office, looking at him and hating him. Fat old John Girty, his boss. A Mudgins man from the old Fifth Precinct days, a man with the lowest phase number in the state.

"Riffraff!" Girty stormed. "A good job is wasted on a bum like you. You wish you were back on relief!"

Rafferty only nodded, his face full of misery, his heart black murder.

"Mark my words, you'll wreck the whole project!" Girty said ominously. "And when the Projects go, the Machine will come back."

Rafferty nodded again. He wasn't listening, although he appeared to be. He was watching his hand on the desk. The

106

hand was moving, crawling slowly over the chipped plastic top like a thick-legged spider. It was crawling toward a letter opener.

"Take warning, Rafferty," said Girty. "You're a trouble-maker. Thank heaven I've got a few loyal workers in the Project, to tell me about skunks like you! Don't let me hear about any complaints from you again. If you don't like your job, you can quit." Of course, he couldn't, and Girty knew it. But it was a way to end the conversation, and he turned and stalked out of the room.

Rafferty sat there, watching his hand, but it was only a hand again. His hand, weak and helpless like himself; and the letter opener was only a letter opener. He got up after a while and leaned absently against the hooded computer that could have unemployed them all—if it weren't for Mudgins and his New Way. You couldn't say he was thinking, exactly, although there was a lot to think about in the silent computer under its sealed plastic cover. But he couldn't be doing that.

Not under the New Way.

It as half an hour before Rafferty opened his books again, before he dipped his pens in the red ink and the black ink and wrote down the figures. If Rafferty was capable of pride he was proud of the way he kept the Project's books. Machines had taught him how to keep books, and even Mudgins granted that machines were useful for that sort of thing. The dark fever inside him slowly receded, and the artist that lived in Rafferty, the creator inside of every man, admired the cool, neat numbers that he made.

He lived with the cool numbers all the long afternoon. (*Vote for Mudgins and the Ten-Hour Day!* the slogans said.) And they calmed him. But when the end of the day came and fat John Girty came out of his office and took down his black hat and walked out, without a smile, without a word—

Then it was that the black heat inside Rafferty surged up again, and the smoke of it bit his nostrils. Not for ten minutes did he get up to leave himself, not until all the others had gone and no one was there to see him tremble as he walked out with a look of utter desperation in his eyes.

Rafferty walked past the lines of tables, walked up the slideway, and to the far corner of the balcony before he put down his tray. All by himself he sat there, as far as he could get from the other people who were eating their Evening Issue meal. He sat down and ate what was before him, not caring what it was or how it tasted, for everything tasted alike to Rafferty. All bitter with the bitterness that is the taste of hatred.

"I hate him," Rafferty said woodenly. "I would like very much to kill him. I think it would be nice to kill him. Fat Girty, some day I will kill you."

Rafferty talked to himself, hardly making a sound, never moving his lips. It wasn't thinking out loud, because it wasn't thinking, only talking, and it was not out loud. Wherever he was, Rafferty talked to himself. No one heard him, no one was meant to hear him.

"I hate your lousy guts," Rafferty would say, and the man beside him would smile and bob his head and never know that Rafferty had said anything at all.

He would talk to people who weren't there. When he first went on the Projects, Rafferty thought that some day he would say those things to people. Now he knew that he would never say them to anyone but himself.

"You are a cow," Rafferty said. He was talking to Girty, who wasn't anywhere near the New Way cafeteria where the Projects personnel ate. "You say I'm a troublemaker, when I only want them to leave me alone. You think I make mistakes with the numbers in the books. I don't. I never make mistakes when I write down numbers and add them. But you think I do."

If Girty had been there, he would have denied it—because how could Rafferty make mistakes after the machines had taught him? But Girty wasn't there, and the rest of the people around Rafferty in the cafeteria went on eating and talking and reading, except for a few as silent and solitary as Rafferty himself. None of them heard him.

Rafferty picked up the big dish and put it away from him, picked up a smaller dish and put it down in front of him, touched a fork to the soggy but vitamin-rich and expertly synthesized pie.

"Your secretary," said Rafferty in his silent voice, "she makes mistakes, though. Perhaps I should kill her too, cow."

Rafferty finished the pie and went down the stairs.

"You blame me for everything," Rafferty said, pushing

silently through the crowd at the coffee-beverage urn. He put a Project-slug in the slot and held the lever down while his cup filled with three streams of fluid, one black, one white, one colorless. "You don't treat me right, cow," he said, and turned away.

A man jostled him and scalding pain ran up Rafferty's wrist as the hot drink slopped over.

Rafferty turned to him slowly. "You are a filthy pig," he said voicelessly, smiling. "Your mother walked the streets."

The man muttered, "Sorry," over his shoulder.

Rafferty sat down at another table with a party of three young Project girls who never looked at him, but talked loudly among themselves.

"I'll kill you, Girty," Rafferty said, as he stirred the coffee-beverage and drank it.

"I'll kill you, Girty," he said, and went home to his dormitory bed.

John Girty said peevishly: "I want you all to try to act like human beings this morning. We have an important visitor from Phase Four."

The Project nodded respectfully and buckled down to work and when the important visitor arrived and stood with Girty, looking over the busy room, not even Rafferty looked up.

But the visitor looked at Rafferty, and said something in an undertone to Girty. "Oh, well, of course," said Girty. "We get all kinds here. That one has a bad record. He was some kind of an artist, or picture painter, or something like that under the Old Way. They take a lot of work, those marginal ones, and, as you see, they're likely to turn out sullen."

The visitor said something again and Girty laughed. "*He* might not like it," he said with heavy, angry humor. "Heaven help us all if we ran this Project the way *he* likes. But come on into my private office. You'll be interested in our overtime schedule—"

They were gone, and Girty was right, Rafferty did not resent the way they talked about him, no more than St. Lawrence, roasting on his grid, would have resented a sneering word from his torturers. Rafferty hadn't the scope left to resent small injuries.

The electronic call-me-up whispered on old Miss Sandburg's desk, and she limped into Girty's office, clutching her stenographer's pad as though it might bite. She was a sour one too, for all she was second in command of the Project office. She had been a wife and a mother once, and they said that she didn't really *want* to work. But she worked, of course.

Rafferty sat hunched over his books, looking at John Girty's door without turning his head. He saw old Ellen Sandburg go in, and saw her come out again ten minutes later, with the spiderweb lines sharper around her eyes, and the white lips pressed hard together. "You are a slave," Rafferty said without a sound. "You let him bully you because you like to be a slave. But I don't."

But he was working with the cool numbers then, and he lost himself. The zeroes and fives and decimals moved in orderly progression, and there was no hate in them, nothing but chill straightness that never changed.

Only at three o'clock in the afternoon when he had to take the Saturday payroll into fat John Girty's office to be checked and verified, did the coolness fall away and leave him burning. "I won't kiss your foot," said Rafferty, and opened the door without knocking. "I'm as good as you are, cow," said Rafferty, and dumped the carton of pay envelopes silently on Girty's desk.

But Girty hardly looked at him, only grunted with his fat, angry cow's grunt and thumbed irritably through the envelopes. But when Rafferty went back to his desk the numbers would not go right. They were hot red and smoldering black, and they swirled and bloated before his stinging eyes. He sat there and watched them swirl and swell as fat as fat John Girty. He just sat there, Rafferty did, holding his pen over the ledger, moving his fingers as though he were writing, but never touching pen to paper until five o'clock, early Saturday quitting time.

Then fat John Girty came out of his office and dumped the pay envelopes on Rafferty's desk again, and took his hat and left. The clerks and the girls put away their papers, and took their coats from where they had hidden them behind the sheeted bookkeeping machines and lined up before Rafferty's desk to get their pay.

"The Project pays you to work, not to collect money." That was what Girty said. "On the Project's time you work. You get paid on your own time. You get off early on Saturdays anyhow."

It wasn't fair. But all Rafferty could do when Girty went out of the office was to stare after him for a second, with his own hot, black heart showing in his eyes, and try to rush through handing out the payroll.

"You're a coward, Girty," he said without a sound, and handed a fat yellow envelope of Project-vouchers and Project-slugs to Ellen Sandburg.

"You know that I hate your guts, so you run away," he said. "But it won't help you, cow. You can run away. But I can catch you."

Fifteen minutes start John Girty had. No more. But it took Rafferty over an hour to make it up. An hour of looking in all the expensive, free-market restaurants where Girty might be, pressing his forehead against the glass like an urchin on Christmas day, only with the blackness coming out of no urchin's eyes.

The streets were packed, and crowds bumped against Rafferty, some careless and impolite, some doddering and apologetic, and once or twice a man as bleak and frozen as Rafferty himself.

It was weekend going-out night, and every street corner had its Mudgins Demonstrator on his flag-draped platform, frightening the passersby with prophecies of the return of Unemployment and the Machine. Rafferty noticed that he was hungry, but he didn't have time to eat, not while he was looking for fat John Girty and while the letter opener was secretly fondled in his pocket.

And then at the end of the search, to see John Girty just as he was coming out of the biggest free-market restaurant of all and get into a taxicab. A taxicab, that cost real money. And there was Rafferty, with two dollar bills of real money in his pocket, hoarded over months, and a pocketful of Project-vouchers and Project-slugs.

He did it. He took another cab to follow Girty, but he sat with his heart in his mouth behind the cab driver, watching the clicking black numbers on the meter and doing something that was close to praying. But of course it wasn't really praying, under the New Way.

Rafferty snarled voiceless curses at the cab driver, who had looked so openly suspicious of his Project suit and his panther's eyes, and so contemptuous of Rafferty's fumbling directions as he tried to keep them on the trail of the fat man in the cab ahead.

"I ought to kill you, too," Rafferty told the driver, but silently. "I ought to cut your throat the way I'm going to cut the fat cow's throat with what I have hidden here."

The driver sat on his little bucket seat, where they had ripped out the automatic control apparatus to make room for a human driver under the New Way, and never knew that murder was right behind him. But it was only a short ride— fortunately for Rafferty's two dollars. The meter said forty cents.

"I ought to kill you," Rafferty said again, not looking at the driver who was fumbling for change but staring at the enormous white Old Way building Girty had gone into. "You deserve to be killed. I'll give you a tip, and you'll go and tell the Mudgin's police that I'm following Girty to cut his throat. Take my money and tell the police, that's what you'll do." He picked up the half dollar from the driver's palm and left the dime. "I ought to kill you, too."

But the driver couldn't tell them what he didn't know, so Rafferty bought a newspaper at a stand and stood looking at the headlines obstinately until he heard the cab drive away. The headlines on the news stories said *Liquidation of 80,000 Wilfully Unemployed* and *Legislators Hail Mudgins Way* and *Project Kitchens to Get New Wonder Yeast Meal,* but it had been a long time since Rafferty had read even a headline in a newspaper, and he didn't read them now. He only looked at them unseeing until the cab was gone, and then he looked up at the big white building. It was a Turkish bath.

"Fat old cow," Rafferty laughed silently. "So fat you go to a place like this to die."

Rafferty tore the newspaper in half and threw it on the street, and then he went in, one hand on the thing in his pocket, although the man in the lobby looked at him oddly.

He had to pay a dollar, real money, to get in, and that left him with 45 cents and the Project-vouchers, the useless Project-vouchers that they wouldn't take in a free-market place like this. But he didn't need even 45 cents, not for what he had in mind.

But there was a problem. He had to put all his clothes in a locker, all of them. He stood there naked, a lean, bent man with panther's eyes, wishing he had a pocket. But there was no pocket in his skin, and he had to leave the long, sharp letter opener in the locker.

Once upon a time, it seemed to Rafferty, a long, long time ago someone who *then* had been that which was Rafferty *now* had been in a place like this. That was during what they called the "Old Way," although it seemed to Rafferty, they hadn't called it that then. There was something there that did no add up neatly in his mind, but he was walking through a hot, steamy corridor of tile, and he didn't bother about that any more. It was damp underfoot, and there were splashing showers alongside. He stepped into a shower and let the water thunder on him.

And he turned his face up into the stream and cowered back, out of sight, as fat old John Girty puffed pinkly past.

Girty was naked as a newborn, soft as a moulted crab, flabby as a pink harem eunuch. "I spit," Rafferty soundlessly told the roaring water. "Fat, soft thing. You're dirty, cow.

"Fat and dirty—

"I'll kill you, Girty."

Rafferty stood in the steam room, peering across the corridor at the massage tables where fat Girty was presenting his flabby pink flesh to be thumped. Rafferty couldn't see through the clouded glass and so he had to keep opening the door, and every time he opened it steam billowed out and drafts knifed in on the men who sat naked on wooden benches in the steam. The metal door burned Rafferty's hand, he noticed, but it was a cool thing compared to the black heat that stung his throat inside him.

Girty was still waddling and puffing around the massage table, talking to the rubber. Rafferty let the door to the steam room close on him, and squinted around the little cube of hell he was in. There were dim, loose shapes sprawled around the walls. Some were fat and many were old, but none was as flabby as John Girty.

There were three lights on the wall of the steam room,

head-high, candle-pale. There was a fourth light that was burned out, and Rafferty sat down in the little dark under it, waiting until it was time.

"I have a knife to kill you with," he crooned soundlessly. "Fat cow. I have a knife to cut you with and stab you with. I'll kill you, Girty."

Rafferty sat there with patient violence, like an avalanche waiting on cue in the wings of a spectacular drama. He was in no hurry; he might perhaps move very fast indeed, fast as lightning or the star rays that shoot across the void, but he would not be hurrying.

There was no time for such as Rafferty, and no longing for waiting to come to an end, and no regret for time lost. Though perhaps there once had been, before Mudgins, and the New Way, and the machines that taught Rafferty and those like Rafferty how to do the work of machines.

It was time to look out the door again, and he got up, squinting his white-hot eyes against the steam, and walked over. In the massage room Girty was on the table now, with a while towel over his ugliness. A tall, brown man in trunks clapped goggles to Girty's eyes and pressed a switch that lit a shimmering violet light overhead.

"Close the door, damn it!" One of the dim white shapes behind Rafferty was sitting up and swearing at him.

"Your mother loved hogs," Rafferty said without voice, but he closed the door and walked out.

This was the part that was hard to do. He walked backward and sidewise like a crab, keeping his face hidden from even the closed, goggled eyes of Girty. He climbed onto a slab next to Girty and lay down with his head turned away.

"Put goggles on me, you filthy pig," he soundlessly ordered the rubber. "Hide my face before Girty looks this way." His averted eyes saw a sign on the wall:

Swedish Rub	$1.00
Salt Rub	.75
Sun Lamp & Massage	1.50

Rafferty had a 25-cent-piece and two dimes. And the Project-vouchers, of course, but not for here. The rubber, came then, and covered Rafferty. He looked at him thoughtfully for a moment before he spoke, but all he said was:

"Good evening, Sir. Swedish rub today?"

Rafferty nodded, looking expressionlessly into the rubber's coarse, tanned face. He could not speak out loud, so close to Girty's fat but listening ears, but he only had to nod. "Anything, filthy pig," he said soundlessly. "One dollar is nothing. Perhaps I will pay you with the same knife I pay Girty with."

The rubber assembled his greases and cloths and Rafferty waited until it was time. He thought about the one dollar of real money that someone in this place would expect him to pay, but of course he would have paid all his bills in full, forever, before he came to the cashier's window again. He thought of the letter opener, lost to him in the locker down below. But the knife was better, eight inches long and carefully honed, with a thin blade that would slash a throat or go between two ribs.

"It will make meat out of Girty," he told the unhearing rubber. "Perhaps it will make meat out of you. I know it will make meat out of me, too, but not until I have finished with fat Girty."

It was good that the knife was there, to solve all his problems at once. He waited until it was time.

Girty's lamp went out, and his rubber rolled him over, and Girty immediately began talking to the man. Rafferty could hear the hard-muscled, cupped-hand slaps on the sagging pink flesh, and Girty's wheezing, jolting voice.

"I'll kill you, Girty," he said, and it was like a hymn. "I'll kill you, Girty," he said without sound.

Girty was saying proudly, "Hell, I've—*ugh*—worked with Mudgins just like—*ugh*—that. Ever since the old Fifth—*ugh* —Precinct days. He and I—"

Rafferty wasn't listening, not exactly. He was letting the words flow over him as unnoticed as his rubber's attentions, waiting for it to be time. There would be some sort of signal, it seemed to him, and then he would make meat out of Girty.

Not exactly listening, he caught a sudden change in Girty's voice and for a second he tensed, thinking perhaps it was the signal. "Easy, sir," said his rubber, thinking he had hit a sore spot.

But Rafferty didn't relax until he realized that the change in Girty's voice was because he was greeting a friend. Rafferty peered and saw another man, as pink as Girty but nothing like as fat, as old but not nearly as flabby, advancing as bare as a baby and talking to Girty.

"Lay down with dogs, you fool," said Rafferty venomously, not making a sound, "and you get up with fleas. I warn you, Girty-lover. I'll kill you, too, with a knife that will hack your heart out before you even see it. Cows."

Rafferty's rubber flopped him over then, and for a plunging moment it seemed to Rafferty the man would surely see the knife. But he didn't say anything, only: "Easy, sir. Let me know if I'm too brisk."

Rafferty lay face down on the slab, watching his fingers crawl across the cloth beside his face. "The hands can kill you, Girty," he said voicelessly. "But the knife is better. Go and run, with your Girty-loving friend. Wherever you go, I'll be there."

They were talking, Girty and the Girty-lover, and Rafferty reached out to taste the conversation. The friend was complaining, while another masseur eased the kinks out of his shoulders. The friend was saying, "Sixty hours? That's a good long workweek, yes. And it keeps them out of trouble, I'm not denying it. But there's a fatigue factor, John. After sixty hours a worker is bound to make mistakes."

Girty said: "Not if he's been disciplined. Give them the New Way treatment, that's all." He laughed, like a pig's squeal. "I'd like to see them make mistakes then."

His friend said: "I don't hold with the treatments."

Girty said, after a moment, in a voice that was still a cow's voice, but the voice of a shocked and stern cow: "*Are you against Mudgins?*"

Rafferty stopped feeling the texture of the conversation then, because what did it matter to him? The Girty-lover was defensive and overemphatic, and Girty himself was hostile and only slowly allowed himself to be soothed. They were talking about full employment and the horrors of the Old Way and the Machines, and the Girty-lover was petulantly insisting that the machine-education treatments had—unspecified—faults.

Rafferty didn't listen. The New Way treatments were machines droning and flashing in your ears and hammering, hammering, hammering at you until you *couldn't* make a mistake, not in the things they taught you to do. Because you were half machine yourself, by the time they finished fluxing and forging your mind. And full employment was overtime at the Project and an end to the—the studio, or whatever the word was, that once had meant something back in the days of the Machine and—and Art, whatever *that* word was.

But what did it matter to Rafferty, that he should listen? Better to lie there with the secret knowledge of eight inches of honed steel, waiting.

John Girty was saying in his hoarse cow's rumble, "I tell you, Mudgins *saved* us from going to hell in a handbasket! You don't remember the Old Way. Love. Churches. And crackpots making speeches—about *anything*. Voting—for anybody, anybody you liked. Mudgins cleaned all that up. 'Keep them busy,' he said, 'and you'll keep them out of trouble.' Get rid of the Machine, put people back to work. If they don't want to work the way they ought to—*make* them! I remember, back in the Fifth—"

Rafferty wasn't listening, not exactly, but the words were fuel to keep him going. But the rubber was through with him, and flopped him right-side-up again, and again there was that moment when the universe stopped, waiting to see if the man would see the knife.

The rubber said cheerfully, "There you are, sir. That'll fix you up. Now how about a little suntan to tone up the skin?" His hand was already on the switch, and the tube overhead flared violent. Rafferty stared ragingly at it through his goggles, hating the darkened, shapeless core of the light.

Girty's oration broke off: "—but that's the way Mudgins always— Hey. Say, excuse me, but— *Hey*."

Rafferty froze. From the corner of his eye he saw John Girty ponderously pushing himself up on one flabby arm, staring at him with doubt in the wrinkled little eyes. Near-sighted Girty—but he had recognized Rafferty!

It was the moment of the knife. Quite slowly Rafferty lowered his legs to the floor. "Dirty cow," he said soundlessly. He felt the knife, keen and ruthless in his hand. Eight slim inches to kill with. "Dirty, dirty, dirty," he chanted—but it was not soundlessly. "Dirty, dirty, I'll kill you, Girty." It was loud now, his own voice.

Oh, they tried to stop him. He could have laughed at that, if he had remembered how. Try to stop Rafferty, with an eight-inch killing knife! They were all shrieking and yowling and running about at once, and they grabbed at him, but he brushed them off like the staining soot of the air. And they got in his way, but it cost them. He hacked and stabbed and sliced and slew.

He was a Spartacus, and a Lizzie Borden, swordsman and butcher. He stabbed every one of them to the heart and ripped them up and down, and for the first time in longer than he could know, Rafferty was Rafferty, *Mister* Rafferty, a man who had once been a human being and, God save the mark, an artist, and not a mere flesh ersatz for a book-keeping machine. Kill and slice and tear! They overturned furniture, squealing and thundering, like a trapped horse kicking at the flaming, booming walls of its stall. But he killed them all, many times, this Rafferty who was Spartacus and Lizzie Borden—

And, at last, a warrior of the Samurai as well.

When he had killed them enough to slake the fever, he killed himself. Into the pit of the stomach and up. He felt the blade slide and slice, too sharp to tear, a warrior's weapon. The eight-inch steel made cat's meat of his bowels and heart and lungs. Rafferty felt himself dying, but it was worth it, it was worth it, it was worth everything in the world . . .

After he committed suicide, he sat there and watched his victims running about. It was several seconds before he noticed that he wasn't dead.

Girty's friend demanded: "Do you still think the machine treatments are good?"

Girty said: "Ow. The ugly son beat me black and blue." He rubbed his bruised pink paunch, staring at the door where they had carried Rafferty out, weeping.

"You're lucky," said Girty's friend. "Suppose he really had a knife, instead of that old cigar butt he picked up. Suppose somebody else on your Project cracks up, only this one gets a gun somewhere."

Girty said petulantly, "Where would anybody get a gun these days?" He was getting his breath back, and his nerve.

"Suppose he did," his friend insisted.

Girty said truculently: "Watch yourself. I don't stand for antiNew Way talk. So Rafferty cracked up. I knew he was a weak one. You can't make an omelette without breaking eggs, and what's it to me if somebody like Rafferty gets broken?"

He measured his words carefully. "People like Rafferty

are troublemakers, they don't want to work, they don't want full employment. They liked the soft, rotting life under the Old Way and the Machine. If you don't give them treatments, they'll make trouble now. Sure, some of them crack up—like sometimes you put a casting in the press and it cracks, because it's brittle. Worthless. Mudgins knows what to do with the worthless ones. Make them fit, or break them."

"But I don't like Mudgins and his treatments," Girty's friend said violently . . . but not out loud. He sat up, wonderingly. He wasn't in the habit of talking to himself and he wondered if other people ever talked like that to themselves.

Girty, unhearing, was brooding: "You'd think even a piece of trash like Rafferty would want to be *part* of something. Why wouldn't he? But no, he has to work up some crazy resentment—try to kill me. Why? What reason could he have?"

Girty's friend could not give him the answer, though he might have had suspicions. Mudgins could have answered him, and a few others around Mudgins or elsewhere. A few in high places who didn't need even touch-up courses under the machines, could have told him Rafferty's reasons. But only a few. The others, the many, many millions, they could never say what the reasons were; because some of them had never known them, and some had had to forget.

I Remember a Winter

I wrote this story on a balcony of the Century Plaza Hotel in Beverly Hills one afternoon, while my wife was taking a nap in our room and, having finished it, could not quite decide what to do next. I was pleased with it, and I thought it was science fiction, but I wasn't at all sure that anyone else would. So I sent it to Damon Knight for an opinion. He never said whether he thought it was sf or not, but he did publish it in Orbit.

I remember a winter when the cold snapped and stung, and it would not snow. It was a very long time ago, and in the afternoons Paulie O'Shaughnessy would come by for me after school and we'd tell each other what we were going to do with our lives. I remember standing with Paulie on the corner, with my breath white and my teeth aching from the cold air, talking. It was too cold to go to the park and we didn't have any money to go anywhere else. We thumbed through the magazines in the secondhand bookstore until the lady threw us out. "Let's hitch downtown," said Paulie; but I could feel how cold the wind would be on the back of the trolley cars and I wouldn't. "Let's sneak in the Carlton," I said, but Paulie had been caught sneaking in to see the Marx Brothers the week before and the usher knew his face. We ducked into the indoor miniature golf course for a while; it had been an automobile showroom the year before and still smelled of gas. But we were the only people there, and conspicuous, and when the man who rented out the clubs started toward us we left.

So we Boy Scout-trotted down Flatbush Avenue to the big old library, walk 50, trot 50, the cold air slicing into the insides of our faces, past the apple sellers and the wine-brick stores, gasping and grunting at each other, and do you know what? Paulie picked a book off those dusty old shelves. We didn't have cards, but he liked it too much to leave it unfinished. He walked out with it under his coat; and 15 years later, shriveled and shrunken and terrified of the priest coming toward his bed, he died of what he read that day. It's true. I saw it happen. And the damn book was only *Beau Geste*.

I remember the summer that followed. I still didn't have any money but I had found girls. That was the summer when Franklin Roosevelt flew to Chicago in an airplane to accept his party's nomination to the Presidency, and it was hotter than you would believe. Standing on the corner, the sparks from the trolley wheels were almost invisible in the bright sun. We hitched to the beach when we could, and Paulie's pale, Jewish-looking face got red and then freckled. He hated that; he wanted to be burned black in the desert sun, or maybe clear-skinned and cleft-chinned with the mark of a helmet strap on his jaw.

But I didn't see much of Paulie that summer. He had finished all the Wren books by then and was moving on to *Daredevil Aces;* he'd wheedled a World War French bayonet out of his uncle and had taken a job delivering suits for a tailor shop, saving his money to buy a .22. I saw much more of his sister. She was 15 then, which was a year older than Paulie and I were. In his British soldier-of-fortune role-playing he cast her as much younger. "Sport," he said to me, eyes a little narrowed, half-smile on his lips, "do what you like. But not with Kitty."

As a matter of fact, in the end I did do pretty much as I liked with Kitty, but we had each married somebody else before that and it was a long way from 1932. But even in 1932 I tried. On a July evening I finally got her to go up on the roof with me; it was no good; somebody else was there ahead of us, and Kitty wouldn't stay with them there. "Let's sit on the stoop," she said. But that was right out in the street, with all the kids playing king-of-the-hill on a pile of sand.

So I took her by the elbow, and I walked her down the Avenue, talking about Life and Courage and War. She had heard the whole thing before, of course, as much as she would listen to, but from Paulie, not from me. She listened.

It was ritual courtship, as formal as a dog lifting his leg. It did not seem to me that it mattered what I said, as long as what I said was masculine.

You can't know how masculine I wanted to be for Kitty. She was without question the prettiest doll around. She looked like—well, like Ginger Rogers, if you remember, with a clean, friendly face and the neatest, slimmest hips. She knew that. She was studying dancing. She was also studying men, and God knows what she thought she was learning from me.

When we got to Dean Street I changed from authority on war to authority on science and told her that the heat was only at ground level. Just a little way above our heads, I told her, the air was always cool and fresh. "Let's go up on the fire escape," I said, nudging her toward the Atlantic Theatre.

The Atlantic was locked up tight that year; Paulie and I were not the only kids who didn't have movie money. But the fire escapes were open, three flights of strap-iron stairs going up to what we called nigger heaven. I don't know why, exactly. The colored kids from the neighborhood didn't sit up there, in fact. I never saw them in the movies at all. The fire escapes made a good place to go. Paulie and I went up there a lot, when he wasn't working, to look down on everybody in the street and not have anyone know we were watching them. So Kitty and I went up to the second landing and sat on the steps, and in a minute I put my arm around her.

And all of this, you know, I'd thought out like two or three months in advance, going up there by myself and experimentally bouncing my tail up and down on the steps to test for discomfort, calculating in a wet morning in May what it would be like right after dark in August, and all. It was a triumph of 14-year-old forethought. Or it would have been if it had come to anything. But somebody coughed, higher up on the fire escape.

Kitty jabbed me with her elbow, and we listened. Somebody was mumbling softly up above us. I don't know if he had heard us coming. I don't think so. I stood up and peered around the landing, and I saw candlelight, and an old man's face, terribly lined and unshaven and sad. He was living there. All around the top landing he had carefully put up sheets of cardboard from grocery cartons, I suppose to keep the rain out. If it rained. Or perhaps just to keep him out of public view. He was sitting on a blanket, leaning his forearm on one knee, looking at the candle, talking to himself.

And that was the end of that. We tiptoed down the stairs, and Kitty said she had to go home. And did. Otherwise, I honestly think that in the long run I would have married her.

I remember the years of the war, the headlines and the blackouts and the crazy way everything was changing under my very eyes. Paulie had it made. He enlisted first thing, and wrote me clipped, concise letters about the joys of close-order drill. I remember buying his old car the last time he came home on furlough, with his cuffs tucked in his paratrooper boots, telling deadpan stories about the hazards of basic training. The car was a 1931 Buick, with a jug cork in the gas tank instead of a cap. I sold it for the price of two train tickets when I ran out of gas-ration coupons in Pittsburgh, on my honeymoon. Not with Kitty. Kitty had gone far out of my life by then. Her dancing lessons had paid off: amateur-night tap dancer to *Film Fun* model to showgirl at the International Casino; and then she'd gone abroad to Paris with a troupe and been caught in the Occupation. Well. Mutatis mutandis and plus ça change and so on. Or, as one might say, things keep getting all screwed up.

I breezed through the war. Barring a company clerk in Jefferson Barracks who I really wanted to kill, there was nothing I couldn't handle; Paulie had lied. Or maybe for me it was a different war. I had got into newspaper work, which let me get into Special Services when my time came. Nobody was shooting at unit managers for USO shows. I went through forty-one months of exaltation and shame. You see, this was the war that really mattered and had to be won; and how I burned, with what a blue-white flame, with pride to be a part of it. And how I groveled before anyone who would listen because my part was mostly chasing enlisted men away from big-breasted starlets. Do you suppose it's really true that somebody had to do that job, too? I couldn't believe it, but it was because of that that I met Kitty again.

She turned up looking for a job as a translator, looking very much as she always had. She was different, though. She was married, to this very nice captain she had met during Occupation days in Paris, and she had become a German national. It was a grand reunion. I took her to dinner and she told me that Paulie had been wounded in the Salerno landing and was still in the hospital. And a little bit later she told me about her husband, the darling, dimpled SS officer, who was now a POW on the Eastern front. And for four months in Wiesbaden she lived in my billet with me, translating day and night; and, actually, that's what happened to that first marriage of mine, because my wife found out about it. I don't think she would have minded a *Fräulein*. She minded my shacking up with a girl I'd known before I knew her.

I remember more consequential causes than I can count. When I look inside my skin I don't see anything but consequences; all I am is the casual aftereffects of, item, an unemployed carpenter evicted from his home and, item, a classification clerk who had been in the newspaper game himself once, and all the other itemized seeds that have now blossomed into 52-year-old me.

I remember more than I absolutely want to, in fact, and some things I remember in the context of a certain time and a certain place when, in fact, I really learned them later on.

The man on the landing. Years after the war, when I had become a TV producer doing a documentary on the Depression, I put one of my research girls on checking him out. She was a good girl, and tracked him down. That's how I know he had been a carpenter. The banks closed and the jobs vanished, and he wound up on the fire escape. It happened that when the police chased him away a reporter was in the precinct house, and he wrote the story my girl found.

And I remember Paulie, 29 years old and weighing a fast 90 pounds, gasping hoarsely as he reached out to shake my hand in the VA hospital ward, the day before he died. He had been there for three years, dying all that time. He looked like his own grandfather. That was a consequence, too: a landing in the second wave at Salerno and a mine the engineers had missed. He got his Purple Heart for a broken spine that kept getting worse until it was so bad that it killed him.

I think I've seen the place where he got it—assuming that I remembered what he said well enough, or understood him well enough, when he was concentrating mostly on dying. I think the place it happened was on the city beach at Salerno, way at the north horn of that crescent, about where there's a little restaurant built out over the water on stilts. I stood there one afternoon on that beach, looking at the floating turds and pizza crusts, trying to see the picture of Paulie hitting the mine and being thrown into the sky in a fountain of saltwater and blood. But it wasn't any good. I can only see what I've seen, not what I've been told about. I couldn't see the causality. All I could do was ask myself questions about it: What made him sign up for his hero suit? Was it really reading that Percival Christopher Wren book when he was 13 years old? Or: What made me alive, and sort of rich, when Paulie was so poor and dead? Was it the four or five really good contacts I made in the USO that turned me into a genius television producer? Is there any of me, or of any of us, that isn't just consequence?

I think, and I've thought it over a lot, that everything that ever happened keeps on happening, extending tendrils of itself endlessly into the moving present tense of time, producing its echoes, and explosions and extinctions forever. Just being careful isn't enough to save us, but we do have to be careful. Smoky Bear wouldn't lie to you about that.

If I'd married Kitty I think we would have had fine kids, even grandchildren by now; but I didn't, not even batting .500 out of my two chances at her. First it was the old man on the fire escape, then it was the kindly Nazi she decided to go back to waiting for. She waited very well and for a long time, all through the years while the Russians were taking their time about letting him go and all through the de-Nazification trials after that. I suppose by then she felt she was too old to want to start a family. And none of my own wives have really wanted the PTA bit.

And think of the consequences of that—I mean, the negative consequences of the babies that Kitty and I didn't have. Did we miss out on a new Mozart? A Lee Harvey Oswald? Maybe just a hell of a solid Brooklyn fireman who might have saved a more largely consequential life than his own, or mine? Think of them. And that's all you can do with those particular consequences, because they didn't get born.

Percival Christopher Wren didn't mean to kill Paulie. The sad old derelict on the fire escape never intended to break up Kitty and me. Intentions don't matter.

We all live in each others' pockets. If I drive my car along Mulholland Drive tonight, I only mean to keep my date with that pretty publicity girl from Paramount. I don't even know you're alive, do I? But the car is burning up the gasoline and pumping out the poison gas that makes the smog; and maybe it's just that little bit of extra exhaust fume in the air that bubbles your lungs out with emphysema. It doesn't matter to you what I mean to do. You're just as dead. I don't suppose I ever in my life really meant to hurt anybody, except possibly that J.B. company clerk. But he got off without a scratch, and meanwhile I may be killing you.

So I walk out on my balcony and stare through the haze at the lights of Los Angeles. I look at where they all live, the black militants and the aerospace engineers, the Desilu sound men and the storefront soul-savers, the kids who go to the Académie Française and the little old ladies with "Back Up Our Boys" bumper stickers on their cars. I remember what they, and you, and each and every one of you have done to me, this half a century I've been battered and bribed into my present shape and status; but what are they, and all of you, doing to each other this night?

The Schematic Man

Playboy *once had an illustration that they liked so well that they wanted to get a story written around it, and they asked me to write it. They were paying, I think, $750 for a very short story at that time, so I did. In fact, I wrote them two stories for the same illustration, and they bought one.*

The other was this one, "The Schematic Man." I really had thought they might buy it, and it puzzled me that they hadn't, so I put it in my file in the hope that time would make clear to me why they hadn't snapped it up, and I forgot it. Until a couple of years later, when I came across it, and read it, and still could not see why they hadn't bought it.

So I retyped it, making a few fairly small revisions, and sent it off to them, and this time they did buy it . . . not for $750, but for $2,000.

I know I'm not really a funny man, but I don't like other people to know it. I do what other people without much sense of humor do: I tell jokes. If we're sitting next to each other at a faculty senate and I want to introduce myself, I probably say: "Bederkind is my name, and computers are my game."

Nobody laughs much. Like all my jokes, it needs to be explained. The joking part is that it was through game theory that I first became interested in computers and the making of mathematical models. Sometimes when I'm explaining it, I say there that the mathematical ones are the only models I've ever had a chance to make. That gets a smile, anyway. I've figured out why: Even if you don't really get much out of the play on words, you can tell it's got something to do with sex, and we all reflexively smile when anybody says anything sexy.

I ought to tell you what a mathematical model is, right? All right. It's simple. It's a kind of picture of something made out of numbers. You use it because it's easier to make numbers move than to make real things move.

Suppose I want to know what the planet Mars is going to do over the next few years. I take everything I know about Mars and I turn it into numbers—a number for its speed in orbit, another number for how much it weighs, another number for how many miles it is in diameter, another number to express how strongly the Sun pulls it toward it and all that. Then I tell the computer that's all it needs to know about Mars, and I go on to tell it all the same sorts of numbers about the Earth, about Venus, Jupiter, the Sun itself—about all the other chunks of matter floating around in the neighbourhood that I think are likely to make any difference to Mars. I then teach the computer some simple rules about how the set of numbers that represents Jupiter say, affects the numbers that represent Mars: the law of inverse squares, some rules of celestial mechanics, a few relativistic corrections —well, actually, there are a lot of things it needs to know. But not more than I can tell it.

When I have done all this—not exactly in English but in a kind of language that it knows how to handle—the computer has a mathematical model of Mars stored inside it. It will then whirl its mathematical Mars through mathematical space for as many orbits as I like. I say to it, "1997 June 18 2400 GMT," and it . . . it . . . well, I guess the word for it is, it *imagines* where Mars will be, relative to my back-yard Questar, at midnight Greenwich time on the 18th of June, 1997, and tells me which way to point.

It isn't real Mars that it plays with. It's a mathematical model, you see. But for the purposes of knowing where to point my little telescope, it does everything that "real Mars" would do for me, only much faster. I don't have to wait for 1997; I can find out in five minutes.

It isn't only planets that can carry on a mathematical metalife in the memory banks of a computer. Take my friend Schmuel. He has a joke, too, and his joke is that he makes 20 babies a day in his computer. What he means by that is that, after six years of trying, he finally succeeded in writing down the numbers that describe the development of a human baby in its mother's uterus, all the way from conception to birth. The point of that is that then it was comparatively easy to write down the numbers for a lot of things that happen to babies before they're born. Momma has high blood pressure. Momma smokes three packs a day. Momma catches scarlet fever or a kick in the belly. Momma keeps making it with Poppa every night until they wheel her into the delivery room. And so on. And the point of *that* is that this way, Schmuel can see some of the things that go wrong and make some babies get born retarded, or blind, or with retrolental fibroplasia or an inability to drink cow's milk. It's easier than sacrificing a lot of pregnant women and cutting them open to see.

O.K., you don't want to hear any more about mathematical models, because what kicks are there in mathematical models for you? I'm glad you asked. Consider a for instance. For instance, suppose last night you were watching the *Late, Late* and you saw Carole Lombard, or maybe Marilyn Monroe with that dinky little skirt blowing up over those pretty thighs. I assume you know that these ladies are dead. I also assume that your glands responded to those cathode-tube flickers as though they were alive. And so you do get some kicks from mathematical models, because each of those great girls, in each of their poses and smiles, was nothing but a number of some thousands of digits, expressed as a spot of light on a phosphor tube. With some added numbers to express the frequency patterns of their voices. Nothing else.

And the point of *that* (how often I use that phrase!) is that a mathematical model not only represents the real thing but sometimes it's as good as the real thing. No, honestly. I mean, do you really believe that if it had been Marilyn or Carole in the flesh you were looking at, across a row of floodlights, say, that you could have taken away any more of them than you gleaned from the shower of electrons that made the phosphors display their pictures?

I did watch Marilyn on the *Late, Late* one night. And I thought those thoughts; and so I spent the next week preparing an application to a foundation for money; and when the grant came through, I took a sabbatical and began turning myself into a mathematical model. It isn't really that hard. Kookie, yes. But not hard.

I don't want to explain what programs like FORTRAN and SIMSCRIPT and SIR are, so I will only say what we all say: They are languages by which people can communicate with machines. Sort of. I had to learn to speak FORTRAN well enough to tell the machine all about myself. It took five graduate students and ten months to write the program that made that possible, but that's not much. It took more than that to teach a computer to shoot pool. After that, it was just a matter of storing myself in the machine.

That's the part that Schmuel told me was kookie. Like everybody with enough seniority in my department, I have a remote-access computer console in my—well, I called it my "playroom." I did have a party there, once, right after I bought the house, when I still thought I was going to get married. Schmuel caught me one night walking in the door and down the stairs and found me methodically typing out my medical history from the ages of four to fourteen. "Jerk," he said, "what makes you think you deserve to be embalmed in a 7094?"

I said, "Make some coffee and leave me alone till I finish. Listen. Can I use your program on the sequelae of mumps?"

"Paranoid psychosis," he said. "It comes on about the age of forty-two." But he coded the console for me and thus gave me access to his programs. I finished and said:

"Thanks for the program, but you make rotten coffee."

"You make rotten jokes. You really think it's going to be *you* in that program. Admit!"

By then, I had most of the basic physiological and environmental stuff on the tapes and I was feeling good. "What's me?" I asked. "If it talks like me, and thinks like me, and remembers what I remember, and does what I would do—who is it? President Eisenhower?"

"Eisenhower was years ago, jerk," he said.

"Turing's question, Schmuel," I said. "If I'm in one room with a teletype. And the computer's in another room with a teletype, programmed to model me. And you're in a third room, connected to both teletypes, and you have a conversation with both of us, and you can't tell which is me and which is the machine—then how do you describe the difference? *Is* there a difference?"

He said, "The difference, Josiah, is I can touch you. And smell you. If I was crazy enough I could kiss you. You. Not the model."

"You could," I said, "if you were a model, too, and were in the machine with me." And I joked with him (Look! It solves the population problem, put everybody in the machine. And, suppose I get cancer. Flesh-me dies. Mathematical-model-me just rewrites its program), but he was really worried. He really did think I was going crazy, but I perceived that his reasons were not because of the nature of the problem but because of what he fancied was my own attitude toward it, and I made up my mind to be careful of what I said to Schmuel.

So I went on playing Turing's game, trying to make the computer's responses indistinguishable from my own. I instructed it in what a toothache felt like and what I remembered of sex. I taught it memory links between people and phone numbers, and all the state capitals I had won a prize for knowing when I was ten. I trained it to spell "rhythm" wrong, as I had always misspelled it, and to say "place" instead of "put" in conversation, as I have always done because of the slight speech impediment that carried over from my adolescence. I played that game; and by God, I won it.

But I don't know for sure what I lost in exchange.

I know I lost something.

I began by losing parts of my memory. When my cousin Alvin from Cleveland phoned me on my birthday, I couldn't remember who he was for a minute. (The week before, I had told the computer all about my summers with Alvin's family, including the afternoon when we both lost our virginity to the same girl, under the bridge by my uncle's farm.) I had to write down Schmuel's phone number, and my secretary's, and carry them around in my pocket.

As the work progressed, I lost more. I looked up at the sky one night and saw three bright stars in a line overhead. It scared me, because I didn't know what they were until I got home and took out my sky charts. Yet Orion was my first and easiest constellation. And when I looked at the telescope I had made, I could not remember how I had figured the mirror.

Schmuel kept warning me about overwork. I really was working a lot, 15 hours a day and more. But it didn't feel like overwork. It felt as though I were losing pieces of myself. I was not merely teaching the computer to be me but putting pieces of me into the computer. I hated that, and it shook me enough to make me take the whole of Christmas week off. I went to Miami.

But when I got back to work, I couldn't remember how to touch-type on the console any more and was reduced to pecking out information for the computer a letter at a time. I felt as though I were moving from one place to another in installments, and not enough of me had arrived yet to be a quorum, but what was still waiting to go had important parts missing. And yet I continued to pour myself into the magnetic memory cores: the lie I told my draft board in 1946, the limerick I made up about my first wife after the divorce, what Margaret wrote when she told me she wouldn't marry me.

There was plenty of room in the storage banks for all of it. The computer could hold all my brain had held, especially with the program my five graduate students and I had written. I had been worried about that, at first.

But in the event I did not run out of room. What I ran out of was myself. I remember feeling sort of opaque and stunned and empty; and that is all I remember until now.

Whenever "now" is.

I had another friend once, and he cracked up while working on telemetry studies for one of the Mariner programs. I remember going to see him in the hospital, and him telling me, in his slow, unworried, coked-up voice, what they had done for him. Or to him. Electroshock. Hydrotherapy.

What worries me is that that is at least a reasonable working hypothesis to describe what is happening to me now.

I remember, or think I remember, a sharp electric jolt. I feel, or think I feel, a chilling flow around me.

What does it mean? I wish I were sure. I'm willing to concede that it might mean that overwork did me in and now I, too, am at Restful Retreat, being studied by the psychiatrists and changed by the nurses' aides. Willing to concede it? Dear God, I *pray* for it. I pray that that electricity was just shock therapy and not something else. I pray that the flow I feel is water sluicing around my sodden sheets and not a flux of electrons in transistor modules. I don't fear the thought of being insane; I fear the alternative.

I do not *believe* the alternative. But I fear it all the same. I can't believe that all that's left of me—my id, my ucs, my *me* —is nothing but a mathematical model stored inside the banks of the 7094. But if I am! If I am, dear God, what will happen when—and how can I wait until—somebody turns me on?

What to Do Until the Analyst Comes

The thing I would like you to note about this story is that, although it is about a sort of tripping, it was written quite a while before the hippies and the beats made dropping out a national conversational topic.

I just sent my secretary out for a container of coffee and she brought me back a lemon Coke.

I can't even really blame her. Who in all the world do I have to blame, except myself? Hazel was a good secretary to me for 15 years, fine at typing, terrific at brushing off people I didn't want to see, and the queen of them all at pumping office gossip out of the ladies' lounge. She's a little fuzzy-brained most of the time now, sure. But after all!

I can say this for myself, I didn't exactly know what I was getting into. No doubt you remember the—Well, let me start that sentence over again, because naturally there is a certain doubt. Perhaps, let's say, *perhaps* you remember the two doctors and their headline report about cigarettes and lung cancer. It hit us pretty hard at VandenBlumer & Silk, because we've been eating off the Mason-Dixon Tobacco account for 20 years. Just figure what our 15 percent amounted to on better than ten million dollars net billing a year, and you'll see that for yourself. What happened first was all to the good, because naturally the first thing that the client did was scream and reach for his checkbook and pour another couple million dollars into special promotions to counteract the bad press, but that couldn't last. And we knew it. V.B. & S. is noted in the trade as an advertising agency that takes the long view; we saw at once that if the client was in danger, no temporary spurt of advertising was going to pull him out of it, and it was time for us to climb up on top

of the old mountain and take a good long look at the country-
side ahead.

The Chief called a special Plans meeting that morning and
laid it on the line for us. "There goes the old fire bell, boys,"
he said, "and it's up to us to put the fire out. I'm listening,
so start talking."

Baggott cleared his throat and said glumly, "It may only
be the paper, Chief. Maybe if they make them without paper . . ." He's the a.e. for Mason-Dixon, so you couldn't really
blame him for taking the client's view.

The Chief twinkled: "If they make them without paper
they aren't cigarettes any more, are they? Let's not wander
off into side issues, boys. I'm still listening."

None of us wanted to wander off into side issues, so we
all looked patronizingly at Baggott for a minute. Finally Ellen
Silk held up her hand. "I don't want you to think," she said,
"that just because Daddy left me a little stock I'm going to
push my way into things, Mr. VandenBlumer, but—well, did
you have in mind finding some, uh, angle to play on that
would take the public's mind off the report?"

You have to admire the Chief. "Is that your recommenda-
tion, my dear?" he inquired fondly, bouncing the ball right
back to her.

She said weakly, "*I* don't know. I'm confused."

"Naturally, my dear," he beamed. "So are we all. Let's see
if Charley here can straighten us out a little. Eh, Charley?"

He was looking at me. I said at once, "I'm glad you asked
me for an opinion, Chief. I've been doing a little thinking,
and here's what I've come up with." I ticked off the points
on my fingers. "One, tobacco makes you cough. Two, liquor
gives you a hangover. Three, reefers and the other stuff—
well, let's just say they're against the law." I slapped the
three fingers against the palm of my other hand. "So what's
left for us, Chief? That's my question. Can we come up with
something new, something different, something that, one, is
not injurious to the health, two, does not give you a hangover,
three, is not habit-forming and therefore against the law?"

Mr. VandenBlumer said approvingly, "That's good thinking, Charley. When you hear that fire bell, you really jump,
boy."

Baggott's hand was up. He said, "Let me get this straight,
Chief. Is it Charley's idea that we recommend to Mason-

Dixon that they go out of the tobacco business and start making something else?"

The old man looked at him blandly for a moment. "Why should it be Mason-Dixon?" he asked softly, and left it at that while we all thought of the very good reasons why it *shouldn't* be Mason-Dixon. After all, loyalty to a client is one thing, but you've got an obligation to your own people, too.

The old man let it sink in, then he turned back to me. "Well, Charley?" he asked. "We've heard you pinpoint what we need. Got any specific suggestions?"

They were all looking at me to see if I had anything concrete to offer.

Unfortunately, I had.

I just asked Hazel to get me the folder on Leslie Clary Cloud, and she came in with a copy of my memo putting him on the payroll two years back. "That's all there was in the file," she said dreamily, her jaw muscles moving rhythmically. There wasn't any use arguing with her, so I handed her the container of lemon Coke and told her to ditch it and bring me back some *coffee*, C-O-F-F-E-E, coffee. I tried going through the files myself when she was gone, but *that* was a waste of time.

So I'll have to tell you about Leslie Clary Cloud from memory. He came in to the office without an appointment and why Hazel ever let him in to see me I'll never know. But she did. He told me right away, "I've been fired, Mr. McGory. Canned. After eleven years with the Wyoming Bureau of Standards as a senior chemist."

"That's too bad, Dr. Cloud," I said, shuffling the papers on my desk. "I'm afraid, though, that our organization doesn't—"

"No, no," he said hastily. "I don't know anything about advertising. Organic chemistry's my field. I have a, well, a suggestion for a process that might interest you. You have the Mason-Dixon Tobacco account, don't you? Well, in my work for my doctorate I—" He drifted off into a fog of long-chain molecules and short-chain molecules and pentose sugars and common garden herbs. It took me a little while, but I listened patiently and I began to see what he was driving at. There was, he was saying, a substance in a common plant which, by cauliflamming the whingdrop and ditricolating the residual glom, or words something like that, you could convert into another substance which appeared to have many features in common with what is sometimes called hop, snow, or joy-dust. In other words, dope.

I stared at him aghast. "Dr. Cloud," I demanded, "do you know what you're suggesting? If we added this stuff to our client's cigarettes we'd be flagrantly violating the law. That's the most unheard-of thing I ever heard of! Besides, we've already looked into this matter, and the cost estimates are—"

"No, no!" he said again. "You don't understand, Mr. McGory. This isn't any of the drugs currently available, it's something new and different."

"Different?"

"Nonhabit-forming, for instance."

"Nonhabit-forming?"

"Totally. Chemically it is entirely unrelated to any narcotic in the pharmacopeia. Legally—well, I'm no lawyer, but I swear, Mr. McGory, this isn't covered by any regulation. No reason it should be. It doesn't hurt the user, it doesn't form a habit, it's cheap to manufacture, it—"

"Hold it," I said, getting to my feet. "Don't go away—I want to catch the boss before he goes to lunch."

So I caught the boss, and he twinkled thoughtfully at me. No, he didn't want me to discuss it with Mason-Dixon just yet, and yes, it did seem to have some possibilities, and certainly, put this man on the payroll and see if he turns up with something.

So we did; and he did.

Auditing raised the roof when the vouchers began to come through, but I bucked them up to the Chief and he calmed them down. It took a lot of money, though, and it took nearly six months. But then Leslie Clary Cloud called up one morning and said, "Come on down, Mr. McGory. We're in."

The place we'd fixed up for him was on the lower East Side and it reeked of rotten vegetables. I made a mental note to double-check all our added-chlorophyll copy and climbed up the two flights of stairs to Cloud's private room. He was sitting at a lab bench, beaming at a row of test tubes in front of him.

"This is it?" I asked, glancing at the test tubes.

"This is it." He smiled dreamily at me and yawned. "Excuse me," he blinked amiably. "I've been sampling the little old product."

I looked him over very carefully. He had been sampling something or other, that was clear enough. But no whiskey breath; no dilated pupils; no shakes; no nothing. He was relaxed and cheerful, and that was all you could say.

"Try a little old bit," he invited, gesturing at the test tubes.

Well, there are times when you have to pay your dues in the club. V.B. & S. had been mighty good to me, and if I had to swallow something unfamiliar to justify the confidence the Chief had in me, why I just had to go ahead and do it. Still, I hesitated for a moment.

"Aw," said Leslie Clary Cloud, "don't be scared. Look, I just had a shot but I'll take another one." He fumbled one of the test tubes out of the rack and, humming to himself, slopped a little of the colorless stuff into a beaker of some other colorless stuff—water, I suppose. He drank it down and smacked his lips. "Tastes awful," he observed cheerfully, "but we'll fix that. Whee!"

I looked him over again, and he looked back at me, giggling. "Too strong," he said happily. "Got it too strong. We'll fix that, too." He rattled beakers and test tubes aimlessly while I took a deep breath and nerved myself up to it.

"All right," I said, and took the fresh beaker out of his hand. I swallowed it down almost in one gulp. It tasted terrible, just as he said, tasted like the lower floors had smelled, but that was all I noticed right away. Nothing happened for a moment except that Cloud looked at me thoughtfully and frowned.

"Say," he said, "I guess I should have diluted that."

I guess he should have. *Wham.*

But a couple of hours later I was all right again.

Cloud was plenty apologetic. "Still," he said consolingly, standing over me as I lay on the lab bench, "it proves one thing. You had a dose about the equivalent of ten thousand normal shots, and you have to admit it hasn't hurt you."

"I do?" I asked, and looked at the doctor. *He* swung his stethoscope by the earpieces and shrugged.

"Nothing organically wrong with you, Mr. McGory—not that I can find, anyway. Euphoria, yes. Temporarily high pulse, yes. Delirium there for a little while, yes—though it was pretty mild. But I don't think you even have a headache now."

"I don't," I admitted. I swung my feet down and sat up, apprehensively. But no hammers started in my head. I had to confess it: I felt wonderful.

Well, between us we tinkered it into what Cloud decided would be a "normal" dosage—just enough to make you feel good—and he saturated some sort of powder and rolled it into pellets and clamped them in a press and came out with what looked as much like aspirins as anything else. "They'd probably work that way, too," he said. "A psychogenic headache would melt away in five minutes with one of those."

"We'll bear that in mind," I said.

What with one thing and another, I couldn't get to the old man that day before he left, and the next day was the weekend and you *don't* disturb the Chief's weekends, and it was Monday evening before I could get him alone for long enough to give him the whole pitch. He was delighted.

"Dear, dear," he twinkled. "So much out of so little. Why, they hardly look like anything at all."

"Try one, Chief," I suggested.

"Perhaps I will. You checked the legal angle?"

"On the quiet. It's absolutely clean."

He nodded and poked at the little pills with his finger. I scratched the back of my neck, trying to be politely inconspicuous, but the Chief doesn't miss much. He looked at me inquiringly.

"Hives," I explained, embarrassed. "I, uh, got an overdose the first time, like I said. I don't know much about these things, but what they told me at the clinic was I set up an allergy."

"Allergy?" Mr. VandenBlumer looked at me thoughtfully. "We don't want to spread allergies with this stuff, do we?"

"Oh, no danger of that, Chief. It's Cloud's fault, in a way; he handed me an undiluted dose of the stuff, and I drank it down. The clinic was very positive about that: Even twenty or thirty times the normal dose won't do you any harm."

"Um." He rolled one of the pills in his finger and thumb and sniffed it thoughtfully. "How long are you going to have your hives?"

"They'll go away. I just have to keep away from the stuff. I wouldn't have them now, but—well, I liked it so much I tried another shot yesterday." I coughed, and added, "It works out pretty well, though. You see the advantages, of course, Chief. I have to give it up, and I can swear that there's no craving, no shakes, no kick-off symptoms, no nothing. I, well, I wish I could enjoy it like anyone else, sure. But I'm here to testify that Cloud told the simple truth: It isn't habit-forming."

"Um," he said again; and that was the end of the discussion.

Oh, the Chief is a cagey man. He gave me my orders: Keep my mouth shut about it. I have an idea that he was waiting to see what happened to my hives, and whether any craving would develop, and what the test series on animals and Cloud's Bowery-derelict volunteers would show. But even more, I think he was waiting until the time was exactly, climactically right.

Like at the Plans meeting, the day after the doctors' report and the panic at Mason-Dixon.

And that's how Cheery-Gum was born.

Hazel just came in with the cardboard container from the drugstore, and I could tell by looking at it—no steam coming out from under the lid, beads of moisture clinging to the sides—that it wasn't the coffee I ordered. "Hey!" I yelled after her as she was dreamily waltzing through the door. "Come back here!"

"Sure 'nough, Massa," she said cheerfully, and two-stepped back. "S'matter?"

I took a grip on my temper. "Open that up," I ordered. "Take a look at what's in it."

She smiled at me and plopped the lid off the container. Half the contents spilled across my desk. "Oh, dear," said Hazel, "excuse me while I get a cloth."

"Never mind the cloth," I said, mopping at the mess with my handkerchief. "What's in there?"

She gazed wonderingly into the container for a moment; then she said, "Oh, *honestly*, boss! I see what you mean. Those idiots in the drugstore, they're gummed up higher than a kite, morning, noon, and night. I always say, if you can't handle it, you shouldn't touch it during working hours. I'm sorry about this, boss. No lemon! How can they call it a lemon Coke when they forget the—"

"Hazel," I said, "what I wanted was coffee. Coffee."

She looked at me. "You mean *I* got it wrong? Oh, I'm sorry, Mr. McGory. I'll go right down and get it now." She smiled repentantly and hummed her way toward the door. With her hand on the knob, she stopped and turned to look at me. "All the same, boss," she said, "that's a funny combination. Coffee *and* Coke. But I'll see what I can do."

And she was gone, to bring me heaven knows what incredible concoction. But what are you going to do?

No, that's no answer. I know it's what *you* would do. But it makes me break out in hives.

The first week we were delighted, the second week we were triumphant, the third week we were millionaires.

The sixth week I skulked along the sidewalks all the way across town and down, to see Leslie Clary Cloud. Even so, I almost got it when a truckdriver dreamily piled into the glass front of a saloon a yard or two behind me.

When I saw Cloud sitting at his workbench feet propped up, hands clasped behind his head, eyes half-closed, I could almost have kissed him. For his jaws were not moving. Alone in New York, except for me, he wasn't chewing Cheery-Gum.

"Thank heaven!" I said sincerely.

He blinked and smiled at me. "Mr. McGory," he said in a pleasant drawl. "Nice of you."

His manner disturbed me, and I looked more closely. "You're not—you're not gummed up, are you?"

He said gently, "Do I look gummed up? I never chew the stuff."

"Good!" I unfolded the newspaper I had carried all the way from Madison Avenue and showed him the inside pages —the ones that were not a mere smear of ink. "See here, Cloud. Planes crashing into Radio City. Buses driving off the George Washington Bridge. Ships going aground at the Battery. We did it, Cloud, you and I!"

"Oh, I wouldn't get upset about it, old man," he said comfortably. "All local, isn't it?"

"Isn't that bad enough? And it isn't local—it can't be. It's just that there isn't any communication outside the city any more—outside of any city, I guess. The shipments of Cheery-

Gum, that's all that ever gets delivered anywhere. Because that's all anybody cares about any more, and we did it, you and I!"

He said sympathetically, "That's too bad, McGory."

"Curse you!" I shrieked at him. "You said it wasn't a drug! You said it wasn't habit-forming! You said—"

"Now, now," he said with gentle firmness. "Why not chew a stick yourself?"

"Because I can't! It gives me hives!"

"Oh, that's right." He looked self-reproachful. "Well," he said dreamily at last, "I guess that's about the size of it, McGory." He was staring at the ceiling again.

"*What* is?"

"What is what?"

"What's about the— Oh, the devil with it. Cloud, you got us into this, you have to get us out of it. There must be some way of curing this habit."

"But there isn't any habit to cure, McGory," he pointed out.

"But there is!"

"Tem-per," he said waggishly, and took a corked test tube out of his workbench. He drank it down, every drop, and tossed the tube in a wastebasket. "You see?" he demanded severely. "*I* don't chew Cheery-Gum."

So I appealed to a Higher Authority.

In the eighteenth century I would have gone to the Church, in the nineteenth, to the State. I went to an office fronting on Central Park where the name on the bronze plaque was *Theodor Yust, Analyst.*

It wasn't easy. I almost walked out on him when I saw that his jaws were chewing as rhythmically as his secretary's. But Cloud's concoction is not, as he kept saying, a drug, and though it makes you relax and makes you happy and, if you take enough of it, makes you drunk, it doesn't make you unfit to talk to. So I took a grip on my temper, the only bad temper left, and told him what I wanted.

He laughed at me—in the friendliest way. "Put a stop to Cheery-Gum? Mr. McGory!"

"But the plane crashes—"

"No more suicides, Mr. McGory!"

"The train wrecks—"

"Not a murder or a mugging in the whole city in a month."

I said hopelessly, "But it's *wrong!*"

"Ah," he said in the tone of a discoverer, "now we come down to it. Why is it wrong, Mr. McGory?"

That was the second time I almost walked out. But I said "Let's get one thing straight: I don't want you digging into my problems. That's not why I'm here. Cheery-Gum *is* wrong, and I am *not* biased against it. You can take a detached view of collisions and sudden death if you want to, but what about slow death? All over the city, all over the country, people are lousing up their jobs. Nobody cares. Nobody does anything but go through the motions. They're happy. What happens when you get hungry because the farmers are feeling too good to put in their crops?"

He sighed patiently. He took the wad of gum out of his mouth, rolled it neatly into a Kleenex and dropped it in the wastebasket. He took a fresh stick out of a drawer and unwrapped it, but stopped when he saw me looking at him. He chuckled. "Rather I didn't, Mr. McGory? Well, why not oblige you? It's not habit-forming, after all." He dropped the gum back into the drawer and said: "Answering your questions, they won't starve. The farmers are farming, the workers are working, the policemen are policing, and I'm analyzing. And you're worrying. Why? Work's getting done."

"But my secretary—"

"Forget about your secretary, Mr. McGory. Sure, she's a little fuzzy-brained, a little absentminded. Who isn't? But she comes to work, because why shouldn't she?"

"Sure she does, but—"

"But she's happy. Let her be happy, Mr. McGory!"

I looked scandalized at him. "You, a doctor! How can you say that? Suppose *you* were fuzzy-brained and so on when a patient desperately needed—"

He stopped me. "In the past three weeks," he said gently, "you're the first to come in that door."

I changed tack: "All right, you're an analyst. What about a G.P. or a surgeon?"

He shrugged. "Perhaps," he conceded, "perhaps in one case out of a thousand—somebody hurt in an accident, say—he'd get to the hospital too late, or the surgeon would make some little mistake. Perhaps. Not even one in a thousand—one in a million, maybe. But Cheery-Gum isn't a drug. A quarter-grain of sodium amytol, and your surgeon's as good as new." Absentmindedly he reached into the drawer for the stick of gum.

"And you say," I said accusingly, "that it's not habit-forming!"

He stopped with his hand halfway to his mouth. "Well," he said wryly, "it *is* a habit. Don't confuse semantics, Mr. McGory. It is not a narcotic addiction. If my supply were cut off this minute, I would feel bad—as bad as if I couldn't play bridge any more for some reason, and no worse." He put the stick of gum away again and rummaged through the bottom drawers of his desk until he found a dusty pack of cigarettes. "Used to smoke three packs a day," he wheezed, choking on the first drag.

He wiped his streaming eyes. "You know, Mr. McGory," he said sharply, "you're a bit of a prig. You don't want people to be happy."

"I—"

He stopped me before I could work up a full explosion. "Wait! Don't think that you're the only person who thinks about what's good for the world. When I first heard of Cheery-Gum, I worried." He stubbed the cigarette out distastefully, still talking. "Euphoria is well and good, I said, but what about emergencies? And I looked around, and there weren't any. Things were getting done, maybe slowly and erratically, but they were getting done. And then I said, on a high moral plane, that's well and good, but what about the ultimate destiny of man? Should the world be populated by cheerful near-morons? And that worried me, until I began looking at my patients." He smiled reflectively. "I had 'em all, Mr. McGory. You name it, I had it coming in to see me twice a week. The worst wrecks of psyches you ever heard of, twisted and warped and destroying themselves; and they stopped. They stopped eating themselves up with worry and fear and tension, and then they weren't my patients any more. And what's more, they weren't morons. Give them a stimulus, they respond. Interest them, they react. I played bridge the other night with a woman who was catatonic last month; we had to put the first stick of gum in her mouth. She beat the hell out of me, Mr. McGory. I had a mathematician coming here who—well, never mind. It was bad. He's happy as a clam, and the last time I saw him he had finished a paper he began ten years ago, and couldn't touch. Stimulate them—

they respond. When things are dull—Cheery-Gum. What could be better?"

I looked at him dully, and said, "So you can't help me."

"I didn't say that. Do you want me to help you?"

"Certainly!"

"Then answer my question: Why don't you chew a stick yourself?"

"Because I can't!" It all tumbled out, the Plans meeting and Leslie Clary Cloud and the beaker that hadn't been diluted and the hives. "A terrific allergy," I emphasized. "Even antihistamines don't help. They said at the clinic that the antibodies formed after a massive initial—"

He said comfortably, "Soma over psyche, eh? Well, what would you expect? But believe me, Mr. McGory, allergies are psychogenic. Now, if you'll just—"

Well, if you can't lick 'em, join 'em, that's what the old man used to say.

But I can't join them. Theodor Yust offered me an invitation, but I guess I was pretty rude to him. And when, at last, I went back, ready to crawl and apologize, there was a scrawled piece of cardboard over the bronze nameplate; it said: *Gone fishing.*

I tried to lay it on the line with the Chief. I opened the door of the Plans room, and there he was with Baggott and Wayber, from Mason-Dixon. They were sitting there whittling out model ships, and so intent on what they were doing that they hardly noticed me. After a while the Chief said idly, "Bankrupt yet?" And moments passed, and Wayber finally replied, in an absentminded tone:

"Guess so. Have to file some papers or something." And they went on with their whittling.

So I spoke sharply to them, and the minute they looked up and saw me, it was like the Rockettes: The hands into the pockets, the paper being unwrapped, the gum into the mouth. And naturally I couldn't make any sense with them after that. So what are you going to do?

No! I can't!

Hazel hardly comes in to see me any more, even. I bawled her out for it—what would happen, I demanded, if I suddenly had to answer a letter. But she only smiled dreamily at me. "There hasn't been a letter in a month," she pointed out amiably. "Don't worry, though. If anything comes up, I'll be with you in a flash. This stuff isn't a habit with me, I can stop it any time, you just say the word and ol' Hazel'll be there . . ."

And she's right because, when you get right down to it, there's the trouble. It isn't a habit.

So how can you break it?

You can stop Cheery-Gum any time. You can stop it this second, or five minutes from now, or tomorrow.

So why worry about it?

It's completely voluntary, entirely under your control; it won't hurt you, it won't make you sick.

I wish Theodor Yust would come back. Or maybe I'll just cut my throat.

Some Joys under the Star

I once wrote a story called "The Plot to Kill Einstein."
Horace Gold changed the title to "Target One" when he
bought it, but he did publish it at a noteworthy time: it
was on the stands the day that Einstein died. This story,
about a comet, was on sale all through the hoo-hah about
Comet Kohoutek, and a dozen of my friends congrat-
ulated me, marveling at my prediction of a future event.
This is what I call the "broken clock" method of predict-
ing the future, from the old French saying: "Even a
broken clock is right twice a day." The hits are note-
worthy but, oh, the dozens and scores of misses!

In a few recognizable ways were Albert Novak—the man
who stalked Myron Landau—and the Secretary of State alike,
but they had this in common: they wanted. They each wanted
something very badly and, as it happens, the thing that each
wanted was not good by the general consensual standards of
your average sensual man.

Let us start with the man who stalked Myron Landau or,
more accurately, with Myron Landau himself. Myron also
wanted, and what he wanted was his girl friend Ellen, with
that masked desperation that characterizes the young man
of seventeen who has never yet made out.

On this night of July in New York City the factors against
Myron were inexperience, self-doubt, and the obstinacy of
Ellen herself, but ranged on his side were powerful allies.
Before him was the great welcoming blackness of Central
Park, where anything might happen, and spread across the
sky was a fine pretext for luring her into the place. So he
bought her a strawberry milkshake in Rumpelmeyer's and

147

strolled with her into the park, chatting of astronomy, beauty, and love.

"Are you sure it's all right?" asked Ellen, looking into the sodium-lit fringes of the undergrowth.

"Cripes, yes," said Myron, in the richly amused tone of a Brown belt in karate from one of the finest academies on the upper West Side, although in fact he had never gone into Central Park at night before. But he had thought everything out carefully and was convinced that tonight there was no danger. Or at any rate not enough danger to scare him off the prize. Overhead was the great beautiful comet that everybody was talking about and it was a clear night. There would be lots of people looking at the sky, he reasoned, and in any case where else could he take her? Not his apartment, with Grandma's ear to the living-room door, just itching for an excuse to come in and start hunting for her glasses. Not Ellen's place, not with her mother and sister remorselessly there. "You can't see the comet well from the middle of the street," he said reasonably, putting his arm around her and nodding to a handsome white-haired gentleman who had first nodded benevolently to them. "There's too much light and anyway, honestly, Ellen, we won't go in very far."

"I never saw a comet before," she conceded, allowing herself to be led down the path. In truth, the comet Ujifusa-McGinnis was not all that hard to see. It spread its tail over a quarter of the sky, drowning out Altair, Vega, and the stars around Deneb, hardly paled even by the lights of New York City. Even a thousand miles south, where NASA technicians were working around-the-clock shifts under the floodlights of the Vehicle Assembly Building, trying to get ready the launch of the probe that would plumb Ujifusa-McGinnis's mysteries, it dominated the sky.

Myron looked upward and allowed himself to be distracted for a moment by the spectacle, but quickly caught himself. "Ah," he said, creeping his fingers toward the lower slope of Ellen's breast, "just think, what you see is all gas. Nothing really there at all. And millions of miles away."

"It's beautiful," Ellen said, looking over her shoulder. She had thought she had heard a noise.

She had. The noise was in fact real. The foot of the handsome white-haired gentleman had broken a stick. He had turned off the flagstone path into the shelter of the dwarf evergreens and was now busy pulling a woman's nylon stocking over his white hair and face. He, too, had planned his evening carefully. In his right-hand coat pocket he had the woolen sock with half a pound of BBs knotted into the toe—that was for Myron. In his left-hand pocket he had the clasp knife with the carefully honed edge. That was for Ellen, first to make sure she didn't scream, then to make sure she never would. He had not known their names when he loaded his pockets and left his ranch house in Waterbury, Connecticut, to go in for an evening's sport to the city, but he had known there would be somebody.

He, too, looked up at the comet, but with irritation. In his Connecticut back yard, as he had shown it to his daughter, it had looked pretty. Here it was an unqualified nuisance. It made the night brighter than he wanted it although, he thought in all fairness, it was not as bad as a full moon.

It would not be more than five minutes, he calculated, before the boy would lead the girl in among the evergreens. But which way? If only they would choose his side of the path! Otherwise it meant he had to cross the walk. That was a small danger and a large annoyance, because it meant scuttling in an undignified way. Still, the fun was worth the trouble. It always had been worth it.

With the weighted sock now ready in his hand, the handsome white-haired gentleman followed them silently. He could feel the gleeful premonitory stirrings of sexual excitement in his private parts. He was as happy as, in his life, he ever was.

At a time approximately two thousand years earlier, when Jesus was a boy in Nazareth and Caesar Augustus was counting up his statues and his gold, a race of creatures resembling soft-shelled crabs on a planet of a star some two hundred light-years away became belatedly aware of the existence of the Great Wall of China.

Although it alone among the then existing works of Man was quite detectable in their telescopes, it was not surprising they had not noticed it before. It had been completed less than 250 years before, and most of that time had been lost in the creeping traverse of light from Earth to their planet. Also they had many, many planets to observe and not a great deal of time to waste on any one. But they expected more of their minions than that, and 10,000 members of a subject race died in great pain as a warning to the others to be more diligent.

The Arrogating Ones, as they called themselves and were called by their subjects, at once took up in their collective councils the question of whether or not to conquer Earth and add humanity to their vassals, now that they had discovered that humanity did exist. This was their eon-long custom. It had made them extremely unpopular over a large volume of the galaxy.

On balance, they decided not to bother at that particular time. What were a few heaped-up rocks, after all? Oh, some sort of civilization no doubt existed, but the planet Earth seemed too distant, too trivial, and too poor to be worth bothering to conquer.

Accordingly they contented themselves with routine precautionary measures. Item, they caused to be abducted in their disc-shaped vessels certain specimens of Earthly human beings and other fauna. These also died in great pain and in the process released much information about their body chemistry, physical structure, and modes of thought. Item, the Arrogating Ones dispatched certain of their servants with a waiting brief. They were instructed to occupy the core of a comet and from it to keep an eye on those endoskeletal, but potentially annoying, creatures who had discovered agriculture, fire, the city, and the wheel, but not as yet even chemical explosive weapons.

They then dismissed Earth from their collective soft-bodied minds, and returned to the more interesting contemplation of measures to be taken against a race of insect-like beings that lived in a steamy high-G planet in quite the other direction from Earth, toward the core of the galaxy. The insects had elected not to be conquered by the Arrogating Ones. In fact, they had destroyed quite a large number of war fleets sent against them.

Nearly a quarter of the collective intelligence of the Arrogating Ones was devoted to plans to defeat these insects in battle. Most of the rest of their intelligence was devoted to the pleasant contemplation of what they would do to the insects after the battle was won to make them wish they hadn't resisted so hard.

While the handsome white-haired gentleman was stalking Myron and Ellen, the second person who wanted, the Secretary of State of the United States of America, was about a hundred miles north of and 40,000 feet above Central Park. He was on board a four-engined jet aircraft with the American flag emblazoned on its prow and he was having a temper tantrum.

The President of the United States was gloomily running his fingers between the toes of his bare feet. "Shoot, Danny," he said, "you're getting yourself all hot about nothing. I'm not saying we *can't* bomb Venezuela. I'm only saying why do we *want* to bomb Venezuela? And I'm saying you ought to watch how you talk to me, too."

"Watch how *you* talk to *me*, Mr. President!" shouted the Secretary of State over the noise of the jets. "I'm pretty fed up with your procrastinations and delays and it wouldn't take much for me to walk right out and dump the whole thing back in your lap. Considering your track record—I am thinking of Iceland—I don't imagine you'd relish that prospect."

"Danny boy," snarled the President, "you've got a bad habit of digging up ancient history. Stick to the point. We've got to have oil, agreed. They have oil, everybody knows that. They don't want to sell it to us at a reasonable price, so you want me to beat on them until they change their minds. Right? Only what you don't see is, there's a right way and a wrong way to do these things. Why can't we just go in with some spooks and Tommy-guns, as usual?"

"But their insolence, Mr. President! The demeaning tone of this document they sent me. It isn't the oil, it is the national credibility of the country that is involved here."

"Right, Danny, right," groaned the President. "You can talk. You don't have Congress breathing down your neck at every little thing." He sighed heavily and opened another can of no-calorie soda. "What I don't see," he said, with a punctuation mark of gas, "is why we have to hit them tonight, with Congress still in session."

The Secretary said petulantly, "I have explained to you, Mr. President, that our communications system is malfunctioning. We've lost global coverage. There is strong dissipation of ionosphere scatter, due to interference from an unprecedentedly strong influx of radiation apparently emanating from—"

"Oh, cut it out," complained the President. "You mean it's that comet that's bollixed up our detection."

The Secretary pursed his lips. "Not precisely the comet, no, Mr. President. No such effect has ever been detected before, although it is possible that there is a connection. Doesn't matter. The situation before us is that we do not have total communication at this time. And so we have no way of knowing whether the Venezuelans are treacherously planning a sneak attack or not. Do you want to take a chance on the security of the Free World, Mr. President? I say preempt now!"

"Yes, you've made your point, Danny," said the President. He swiveled his armchair and gazed out at the bright spray of white light across the eastern horizon where Comet Ujifusa-McGinnis lay. "I've heard worse excuses for starting a war," he mused, "but I can't remember exactly when. All right, Danny. We'll do what you say. Get me Charlie on the scrambler and I'll put in the attack in two hours."

The watchers for the Arrogating Ones, hiding inside the pebbly core of the comet named after the two amateur astronomers who had simultaneously discovered it, studied the results of their radar-like scan of the Earth. This was routine. They were not aware that their scanning had damaged mankind's communications, but that was not their problem. Their only task was to spray out a shower of particles and catch the returning ones to study—this they did, and what their study told them was that the planet Earth had reached redpoint status. It was now well ino a technological age and was thus an active, rather than merely a potential, threat to their masters.

The Arrogating Ones were no longer quite as effectively arrogant as they had once been. They had been creamed rather frequently in their millennia-long struggle against the insectoids. The score was, roughly, Arrogating Ones 53, Insectoids 23,724. The watchers, knowing this, were aware that at least their task would not under these circumstances involve the actual physical conquest of the Earth. It would simply be destroyed.

This was no big deal. Plenty of mechanisms for wiping out a populated planet were stockpiled in the arsenals of the Arrogating Ones. They had not worked very well against the insectoids, unfortunately, but they would be plenty powerful enough to deal with, say, mankind. The weapons for accomplishing this were readily available at any time, but not to the watchers, who were far too low in the hierarchy of authority to be trusted with anything like that.

Their task was much simpler. They were only required to report what they saw and then to soften up the human race so that it would not be able to offer resistance, even ineffectual resistance, to the clean-up teams when they arrived with their planet-busters.

Softening up was a technical problem of some magnitude, but it had been solved long ago. The abducted humans had died messily but not in vain. At least, from the point of view of the Arrogating Ones their deaths had not been in vain, for in their dying agonies they had supplied information about themselves which had enabled the Arrogating Ones to devise appropriate softening-up mechanisms. The watchers had been equipped with these on a standby basis ever since.

Of course, from the point of view of the abducted humans the question of whether their deaths had been in vain might have had a different answer. No one had troubled to ask them.

At any rate, the watchers now energized the generators which would soften up mankind for its destruction.

While they were waiting for a charge to build up they looked up the coordinates and call signal for the nearest cruising superdreadnaught of the Arrogating Ones and transmitted a request for it to come in and finish up the job with a core-bomb. They then discussed among themselves the prospects of what their next assignment would be. It was not a fruitful discussion. Core-bombs are messy and there was not much chance that Comet Ujifusa-McGinnis's orbit would get them far enough away to be out of its range when it went off. Even if they survived, none of them had any idea what the Arrogating Ones' future plans for the watchers were. All they were sure of was that they were certain not to enjoy them.

We now turn to Albert Novak. He was in another four-engined jet, climbing to cruising altitude out of Kennedy en route to Los Angeles International. He was a crew-cut young man, with something on his mind. His neighbor was a short, white-haired, dark-tanned Westerner with the face of a snapping turtle, who offered his hand and said aggressively, jerking his head toward the window, "That confounded thing! Do you know the space agency wants to spend thirty million dollars of your tax money just to go sniff around it? Thirty million dollars! Just to sniff some marsh gas! Not as long as I'm on the Aeronautics and Space Committee. Let me introduce myself. I'm Congressman—" But he was talking to gas himself. Albert Novak had not accepted his hand, had not even met his eyes. Although the "Fasten Seat Belts" sign was still lighted in three languages, he unstrapped himself and walked down the aisle. Hostesses hissed at him and tardily began to unsnap themselves to make him return to his seat. He ignored them. He had no intention of ever arriving at L.A. International and when he wanted to talk to a hostess he would do so on his own terms. He carried a cassette recorder into a toilet and locked the door against everyone.

The cassette recorder could no longer be used to record or play. He had removed its insides the day before, replacing them with more batteries and a coil of fine wire, which he now carefully connected to 30 Baggies full of dynamite and firing caps he had sewn into the lining of his trenchcoat while his mother nearsightedly smiled on him from across the room.

Although Novak thought of himself as a hijacker, it was not his intention to cause the jet to head for Cuba, Caracas, or even Algiers. He did not want the airplane. He didn't even want the one hundred million dollars' ransom he planned to ask for.

What Novak wanted, mostly, was to matter to somebody. As far as he had thought out his plan of action, it was to walk up to a stewardess with his hand on the detonating switch, show her the ingenious arrangement he had gotten past the metal detectors, be escorted to the flight deck in the traditional manner and then, after the airline had begun trying to get together the 5,000,000 unmarked twenty-dollar bills he intended to demand and the maximum of annoyance and confusion had been caused, to close the switch and explode the dynamite.

He knew that in destroying the airplane he would die. That was not very important to him. The one important failure that he regretted very much was that he would not be able to see his mother's face when the reporters and TV crew began to swarm around her and she learned he had been pushing around all kinds of people and thirty million dollars' worth of airplane.

The generators at the core of Comet Ujifusa-McGinnis were now up to full charge.

Disgruntledly, the watchers of the Arrogating Ones sighted the beam in on the planet Earth. They were quite careful to get it aligned properly, for they remembered very well what the consequences were for slipshod work. When it was locked in, they released the safety switch that allowed the contact to close that discharged the beam.

More than three million watts of beamed power surged out toward the near hemisphere of the planet. Certain chemical changes at once took place in the atmosphere and were borne by jet stream, trade winds, and the aimless migration of air masses all around the Earth.

The equipment used was highly directional, but the watchers who operated it were very close and large magnitudes of energy were involved. Some of the radiation sprayed them. There was some loss from corona points, some reflection even from the tenuous gases of the comet's halo.

As the radiation had been designed specifically for use against mankind, on the basis of the experiments conducted on the kidnappees of 2,000 years before, it was only of limited effect on the watchers. But they happened to be warm-blooded oxygen-breathers with two sexes and many of humanity's hangups, so that the weapon did do to them much what it was intended to do to mankind.

First they felt a sudden, sharp pang of an emotion which they identified (but only by logical deduction) as joy. The diagnosis was not simple, for they had little in their lives that would enable them to recognize such a state. But they looked at each other with fatuous fondness and, in their not really very human ways, shared pleasure.

The next thing they shared was serious physical pain, accompanied by vomiting, dizziness, and a feeling of weakness, for they were receiving a great deal more of the radiation than was necessary for the mere task of turning them into pussycats to receive the knockout blow of the Arrogating Ones. They recognized that, too. They deduced that they were dying, and doing it pretty fast.

They did not mind that any more than Albert Novak minded blowing himself up with the airliner. It was worthwhile. They were happy. It was what the ray was intended to do to people and it did its work very well.

And all over the near side of the Earth, as the radiation searched out and saturated humanity, joy replaced fear, peace replaced tension, love replaced anger.

In Central Park three slum youths released the girl they had lured behind the 72d Street boat house and decided to apply for Harvard, while a member of the Tactical Patrol Force lay down on Umpire Rock and gazed jubilantly at the comet. At the park's southern margin the white-haired gentleman came leaping out at Myron Landau and his girl. "My dear children!" he cried, tugging the women's stocking off his face. "How sweet and tender you are. You remind me so much of my own beloved son and daughters that you must let me stand you to the best hotel room in New York, with unlimited room service."

This spectacle would normally have disconcerted Myron Landau, especially as he had just succeeded in solving the puzzle of Ellen's bra snap. But he was so filled with the sudden rapture himself that he could only say, "You bet you can, friend. But only if you come with us. Ellen and I wouldn't have it any other way."

And Ellen chimed in sweetly: "What do we need a motel room for, mister? Why don't we just get out of these clothes?"

Forty thousand feet directly overhead, as the Presidential jet sped back from the Summer White House near Boothbay Harbor, Maine, the Secretary of State lifted eyes streaming with joy and said, "Dear Mr. President, let's give the spics another chance. It's too nice a night to be H-bombing Caracas." And the President, flinging an arm around him, sobbed, "Danny, as a diplomat you're not worth a bucket of warm snot, but I've always said you've got the biggest damn heart in the cabinet."

A great bubble of orange-yellow flame off on the western horizon disconcerted them for a moment, but it did not seem relevant to their transcendental joy. They began singing all the good old favorites like "Down by the Old Mill Stream," "Sweet Adeline," and "I've Been Working on the Railroad," and had so much fun doing it that the President quite forgot

to radio the message that would cancel his strike order against
Caracas. It did not matter very much. The B-52 ordnance
crews had dumped the bombs from the fork lifts and were
now giving each other rides on them, while the commanding
general of the strike, Curtis T. "Vinegar Ass" Pinowitz, had
decided he preferred going fishing to parachuting into Venezuela in support of the bombing. He was looking for his
spinning reel, oblivious to the noise on the hardstand where
the 101st Airborne was voting whether to fly to Disneyland
or the Riviera. (In any event, the Venezuelans, or those
members of the Venezuelan government who were bothering
to answer their telephones, had just voted to give the Yankees
all the oil they wanted and were seriously considering scent-
ing it with jasmine.)

The ball of flame on the horizon, however, was not without
its importance.

Arnold Novak had released the armlock he had got around
the little brown-eyed stewardess's neck and had begun to
try to explain to her that his intention to blow up the jet
meant nothing personal, but was only a way of inducing his
mother to pay as much attention to him as she had, all
through their lives, to his brother, Dick. Although he stam-
mered so that he was almost incoherent, the stew understood
him at once. She, too, had had both a mother and an older
brother. Her pretty brown eyes filled with tears of sympathy
and with a rush of love she flung her arms around him. "You
poor boy," she cried, covering his stubbly face with kisses.
"Here, honey! Let me help you." And she caught the cassette
from his hand, careful not to pull the wires loose, and closed
the switch that touched off the caps in all the 30 Baggies.

One hundred and thirty-one men, women, and children
simultaneously were converted into maltreated chunks of
barbecued meat falling through the sky. Their roster included
the pilot, the co-pilot, the third pilot, and 8 other members
of the flight crew; plus, among the passengers, mothers, in-
fants, honeymooning couples, nonhoneymooning but equally
amorous couples who did not happen to be married to each
other, a middle-aged grape picker returning home after a
5-days-4-nights all-expense tour of Sin City (which he had
found disappointing), a defrocked priest, a disbarred lawyer,
and a Congressman from Oregon who would never now
achieve his dream of dismantling NASA and preventing the

further waste of the taxpayer's funds on space, which he held to be empty and uninteresting.

Whoever they had been when whole, the pieces of barbecue all looked pretty much alike now. It did not matter. Not one of the passengers or crew had died unhappy, since they had all been touched by the comet.

And deep inside the core of the comet Ujifusa-McGinnis, the device which was meant to display the wave forms signifying receipt of the destruction order for Earth remained blank. No signal was received. No one would have observed it if it had been, certainly not the watchers, but it was unprecedented that a response should not be received.

The reason was quite simple. It was that that particular superdreadnaught of the Arrogating Ones, like most of the others in their galactic fleet, had long since been hurled against the fortresses of the insectoids of the core. There, like the others, it had been quickly destroyed, so that the message sent by the watchers had never reached its destination.

It was, in a way, too bad, to think of all that strength and sagacity spent with no more tangible visible result than to give pleasure to a few billion advanced primates. Although this was regrettable, it did not much bother the Arrogating Ones. They had plenty of other regrets to work on. What remained of their collective intelligence was fully taken up with the problem of bare survival against the insectoid fleets —plus, to be sure, a good deal of attention given to mutual recrimination.

The watchers did not mind; they had long since perished of acute terminal pleasure.

And, as it turned out, they had not died entirely in vain.

Because the Oregon congressman did not live to complete his plan to dismantle NASA, all his seniority and horse-trading power having perished with him, the projected comet-study mission was not canceled. To be sure, the bird did not fly on schedule. The effects of the joy beams from the comet did not begin to wear off for several days and the NASA technicians simply could not be bothered while their joy was in its manic phase.

But gradually the world returned to—normal? No. It was definitely not normal for everyone to be feeling rather cheerful most of the time. But the world settled down, sweetly and fondly, to something not unlike its previous condition of work and play. So the astronauts found another launch window and made rendezvous with the comet; and what they found there made quite a difference in the history of both the human race and the galaxy. The watchers were gone, but they had left their weaponry behind.

When the astronauts returned with the least and weakest of the weapons, all they could cram into their ship, the President of the United States gave up his shuffleboard game to fly to the deck of the *Independence* and stare at it. "Oh, boy!" he chortled, awed and thrilled. "If that'd turned up two months ago Brazil would've had a seaport on the Caribbean!" But Venezuela went about its business untouched. The President was tempted. Even cheerful and at peace with himself and the world, he was tempted—old habits die hard. But he had several thoughts and the longest and most persuasive of them was that weaponry like this meant that somewhere there was an enemy who had constructed and deployed it and someday might return to use it. So with some misgivings, but without any real freedom of choice, he flew back to Washington, summoned the ambassadors of Venezuela, Cuba, Canada, the U.S.S.R., the People's Republic of China, and the United Irish Republics of Great Britain and laid everything before them.

Although politicians, too, were residually cheerful still from the effect of the comet, they had not lost their intelligence. They quickly saw that there was an external foe—somewhere —which made each of them look like a very good friend. Nobody was in a mood to fool with little international wars. So treaties were signed, funds were appropriated, construction was begun.

And the human race, newly armed and provided with excellent spaceships, went looking for the Arrogating Ones.

They did not, of course, find them. By the time they were ready to make their move, the last of the Arrogating Ones had gone resentfully to his death. But a good many generations later, humans found the insectoids of the core instead and what then happened to the insectoids would have satisfied even the Arrogating Ones.

The Man Who Ate the World

During the presidential election of 1948 I was spending a lot of time with an enchantingly beautiful girl, all of five years old, named Merril Zissman. She knew what an election was, and she knew that Harry Truman was battling for survival against the favorite contender, Tom Dewey; but she had a little trouble remembering which was which. So she called them both "Trumie." It wasn't until I had actually written "The Man Who Ate the World," and sold it, and seen it in print that I realized where the name of the lead character had come from, tucked away for years in my subconscious and emerging through my fingertips onto the typewriter paper with no intervention at all of the conscious mind.

I

He had a name but at home he was called "Sonny," and he was almost always at home. He hated it. Other boys his age went to school. Sonny would have done anything to go to school, but his family was, to put it mildly, not well off. It was not Sonny's fault that his father was so unsuccessful. But it meant no school for Sonny, no boys of his own age for Sonny to play with. All childhoods are tragic (as all adults forget), but Sonny's was misery all the way through.

The worst time was at night, when the baby sister was asleep and the parents were grimly eating and reading and dancing and drinking, until they were ready to drop. And of all bad nights, the night before his twelfth birthday was perhaps Sonny's worst. He was old enough to know what a birthday party was like.

It would be cake and candy, shows and games.

It would be presents, presents, presents.

It would be a terrible, endless day.

He switched off the color-D television and the recorded tapes of sea chanteys and, with an appearance of absent-mindedness, walked toward the door of his playroom.

Davey Crockett got up from beside the model rocket field and said, "Hold on thar, Sonny. Mought take a stroll with you." Davey, with a face as serene and strong as a Tennessee crag, swung its long huntin' rifle under one arm and put its other arm around Sonny's shoulders. "Where you reckon the two of us ought to head?"

Sonny shook Davey Crockett's arm off. "Get lost," he said petulantly. "Who wants you around?"

Long John Silver came out of the closet, hobbling on its wooden leg, crouched over its knobby cane. "Ah, young master," it said reproachfully, "you shouldn't ought to talk to old Davey like that! He's a good friend to you, Davey is. Many's the weary day Davey and me has been a-keepin' of your company. I asks you this, young master: Is it fair and square that you should be a-tellin' him to get lost? Is it fair, young master? Is it square?"

Sonny looked at the floor stubbornly and didn't answer. What was the use of answering dummies like them? He stood rebelliously silent and still until he just felt like saying something. And then he said: "You go in the closet, both of you. I don't want to play with you. I'm going to play with my trains."

Long John said unctuously: "Now there's a good idea, that is! You just be a-havin' of a good time with your trains and old Davey and me'll—"

"Go ahead!" shouted Sonny. He kept stamping his foot until they were out of sight.

His fire truck was in the middle of the floor; he kicked at it, but it rolled quickly out of reach and slid into its little garage under the tanks of tropical fish.

He scuffed over to the model railroad layout and glared at it. As he approached, the Twentieth Century Limited came roaring out of a tunnel, sparks flying from its stack. It crossed a bridge, whistled at a grade crossing, steamed into the Union Station. The roof of the station glowed and suddenly became transparent, and through it Sonny saw the bustling crowds of redcaps and travelers—

"I don't want that," he said. "Casey, crack up old Number Ninety-Nine again."

Obediently the layout quivered and revolved a half-turn. Old Casey Jones, one and an eighth inches tall, leaned out of the cab of the S.P. locomotive and waved good-bye to Sonny. The locomotive whistled shrilly twice and picked up speed—

It was a good crackup. Little old Casey's body, thrown completely free, developed real blisters from the steam and bled real blood. But Sonny turned his back on it. He had liked that crackup for a long time—longer than he liked almost any other toy he owned. But he was tired of it.

He looked around the room.

Tarzan of the Apes, leaning against a foot-thick tree trunk, one hand on a vine, lifted its head and looked at him; but Tarzan was clear across the room. The others were in the closet.

Sonny ran out and slammed the door. He saw Tarzan start to come after him, but even before Sonny was out of the room, Tarzan slumped and stood stockstill.

It wasn't fair, Sonny thought angrily. They wouldn't even *chase* him, so that at least he could have some kind of chance to get away by himself. They'd just talk to each other on their little radios, and in a minute one of the tutors, or one of the maids, or whatever else happened to be handy would vector in on him—

But, for the moment, he was free.

He slowed down and walked along the Great Hall toward his baby sister's room. The fountains began to splash as he entered the hall; the mosaics on the wall began to tinkle music and sparkle with moving colors.

"Now, chile, whut you up to?"

He turned around, but he knew it was Mammy coming toward him. It was slapping toward him on big, flat feet, its pink-palmed hands lifted to its shoulders. The face under the red bandanna was frowning, its gold tooth sparkling as Mammy scolded: "Chile, you is got usns so worried, we's fit to *die!* How you 'speck us to take good keer of you efn you run off lak that? Now you jes come on back to your nice room with Mammy an' we'll see if there ain't some real nice program on the TV."

Sonny stopped and waited for it, but he wouldn't give it the satisfaction of looking at it. Slap-slap, the big feet waddled cumbersomely toward him; but he didn't have any illusions. Waddle, big feet, 300 pounds and all, Mammy could catch him in 20 yards with a ten-yard start. Any of them could.

He said in his best icily indignant voice: "I was just going in to look at my baby sister."

Pause. "You was?" The plump black face looked suspicious.

"Yes, I was. Doris is my own sister and I love her."

Pause—long pause. "Dat's nice," said Mammy, but its voice was still doubtful. "I 'speck I better come 'long with you. You wouldn't want to wake your lil baby sister up. Ef I come, I'll he'p you keep real quiet."

Sonny shook free of it—they were always putting their hands on kids! "I don't *want* you to come with me, Mammy!"

"Aw, now, honey! Mammy ain't gwine bother nothin', you knows that!"

Sonny turned his back on it and marched grimly toward his sister's room. If only they would leave him *alone!* But they never did.

It was always that way, always one darn old robot—yes, *robot*, he thought, savagely tasting the naughty word. Always one darn *robot* after another. Why couldn't Daddy be like other daddies, so they could live in a decent little house and get rid of those darn *robots*—so he could go to a real school and be in a class with other boys, instead of being taught at home by Miss Brooks and Mr. Chips and all those other *robots?*

They spoiled everything. And they would spoil what he wanted to do now. But he was going to do it all the same, because there was something in Doris's room that he wanted very much.

It was probably the only tangible thing he wanted in the world.

As he and Mammy passed the imitation tumbled rocks of the Bear Cave, Mama Bear poked its head out and growled: "Hello, Sonny. Don't you think you ought to be in bed? It's nice and warm in our bear bed, Sonny."

He didn't even look at it. Time was when he had liked that sort of thing, too, but he wasn't a four-year-old like Doris any more. All the same, there was one thing a four-year-old had—

He stopped at the door of her room. "Doris?" he whispered.

Mammy scolded: "Now, chile, you knows that lil baby is asleep! How come you tryin' to wake her up?"

"I won't wake her up." The furthest thing from Sonny's mind was to wake his sister up. He tiptoed into the room and stood beside the little girl's bed. *Lucky kid!* he thought enviously. Being four, she was allowed to have a tiny little room and a tiny bed—while Sonny had to wallow around in a 40-foot bedchamber and a bed eight feet long.

He looked down at his sister. Behind him, Mammy clucked approvingly. "Dat's nice when chilluns loves each other lak you an' that lil baby," it whispered.

Doris was sound asleep, clutching her teddy bear. It wriggled slightly and opened an eye to look at Sonny, but it didn't say anything.

Sonny took a deep breath, leaned forward and gently slipped the teddy bear out of the bed.

It scrambled pathetically, trying to get free.

Mammy whispered urgently: "Sonny! Now you let dat old teddy bear alone, you heah me?"

Sonny whispered: "I'm not hurting anything. Leave me alone, will you?"

"Sonny!"

He clutched the little furry robot desperately around its middle. The stubby arms pawed at him, the furred feet scratched against his arms. It growled a tiny doll-bear growl, and whined, and suddenly his hands were wet with its real salt tears.

"Sonny! Come on now, honey, you knows that's Doris's Teddy. Aw, chile!"

He said: "It's mine!" It wasn't his. He knew it wasn't. His was long gone, taken away from him when he was six because it was *old*, and because he had been six, and six-year-olds had to have bigger, more elaborate companion-robots. It wasn't even the same color as his—it was brown and his had been black and white. But it was cuddly and gently warm and he had heard it whispering little bedtime stories to Doris. And he wanted it very much.

Footsteps in the hall outside. A low-pitched pleading voice from the door: "Sonny, you must not interfere with your sister's toys. One has obligations."

He stood forlornly, holding the teddy bear. "Go away, Mr. Chips!"

"Really, Sonny! This isn't proper behavior. Please return the toy."

"I won't!"

Mammy, dark face pleading in the shadowed room, leaned toward him and tried to take it away from him. "Aw, honey, now you know that's not—"

"Leave me alone!" he shouted. There was a gasp and a little whimper from the bed, and Doris sat up and began to cry.

The little girl's bedroom was suddenly filled with robots— and not only robots, for in a moment the butler appeared, leading Sonny's actual flesh-and-blood mother and father.

Sonny made a terrible scene. He cried, and he swore at them childishly for being the unsuccessful clods they were, and they nearly wept, too, because they were aware that their lack of standing was bad for the children. But he couldn't keep Teddy.

They marched him back to his room, where his father lectured him while his mother stayed behind to watch Mammy comfort the little girl.

His father said: "Sonny, you're a big boy now. We aren't as well off as other people, but you have to help us. Don't you know that, Sonny? We all have to do our part. Your mother and I'll be up till midnight now, consuming, because you've made this scene. Can't you at least *try* to consume something bigger than a teddy bear? It's all right for Doris because she's so little, but a big boy like you—"

"I hate you!" cried Sonny, and he turned his face to the wall.

They punished him, naturally. The first punishment was that they give him an extra birthday party the week following.

The second punishment was even worse.

II

Later—much, much later, nearly a score of years—a man named Roger Garrick in a place named Fisherman's Island walked into his hotel room.

The light didn't go on.

The bellhop apologized, "We're sorry, sir. We'll have it attended to, if possible."

"If possible?" Garrick's eyebrows went up. The bellhop made putting in a new light tube sound like a major industrial operation. "All right." He waved the bellhop out of the room. It bowed and closed the door.

Garrick looked around him, frowning. One light tube more or less didn't make a lot of difference; there was still the light from the sconces at the walls, from the reading lamps at the chairs and chaise lounge and from the photomural on the long side of the room—to say nothing of the fact that it was broad, hot daylight outside and light poured through the windows. All the same, it was a new sensation to be in a room where the central lighting wasn't on. He didn't like it. It was —creepy.

A rap on the door. A girl was standing there, young, attractive, rather small. But a woman grown, it was apparent. "Mr. Garrick? Mr. Roosenburg is expecting you on the sun deck."

"All right." He rummaged around in the pile of luggage, looking for his briefcase. It wasn't even sorted out! The bell-hop had merely dumped the stuff and left.

The girl said: "Is that what you're looking for?" He looked where she was pointing; it was his briefcase, behind another bag. "You'll get used to that around here. Nothing in the right place, nothing working right. We've all gotten used to it."

We. He looked at her sharply, but she was no robot; there was life, not the glow of electronic tubes, in her eyes. "Pretty bad, is it?"

She shrugged. "Let's go see Mr. Roosenburg. I'm Kathryn Pender, by the way. I'm his statistician."

He followed her out into the hall. "Statistician, did you say?"

She turned and smiled—a tight, grim smile of annoyance. "That's right. Surprised?"

Garrick said uneasily: "Well, it's more a robot job. Of course, I'm not familiar with the practice in this sector—"

"You will be," she promised bluntly. "No, we aren't taking the elevator. Mr. Roosenburg's in a hurry to see you."

"But—"

She actually glared at him. "Don't you understand? Day

before yesterday, I took the elevator and I was hung up between floors for an hour and a half. Something was going on at North Guardian and it took all the power in the lines. Would it happen again today? I don't know. But, believe me, an hour and a half is a long time to be stuck in an elevator."

She turned and led him to the fire stairs. Over her shoulder, she said: "Get it straight once and for all, Mr. Garrick. You're in a disaster area here . . . Anyway, it's only ten more flights."

Ten flights. *Nobody* climbed ten flights of stairs any more! Garrick was huffing and puffing before they were halfway, but the girl kept on ahead, light as a gazelle. Her skirt reached between hip and knees, and Garrick had plenty of opportunity to observe that her legs were attractively tanned. Even so, he couldn't help looking around him.

It was a robot's eye view of the hotel that he was getting; this was the bare wire armature that held up the confectionery suites and halls where the humans went. Garrick knew, as everyone absently knew, that there were places like this behind the scenes everywhere. Belowstairs, the robots worked; behind scenes, they moved about their errands and did their jobs. But nobody *went* there.

It was funny about the backs of this girl's knees. They were paler than the rest of the leg—

Garrick wrenched his mind back to his surroundings. Take the guardrail along the steps, for instance. It was wire-thin, frail-looking. No doubt it could bear any weight it was required to, but why couldn't it *look* that strong?

The answer, obviously, was that robots did not have humanity's built-in concepts of how strong a rail should look before they could believe it really was strong. If a robot should be in any doubt—and how improbable that a robot should be in doubt!—it would perhaps reach out a sculptured hand and test it. Once. And then it would remember, and never doubt again, and it wouldn't be continually edging toward the wall, away from the spider-strand between it and the vertical drop—

He conscientiously took the middle of the steps all the rest of the way up.

Of course, that merely meant a different distraction, when he really wanted to do some thinking. But it was a pleasurable distraction. And by the time they reached the top, he had solved the problem. The pale spots at the back of Miss Pender's knees meant she had got her tan the hard way—walking in the Sun, perhaps working in the Sun, so that the bending knees kept the Sun from the patches at the back; not, as anyone else would acquire a tan, by lying beneath a normal, healthful sunlamp held by a robot-masseur.

He wheezed: "You don't mean we're all the way up!"

"All the way up," she said, and looked at him closely. "Here, lean on me if you want to."

"No, thanks!" He staggered over to the door, which opened naturally enough as he approached it, and stepped out into the flood of sunlight on the roof, to meet Mr. Roosenburg.

Garrick wasn't a medical doctor, but he remembered enough of his basic pre-specialization to know there was something in that fizzy golden drink. It tasted perfectly splendid—just cold enough, just fizzy enough, not quite too sweet. And after two sips of it, he was buoyant with strength and well-being.

He put the glass down and said: "Thank you for whatever it was. Now let's talk."

"Gladly, gladly!" boomed Mr. Roosenburg. "Kathryn, the files!"

Garrick looked after her, shaking his head. Not only was she a statistician, which was robot work, she was also a file clerk—and that was barely robot work. It was the kind of thing handled by a semisentient punchcard sorter in a decently run sector.

Roosenburg said sharply: "Shocks you, doesn't it? But that's why you're here." He was a slim, fair little man and he wore a golden beard cropped square.

Garrick took another sip of the fizzy drink. It was good stuff; it didn't intoxicate, but it cheered. He said: "I'm glad to know why I'm here."

The golden beard quivered. "Area Control sent you down and didn't tell you this was a disaster area?"

Garrick put down the glass. "I'm a psychist. Area Control said you needed a psychist. From what I've seen, it's a supply problem, but—"

"Here are the files," said Kathryn Pender, and stood watching him.

Roosenburg took the spools of tape from her and dropped them in his lap. He asked tangentially: "How old are you, Roger?"

Garrick was annoyed. "I'm a qualified psychist! I happen to be assigned to Area Control and—"

"How old are you?"

Garrick scowled. "Twenty-four."

Roosenburg nodded. "Umm. Rather young," he observed. "Maybe you don't remember how things used to be."

Garrick said dangerously: "All the information I need is on that tape. I don't need any lectures from you."

Roosenburg pursed his lips and got up. "Come here a minute, will you?"

He moved over to the rail of the sun deck and pointed. "See those things down there?"

Garrick looked. Twenty stories down, the village straggled off toward the sea in a tangle of pastel oblongs and towers. Over the bay, the hills of the mainland were faintly visible through mist and, riding the bay, the flat white floats of the solar receptors.

"It's a power plant. That what you mean?"

Roosenburg boomed: "A power plant. All the power the world can ever use, out of this one and all the others, all over the world." He peered out at the bobbing floats, soaking up energy from the Sun. "And people used to try to wreck them," he added.

Garrick said stiffly: "I may only be twenty-four years old, Mr. Roosenburg, but I *have* completed school."

"Oh, yes. Of course you have, Roger. But maybe schooling isn't the same thing as living through a time like that. I grew up in the Era of Plenty, when the law was *Consume!* My parents were poor and I still remember the misery of my childhood. Eat and consume, wear and use. I never had a moment's peace, Roger! For the very poor, it was a treadmill; we had to consume so much that we could never catch up, and the further we fell behind, the more the Ration Board forced on us—"

"That's ancient history, Mr. Roosenburg. Morey Fry liberated us from all that."

The girl said softly: "Not all of us."

The man with the golden beard nodded. "Not all of us—as you should know, Roger, being a psychist."

Garrick sat up straight and Roosenburg went on: "Fry showed us that the robots could help at both ends—by producing and by consuming. But it came a little late for some of us. The patterns of childhood do linger on."

Kathryn Pender leaned toward Garrick. "What he's trying to say, Mr. Garrick, is that we've got a compulsive consumer on our hands."

III

North Guardian Island—nine miles away. It wasn't as much as a mile wide and not much more than that in length, but it had its city and its bathing beaches, its parks and theaters. It was possibly the most densely populated island in the world ... for the number of its inhabitants.

The President of the Council convened their afternoon meeting in a large and lavish room. There were 19 councilmen around a lustrous mahogany table. Over the President's shoulder, the others could see the situation map of North Guardian and the areas surrounding. North Guardian glowed blue, cold, impregnable. The sea was misty green; the mainland, Fisherman's Island, South Guardian and the rest of the little archipelago were hot, hostile red.

Little flickering fingers of red attacked the blue. Flick, and a ruddy flame wiped out a corner of a beach. Flick, and a red spark appeared in the middle of the city, to grow and blossom, and then to die. Each little red whip-flick was a point where, momentarily, the defenses of the island were down; but always and always, the cool blue brightened around the red and drowned it.

The President was tall, stooped, old. It wore glasses, though robot eyes saw well enough without. It said, in a voice that throbbed with power and pride: "The first item of the order of business will be a report of the Defense Secretary."

The Defense Secretary rose to its feet, hooked a thumb in its vest and cleared its throat. "Mr. President—"

"Excuse me, sir." A whisper from the sweet-faced young blonde taking down the minutes of the meeting. "Mr. Trumie has just left Bowling Green, heading north."

The whole council turned to glance at the situation map, where Bowling Green had just flared red.

The President nodded stiffly, like the crown of an old redwood nodding. "You may proceed, Mr. Secretary," it said after a moment.

"Our invasion fleet," began the Secretary, in its high, clear voice, "is ready for sailing on the first suitable tide. Certain units have been, ah, inactivated, at the, ah, instigation of Mr. Trumie. But on the whole, repairs have been completed and the units will be serviceable within the next few hours." Its lean, attractive face turned solemn. "I am afraid, however, that the Air Command has sustained certain, ah, increments of attrition—due, I should emphasize, to chances involved in certain calculated risks—"

"Question! Question!" It was the Commissioner of Public Safety, small, dark, fire-eyed, angry.

"Mr. Commissioner?" the President began, but it was interrupted again by the soft whisper of the recording stenographer, listening intently to the earphones that brought news from outside.

"Mr. President," it whispered, "Mr. Trumie has passed the Navy Yard."

The robots turned to look at the situation map. Bowling Green, though it smoldered in spots, had mostly gone back to blue. But the jagged oblong of the Yard flared red and bright. There was a faint electronic hum in the air, almost a sigh.

The robots turned back to face each other. "Mr. President! I demand that the Defense Secretary explain the loss of the *Graf Zeppelin* and the 456th Bomb Group!"

The Defense Secretary nodded to the Commissioner of Public Safety. "Mr. Trumie threw them away," it said sorrowfully.

Once again, that sighing electronic drone from the assembled robots.

The Council fussed and fiddled with its papers, while the situation map on the wall flared and dwindled, flared and dwindled.

The Defense Secretary cleared its throat again. "Mr. President, there is no question that the, ah, absence of an effective air component will seriously hamper, not to say endanger, our prospects of a suitable landing. Nevertheless—and I say this, Mr. President, in full knowledge of the conclusions that may —indeed, should!—be drawn from such a statement—nevertheless, Mr. President, I say that our forward elements will successfully complete an assault landing—"

"Mr. President!" The breathless whisper of the blonde stenographer again. "Mr. President, Mr. Trumie is in the building!"

On the situation map behind it, the Pentagon—the building they were in—flared scarlet.

The Attorney General, nearest the door, leaped to its feet. "Mr. President, I hear him!"

And they could all hear now. Far off, down the long corridors, a crash. A faint explosion, and another crash, and a raging, querulous, high-pitched voice. A nearer crash, and a sustained, smashing, banging sound, coming toward them.

The oak-paneled doors flew open with a crash, splintering.

A tall, dark male figure in gray leather jacket, rocket-gun holsters swinging at its hips, stepped through the splintered doors and stood surveying the Council. Its hands hung just below the butts of the rocket guns.

It drawled: "Mistuh Anderson Trumie!"

It stepped aside. Another male figure—shorter, darker, hobbling with the aid of a stainless steel cane that concealed a ray-pencil, wearing the same gray leather jacket and the same rocket-gun holsters—entered, stood for a moment, and took position on the other side of the door.

Between them, Mr. Anderson Trumie shambled ponderously into the Council Chamber to call on his Council.

Sonny Trumie, come of age. He wasn't much more than five feet tall, but his weight was close to 400 pounds. He stood there in the door, leaning against the splintered oak, quivering jowls obliterating his neck, his eyes nearly swallowed in the fat that swamped his skull, his thick legs trembling as they tried to support him.

"You're all under arrest!" he screeched. "Traitors! Traitors!"

He panted ferociously, glowering at them. They waited with bowed heads. Beyond the ring of councilmen, the situation map slowly blotted out the patches of red as the repair robots worked feverishly to fix what Sonny Trumie had destroyed.

"Mr. Crockett!" Sonny cried shrilly. "Slay me these traitors!"

Wheep-wheep, and the guns whistled out of their holsters

into the tall bodyguard's hands. *Rata-tat-tat,* and two by two, the 19 councilmen leaped, clutched at air and fell as the rocket pellets pierced them through.

"That one, too!" Mr. Trumie pointed at the sweet-faced blonde.

Bang. The sweet young face convulsed and froze; it fell, slumping across its little table.

On the wall, the situation map flared red again, but only faintly—for what were 20 robots?

Sonny gestured curtly to his other bodyguard. It leaped forward, tucking the stainless steel cane under one arm, putting the other around the larded shoulders of Sonny Trumie. "Ah, now, young master," it crooned. "You just get ahold o' Long John's arm now—"

"Get them fixed," Sonny ordered abruptly. He pushed the President of the Council out of its chair and, with the robot's help, sank into it himself. "Get them fixed *right,* you hear? I've had enough traitors! I want them to do what I tell them!"

"Sartin sure, young master. Long John'll be pleased to—"

"Do it *now!* And you, Davey, I want my lunch!"

"Reckoned you would, Mistuh Trumie. It's right hyar." The Crockett robot kicked the fallen councilmen out of the way as a procession of waiters filed in from the corridor.

Sonny ate.

He ate until eating was pain, and then he sat there sobbing, his arms braced against the tabletop, until he could eat more.

The Crockett robot said worriedly: "Mistuh Trumie, moughtn't you rear back a mite? Old Doc Aeschylus, he don't hold with you eatin' too much, you know."

"I hate Doc!" Trumie said bitterly.

He pushed the plates off the table. They fell with a rattle and a clatter, and they went spinning away as he heaved himself up and lurched alone over to the window.

"I hate Doc!" he brayed again, sobbing, staring through tears out the window at his kingdom with its hurrying throngs and marching troops and roaring waterfront. The tallow shoulders tried to shake with pain. He felt as though hot cinderblocks were being thrust down his throat, the ragged edges cutting, the hot weight crushing.

"Take me back," he wept to the robots. "Take me away from these traitors. Take me to my Private Place!"

IV

"As you see," said Roosenburg, "he's dangerous."

Garrick looked out over the water, toward North Guardian. "I'd better look at his tapes," he said.

The girl swiftly picked up the reels and began to thread them into the projector. Dangerous. This Trumie indeed was dangerous, Garrick conceded. Dangerous to the balanced, stable world, for it only took one Trumie to topple its stability. It had taken thousands and thousands of years for society to learn its delicate tightrope walk. It was a matter for a psychist, all right.

And Garrick was uncomfortably aware that he was only 24.

"Here you are," said the girl.

"Look them over," Roosenburg suggested. "Then, after you've studied the tapes on Trumie, we've got something else. One of his robots. But you'll need the tapes first."

"Let's go," said Garrick.

The girl flicked a switch and the life of Anderson Trumie appeared before them, in color, in three dimensions—in miniature.

Robots have eyes; and where the robots go, the eyes of Robot Central go with them. And the robots go everywhere. From the stored files of Robot Central came the spool of tape that was the frightful life story of Sonny Trumie.

The tapes played into the globe-shaped viewer, ten inches high, a crystal ball that looked back into the past. First, from the recording eyes of the robots in Sonny Trumie's nursery. The lonely little boy, 20 years before, lost in the enormous nursery.

"Disgusting!" breathed Kathryn Pender, wrinkling her nose. "How could people live like that?"

Garrick said: "Please, let me watch this. It's important."

In the gleaming globe, the little boy kicked at his toys, threw himself across his huge bed, sobbed. Garrick squinted, frowned, reached out, tried to make contact. It was hard. The tapes showed the objective facts, but for a psychist, it was the subjective reality behind the facts that mattered.

Kicking at his toys. Yes, but why? Because he was tired of them—and why was he tired? Because he feared them? *Kicking at his toys.* Because—because they were the wrong toys? *Kicking—hate them! Don't want them! Want—*

A bluish flare in the viewing globe. Garrick blinked and jumped, and that was the end of that section.

The colors flowed and suddenly jelled into bright life. Garrick recognized the scene after a moment—it was right there in Fisherman's Island, some pleasure spot overlooking the water. A bar, and at the end of it was Anderson Trumie at 20, staring somberly into an empty glass. The view was through the eyes of the robot bartender.

Anderson Trumie was weeping.

Once again, there was the objective fact—but the fact behind the fact, what was it? Trumie had been drinking, drinking. Why?

Drinking, drinking.

With a sudden sense of shock, Garrick saw what the drink was—the golden, fizzy liquor. Not intoxicating. Not habit-forming! Trumie had become no drunk. It was something else that kept him *drinking, drinking, must drink, must keep on drinking, or else—*

And again the bluish flare.

There was more—Trumie feverishly collecting objects of art, Trumie decorating a palace, Trumie on a world tour, and Trumie returned to Fisherman's Island.

And then there was no more.

"That," said Roosenburg, "is the file. Of course, if you want the raw, unedited tapes, we can try to get them from Robot Central, but—"

"No." The way things were, it was best to stay away from Robot Central; there might be more breakdowns and there wasn't much time. Besides, something was beginning to suggest itself.

"Run the first one again," said Garrick. "I think maybe I'll find something there."

Garrick made out a quick requisition slip and handed it to Kathryn Pender, who looked at it, raised her eyebrows, shrugged and went off to have it filled.

By the time she came back, Roosenburg had escorted Garrick to the room where the captured Trumie robot lay chained.

"He's cut off from Robot Central," Roosenburg was saying. "I suppose you figured that out. Imagine! Not only has Trumie built a whole city for himself—but even his own Robot Central!"

Garrick looked at the robot. It was a fisherman, or so

Roosenburg has said. It was small, dark, black-haired; possibly the hair would have been curly, if the sea water hadn't plastered the curls to the scalp. It was still damp from the tussle that had landed it in the water and eventually into Roosenburg's hands.

Roosenburg was already a work. Garrick tried to think of the robot as a machine, but it wasn't easy. The thing looked very nearly human—except for the crystal and copper that showed where the back of its head had been removed.

"It's as bad as a brain operation," said Roosenburg, working rapidly without looking up. "I've got to short out the input leads without disturbing the electronic balance—"

Snip, snip. A curl of copper fell free, to be grabbed by Roosenburg's tweezers. The fisherman's arms and legs kicked sharply like a dissected, galvanized frog's.

Kathryn Pender said: "They found him this morning, casting nets into the bay and singing '*O Sole Mio*.' He's from North Guardian, all right."

Abruptly the lights flickered and turned yellow, then slowly returned to normal brightness. Roger Garrick got up and walked over to the window. North Guardian was a haze of light in the sky, across the water.

Click, snap. The fisherman robot began to sing:

> *Tutte le serre, dopo quel fanal,*
> *Dietro la caserma, ti staró ed—*
> *Click.*

Roosenburg muttered under his breath and probed further. Kathryn Pender joined Garrick at the window.

"Now you see," she said.

Garrick shrugged. "You can't blame him."

"*I* blame him!" she said hotly. "I've lived here all my life. Fisherman's Island used to be a tourist spot—why, it was lovely here. And look at it now. The elevators don't work. The lights don't work. Practically all of our robots are gone. Spare parts, construction material, everything—it's all gone to North Guardian! There isn't a day that passes, Garrick, when half a dozen bargeloads of stuff don't go north, because *he* requisitioned them. Blame him? I'd like to kill him!"

Snap. Sputtersnap. The fisherman lifted its head and caroled:

Forse dommani, piangerai,
E dopo tu, sorriderai—

Roosenburg's probe uncovered a flat black disc. "Kathryn, look this up, will you?" He read the serial number from the disc and then put down the probe. He stood flexing his fingers, looking irritably at the motionless figure.

Garrick joined him. Roosenburg jerked his head at the fisherman.

"That's robot repair work, trying to tinker with their insides. Trumie has his own Robot Central, as I told you. What I have to do is recontrol this one from the substation on the mainland, but keep its receptor circuits open to North Guardian on the symbolic level. You understand what I'm talking about? It'll think from North Guardian, but act from the mainland."

"Sure," said Garrick.

"And it's damned close work. There isn't much room inside one of those things—" He stared at the figure and picked up the probe again.

Kathryn Pender came back with a punchcard in her hand. "It was one of ours, all right. Used to be a busboy in the cafeteria at the beach club." She scowled. "That Trumie!"

"You can't blame him," Garrick said reasonably. "He's only trying to be good."

She looked at him queerly. "He's only—"

Roosenburg interrupted with an exultant cry. "Got it! Okay, you—sit up and start telling us what Trumie's up to now!"

The fisherman figure said obligingly, "Yes, Boss. What you wanna know?"

What they wanted to know, they asked; and what they asked, it told them, volunteering nothing, concealing nothing.

There was Anderson Trumie, king of his island, the compulsive consumer.

It was like an echo of the bad old days of the Age of Plenty, when the world was smothering under the endless, pounding flow of goods from the robot factories and the desperate race between consumption and production strained the whole society. But Trumie's orders came not from society, but from within. *Consume!* commanded something inside him, and *Use!* it cried, and *Devour!* it ordered. And Trumie obeyed, heroically.

They listened to what the fisherman robot had to say, and the picture was dark. Armies had sprung up on North Guardian; navies floated in its waters. Anderson Trumie stalked among his creations like a blubbery god, wrecking and ruling. Garrick could see the pattern in what the fisherman had to say. In Trumie's mind, he was dictator, building a war machine. He was supreme engineer, constructing a mighty state. He was warrior.

"He was playing tin soldiers," said Roger Garrick, and Roosenburg and the girl nodded.

"The trouble is," Roosenburg said, "he has stopped playing. Invasion fleets, Garrick! He isn't content with North Guardian any more. He wants the rest of the country, too!"

"You can't blame him," said Roger Garrick for the third time, and stood up. "The question is, what do we do about it?"

"That's what you're here for," Kathryn told him.

"All right. We can forget about the soldiers—as soldiers, that is. They won't hurt anyone. Robots can't."

"I know that," Kathryn snapped.

"The problem is what to do about Trumie's drain on the world's resources." Garrick pursed his lips. "According to my directive from Area Control, the first plan was to let him alone—there is still plenty of everything for anyone, so why not let Trumie enjoy himself? But that didn't work out too well."

"Didn't work out too well," repeated Kathryn Pender bitterly.

"No, no—not on your local level," Garrick explained quickly. "After all, what are a few thousand robots, a few hundred million dollars' worth of equipment? We could resupply this area in a week."

"And in a week," said Roosenburg, "Trumie would have us cleaned out again!"

"That's the trouble," Garrick declared. "He doesn't seem to have a stopping point. Yet we can't refuse his orders. Speaking as a psychist, that would set a very bad precedent. It would put ideas in the minds of a lot of persons—minds that, in some cases, might not prove stable in the absence of a completely reliable source of everything they need, on request. If we say no to Trumie, we open the door on some mighty dark corners of the human mind. Covetousness. Greed. Pride of possession—"

"So what are you going to do?" demanded Kathryn Pender.

Garrick said resentfully: "The only thing there is *to* do. I'm going to look over Trumie's folder again. And then I'm going to North Guardian Island."

V

Roger Garrick was all too aware of the fact that he was only 24. But his age couldn't make a great deal of difference. The oldest and wisest psychist in Area Control's wide sphere might have been doubtful of success in as thorny a job as the one ahead.

He and Kathryn Pender warily started out at daybreak. Vapor was rising from the sea about them, and the little battery-motor of their launch whined softly beneath the keelson. Garrick sat patting the little box that contained their invasion equipment, while the girl steered.

The workshops of Fisherman's Island had been all night making some of the things in that box—not because they were so difficult to make, but because it had been a bad night. Big things were going on at North Guardian; twice, the power had been out entirely for an hour, while the demand on the lines from North Guardian took all the power the system could deliver.

The Sun was well up as they came within hailing distance of the Navy Yard.

Robots were hard at work; the Yard was bustling with activity. An overhead traveling crane, eight feet tall, laboriously lowered a prefabricated fighting top onto an 11-foot aircraft carrier.

A motor torpedo boat—full-sized, this one was, not to scale—rocked at anchor just before the bow of their launch. Kathryn steered around it, ignoring the hail from the robot lieutenant-j.g. at its rail.

She glanced at Garrick over her shoulder, her face taut. "It's—it's all mixed up."

Garrick nodded. The battleships were model-sized, the small boats full-scale. In the city beyond the Yard, the pinnacle of the Empire State Building barely cleared the Pentagon, right next door. A soaring suspension bridge leaped out from the shore a quarter of a mile away and stopped short a thousand yards out, over empty water.

It was easy to understand—even for a psychist just out of school, on his first real assignment. Trumie was trying to run a world singlehanded, and where there were gaps in his conception of what his world should be, the results showed.

"Get me battleships!" he ordered his robot supply clerks, and they found the only battleships there were in the world to copy, the child-sized, toy-scaled play battleships that still delighted kids.

"Get me an Air Force!" And a thousand model bombers were hastily put together.

"Build me a bridge!" But perhaps he had forgotten to say to where.

Garrick shook his head and focused on the world around him. Kathryn Pender was standing on a gray steel stage, the mooring line from their launch secured to what looked like a coast defense cannon—but only about four feet long. Garrick picked up the little box and leaped up to the stage beside her. She turned to look at the city.

"Hold on a second." He was opening the box, taking out two little cardboard placards. He turned her by the shoulder and, with pins from the box, attached one of the cards to her back. "Now me," he said, turning his back to her.

She read the placard dubiously:

I
AM A
SPY!

"Garrick," she said, "you're sure you know what you're doing?"

"Put it on!" She shrugged and pinned it to the back of his jacket.

Side by side, they entered the citadel of the enemy.

According to the fisherman robot, Trumie lived in a gingerbread castle south of the Pentagon. Most of the robots got no chance to enter it. The city outside the castle was Trumie's kingdom, and he roamed about it, overseeing, changing, destroying, rebuilding. But inside the castle was his Private

Place; the only robots that had both an inside- and outside-the-castle existence were the two bodyguards of his youth, Davey Crockett and Long John Silver.

"That," said Garrick, "must be the Private Place."

It was decidedly a gingerbread castle. The "gingerbread" was stonework, gargoyles, and columns; there were a moat and a drawbridge, and there were robot guards with crooked little rifles, wearing scarlet tunics and fur shakos three feet tall. The drawbridge was up and the guards stood at stiff attention.

"Let's reconnoiter," said Garrick. He was unpleasantly conscious of the fact that every robot they passed—and they had passed thousands—had turned to look at the signs on their backs.

Yet it was right, wasn't it? There was no hope of avoiding observation in any event. The only hope was to fit somehow into the pattern—and spies would certainly be a part of the military pattern.

Wouldn't they?

Garrick turned his back on doubts and led the way around the gingerbread palace.

The only entrance was the drawbridge.

They stopped out of sight of the ramrod-stiff guards. Garrick said: "We'll go in. As soon as we get inside, you put on your costume." He handed her the box. "You know what to do. All you have to do is keep him quiet for a while and let me talk to him."

"Garrick, will this work?"

Garrick exploded: "How the devil do I know? I had Trumie's dossier to work with. I know everything that happened to him when he was a kid—when this trouble started. But to reach him takes a long time, Kathryn. And we don't have a long time. So—"

He took her elbow and marched her toward the guards. "So you know what to do," he said.

"I hope so," breathed Kathryn Pender, looking very small and very young.

They marched down the wide white pavement, past the motionless guards—

Something was coming toward them. Kathryn held back.

"Come on!" Garrick muttered.

"No, look!" she whispered. "Is that—is that Trumie?"

He looked, then stared.

It was Trumie, larger than life. It was Anderson Trumie, the entire human population of the most-congested-island-for-its-population in the world. On one side of him was a tall dark figure, on the other side a squat dark figure, helping him along. His face was horror, drowned in fat. The bloated cheeks shook damply, wet with tears. The eyes squinted out with fright on the world he had made.

Trumie and his bodyguards rolled up to them and past. And then Anderson Trumie stopped.

He turned the blubbery head and read the sign on the back of the girl. I AM A SPY. Panting heavily, clutching the shoulder of the Crockett robot, he gaped wildly at her.

Garrick cleared his throat. This far his plan had gone, and then there was a gap. There had to be a gap. Trumie's history, in the folder that Roosenburg had supplied, had told him what to do with Trumie; and Garrick's own ingenuity had told him how to reach the man. But a link was missing. Here was the subject, and here was the psychist who could cure him, and it was up to Garrick to start the cure.

Trumie cried out in a staccato bleat: "You! What are you? Where do you belong?"

He was talking to the girl. Beside him, the Crockett robot murmured: "Reckon she's a spy, Mistuh Trumie. See thet sign a-hangin' on her back?"

"Spy? Spy?" The quivering lips pouted. "Curse you, are you Mata Hari? What are you doing out here? It's changed its face," Trumie complained to the Crockett robot. "It doesn't belong here. It's supposed to be in the harem. Go on, Crockett, get her back!"

"Wait!" said Garrick, but the Crockett robot was ahead of him. It took Kathryn Pender by the arm.

"Come along thar," it said soothingly, and urged her across the drawbridge. She glanced back at Garrick, and for a moment it looked as though she were going to speak. Then she shook her head, as if giving an order.

"Kathryn!" yelled Garrick. "Trumie, wait a minute! That isn't Mata Hari!"

No one was listening. Kathryn Pender disappeared into the Private Place. Trumie, leaning heavily on the hobbling Long John Silver robot, followed.

Garrick, coming back to life, leaped after them.

The scarlet-coated guards jumped before him, their shakos bobbing, their crooked little rifles crossed to bar his way.

He ordered: "One side! Out of my way! I'm a human, don't you understand? You've got to let me pass!"

They didn't even look at him; trying to get by them was like trying to walk through a wall of moving, thrusting steel. He shoved and they pushed him back; he tried to dodge and they were before him. It was hopeless.

And then it was hopeless indeed, because behind them, he saw, the drawbridge had gone up.

VI

Sonny Trumie collapsed into a chair like a mound of blubber falling to the deck of a whaler.

Though he made no signal, the procession of serving robots started at once. In minced the maitre d', bowing and waving its graceful hands. In marched the sommelier, clanking its necklace of keys, bearing its wines in their buckets of ice. In came the lovely waitress robots and the sturdy steward robots, with the platters and tureens, the plates and bowls and cups.

They spread a meal—a dozen meals—before him, and he began to eat.

He ate as a penned pig eats, gobbling until it chokes, forcing the food down because there is nothing to do *but* eat. He ate, with a sighing accompaniment of moans and gasps, and some of the food was salted with the tears of pain he wept into it, and some of the wine was spilled by his shaking hand. But he ate. Not for the first time that day, and not for the tenth.

Sonny Trumie wept as he ate. He no longer even knew he was weeping. There was the gaping void inside him that he had to fill, had to fill; there was the gaping world about him that he had to people and build and furnish . . . and *use*.

He moaned to himself. Four hundred pounds of meat and lard, and he had to lug it from end to end of his island, every hour of every day, never resting, never at peace! There should have been a place somewhere, there should have been a time, when he could rest. When he could sleep without dreaming, sleep without waking after a scant few hours with the goading drive to eat and to use, to use and to eat . . .

And it was all so *wrong!*

The robots didn't understand. They didn't try to understand; they didn't think for themselves. Let him take his eyes from any one of them for a single day and everything went *wrong*. It was necessary to keep after them, from end to end of the island, checking and overseeing and ordering—yes, and destroying to rebuild, over and over!

He moaned again and pushed the plate away.

He rested, with his tallow forehead flat against the table, waiting, while inside him the pain ripped and ripped, and finally became bearable again. And slowly he pushed himself up, and rested for a moment, and pulled a fresh plate toward him, and began again to eat.

After a while, he stopped. Not because he didn't want to go on, but because he absolutely couldn't.

He was bone-tired, but something was bothering him—one more detail to check, one more thing that was *wrong*. Mata Hari. The houri at the drawbridge. It shouldn't have been out of the Private Place. It should have been in the harem, of course. Not that it mattered, except to Sonny Trumie's never-resting sense of what was right.

Time was when the houris of the harem had their uses, but that time was long and long ago; now they were property, to be fussed over and made to be *right,* to be replaced if they were worn, destroyed if they were *wrong.* But only property, as all of North Guardian was property—as all of the world would be his property, if only he could manage it.

But property shouldn't be *wrong.*

He signaled to the Crockett robot and, leaning on it, walked down the long terrazzo hall toward the harem. He tried to remember what the houri had looked like. The face didn't matter; he was nearly sure it had changed it. It had worn a sheer red blouse and a brief red skirt, he was almost certain, but the face—

It had had a face, of course. But Sonny had lost the habit of faces. This one had been somehow different, but he couldn't remember just why. Still—the blouse and skirt were red, he was nearly sure. And it had been carrying something in a box. And that was odd, too.

He waddled a little faster, for now he was positive it was *wrong.*

"Thar's the harem, Mistuh Trumie," said the robot at his

side. It disengaged itself gently, leaped forward and held the door to the harem for him.

"Wait for me," Sonny commanded, and waddled forward into the harem halls.

Once he had so arranged the harem that he needed no help inside it; the halls were railed, at a height where it was easy for a pudgy hand to grasp the rail; the distances were short, the rooms close together.

He paused and called over his shoulder: "Stay where you can hear me." It had occurred to him that if the houri robot was *wrong*, he would need Crockett's guns to make it right.

A chorus of female voices sprang into song as he entered the main patio. They were a bevy of beauties, clustered around a fountain, diaphanously dressed, languorously glancing at Sonny Trumie as he waddled inside.

"Shut up!" he shrieked. "Go back to your rooms!"

They bowed their heads and, one by one, slipped into the cubicles.

No sign of the red blouse and the red skirt. He began the rounds of the cubicles, panting, peering into them.

"Hello, Sonny," whispered Theda Bara, lithe on a leopard rug, and he passed on. "I love you!" cried Nell Gwynn, and, "Come to me!" commanded Cleopatra, but he passed them by. He passed Du Barry and Marilyn Monroe, he passed Moll Flanders and he passed Troy's Helen. No sign of the houri in red—

Yes, there was. He didn't see the houri, but he saw the signs of the houri's presence: the red blouse and the red skirt, lying limp and empty on the floor.

Sonny gasped: "Where are you? Come out here where I can see you!"

Nobody answered Sonny.

"Come out!" he bawled.

And then he stopped. A door opened and someone came out; not an houri, not female; a figure without sex but loaded with love, a teddy bear figure, as tall as pudgy Sonny Trumie himself, waddling as he waddled, its stubby welcoming arms stretched out to him.

He could hardly believe his eyes. Its color was a little darker than Teddy. It was a good deal taller than Teddy. But unquestionably, undoubtedly, in everything that mattered, it was—

"Teddy," whispered Sonny Trumie, and let the furry arms go around his 400 pounds.

Twenty years disappeared. "They wouldn't let me have you," Sonny told the teddy bear.

It said, in a voice musical and warm: "It's all right, Sonny. You can have me now, Sonny. You can have everything, Sonny."

"They took you away," he whispered, remembering.

They took the teddy bear away; he had never forgotten. They took it away and Mother was wild and Father was furious. They raged at the little boy and scolded him and threatened him. Didn't he know they were *poor*, and Did he want to ruin them all, and What was wrong with him, anyway, that he wanted his little sister's silly stuffed robots when he was big enough to use nearly grown-up goods?

The night had been a terror, with the frowning, sad robots ringed around, and the little girl crying; and what had made it terror was not the scolding—he'd had scoldings—but the *worry*, the *fear* and almost the *panic* in his parents' voices. For what he did, he came to understand, was no longer a childish sin. It was a *big* sin, a failure to consume his quota—

And it had to be punished.

The first punishment was the extra birthday party.

The second was—shame.

Sonny Trumie, not quite 12, was made to feel shame and humiliation. Shame is only a little thing, but it makes the victim of it little, too.

Shame.

The robots were reset to scorn him. He woke to mockery and went to bed with contempt. Even his little sister lisped the catalog of his failures.

You aren't trying, Sonny, and You don't care, Sonny, and You're a terrible disappointment to us, Sonny.

And finally all the things were true, because Sonny at 12 was what his elders made him.

And they made him . . . "neurotic" is the term; a pretty-sounding word that means ugly things like fear and worry and endless self-reproach . . .

"Don't worry," whispered the Teddy. "Don't worry, Sonny. You can have me. You can have what you want. You don't have to have anything else."

VII

Garrick raged through the halls of the Private Place like a tiger. "Kathryn!" he shouted. "Kathryn Pender!"

The robots peeped out at him worriedly and sometimes they got in his way and he bowled them aside. They didn't fight back, naturally—what robot would hurt a human? But sometimes they spoke to him, pleading, for it was not according to the wishes of Mr. Trumie that anyone but him rage destroying through North Guardian Island. Garrick passed them by.

"Kathryn!" he called. "Kathryn!"

He told himself fiercely: Trumie was *not* dangerous. Trumie was laid bare in his folder, the one that Roosenburg had supplied, and he couldn't be blamed; he meant no harm. He was once a little boy who was trying to be good by consuming, consuming, and he wore himself into neurosis doing it; and then they changed the rules on him. End of the ration, end of forced consumption, as the robots took over for mankind at the other end of the farm-and-factory cornucopia. It wasn't necessary to struggle to consume, so the rules were changed.

And maybe Trumie knew that the rules had been changed, but Sonny didn't. It was Sonny, the little boy trying to be good, who had made North Guardian Island.

And it was Sonny who owned the Private Place and all it held—including Kathryn Pender.

Garrick called hoarsely: "Kathryn! If you hear me, *answer me!*"

It had seemed so simple. The fulcrum on which the weight of Trumie's neurosis might move was a teddy bear. Give him a teddy bear—or, perhaps, a teddy-bear suit, made by night in the factories of Fisherman's Island, with a girl named Kathryn Pender inside—and let him hear, from a source he could trust, the welcome news that it was no longer necessary to struggle, that compulsive consumption could have an end. Then Garrick or any other psychist would clear it all up, but only if Trumie would listen.

"Kathryn!" roared Roger Garrick, racing through a room of mirrors and carved statues. Because, just in case Trumie didn't listen, just in case the folder was wrong and Teddy wasn't the key—

Why, then, Teddy to Trumie would be only a robot. And Trumie destroyed them by the score.

"Kathryn!" bellowed Roger Garrick, trotting through the silent palace, and at last he heard what might have been an answer. At least it was a voice—a girl's voice, at that. He was before a passage that led to a room with a fountain and silent female robots, standing and watching him. The voice came from a small room. He ran to the door.

It was the right door.

There was Trumie, 400 pounds of lard, lying on a marble bench with a foam-rubber cushion, the jowled head in the small lap of—

Teddy. Or Kathryn Pender in the teddy-bear suit, the stick-like legs pointed straight out, the sticklike arms clumsily patting him. She was talking to him, gently and reassuringly. She was telling him what he needed to know—that he had eaten *enough*, that he had used *enough*, that he had consumed *enough* to win the respect of all, and an end to consuming.

Garrick himself could not have done better.

It was a sight from Mother Goose, the child being soothed by his toy. But it was not a sight that fitted in well with its surroundings, for the seraglio was upholstered in mauve and pink, and the paintings that hung about were wicked.

Sonny Trumie rolled the pendulous head and looked squarely at Garrick. The worry was gone from the fear-filled little eyes.

Garrick stepped back.

No need for him just at this moment. Let Trumie relax for a while, as he had not been able to relax for a score of years. Then the psychist could pick up where the girl had been unable to proceed, but in the meantime, Trumie was finally at rest.

The Teddy looked up at Garrick and in its bright blue eyes, the eyes that belonged to the girl named Kathryn, he saw a queer tincture of triumph and compassion.

Garrick nodded, and left, and went out to the robots of North Guardian, and started them clearing away the monstrous child's-eye conception of an empire.

Sonny Trumie nestled his head in the lap of the teddy bear. It was talking to him nicely, so nicely. It was droning away:

"Don't worry, Sonny. Don't worry. Everything's all right. Everything's all right." Why, it was almost as though it were real.

It had been, he calculated with the part of his mind that was razor-sharp and never relaxed, nearly two hours since he had eaten. Two hours! And he felt as though he could go another hour at least, maybe two. Maybe—maybe even not eat at all again that day. Maybe even learn to live on three meals. Perhaps two. Perhaps—

He wriggled—as well as 400 greasy pounds can wriggle—and pressed against the soft warm fur of the teddy bear. It was so soothing.

You don't have to eat so much, Sonny. You don't have to drink so much. No one will mind. Your father won't mind, Sonny. Your mother won't mind . . ."

It was very comfortable to hear the teddy bear telling him those things. It made him drowsy. So deliciously drowsy! It wasn't like going to sleep, as Sonny Trumie had known going to sleep for a dozen or more years, the bitterly-fought surrender to the anesthetic weariness. It was just drowsy.

And he did want to go to sleep.

And finally he slept. All of him. Not just the 400 pounds of blubber and the little tormented eyes, but even the razor-sharp mind-Trumie that lived in the sad, obedient hulk.

It slept.

It had not slept all these 20 years.

SF: The Game-Playing Literature

Science fiction is fun, otherwise it wouldn't exist at all. But sometimes, I think, it is more than fun, it is a way of looking at the world that cannot be duplicated in any other way, or improved on in some very important respects. And this short essay tells why I believe that.

My late collaborator, Cyril Kornbluth, once wrote a story called "The Only Thing We Learn." He didn't think it necessary to complete the quotation, or indeed to attribute it. He was, after all, writing for a science-fiction audience. Ess Effers are usually cynics and always time-binders. The message that the only thing to be learned from history is that no one ever learns anything from history is not news to them. In fact, the only quarrel an sf writer or reader might have with the statement would be that it is incomplete, and should properly read: "The only thing we learn from history is that we learn nothing from history—unless we view history, both past and present, as a science-fiction story."

In order to see why this statement is true we must first explain what we mean by a "science-fiction story." This isn't easy, since the defining of the term "science fiction" has never been done in a really satisfactory fashion. Science fiction may be a story about the future, or a story about space travel, or a Japanese monster movie, or a political parable. It may also be none of those things. It may be *about* anything, anything at all, because that quality which most clearly distinguishes sf from non-sf writing has to do not with content but with method.

This is true, of course, not only of science fiction but of its collateral relative science. Most of us rather hastily and thoughtlessly regard "science" as a sort of collection of linear accelerators and space vehicles and organic chemistry models. In fact it is not any of these things; it is only a systematic method of gathering and testing knowledge, involving certain formal procedures: gathering information, forming a theory to explain the information, predicting certain consequences of the theory and performing an experiment to test the prediction. If you investigate any area of knowledge (whether it is stellar physics or the number of angels who can dance on the head of a pin) by this method, you are doing science. If you use any other method, you are doing something else.

In the same way, science fiction has to do with methodology, and "the science-fiction method"* is that quality in the creative process of the science-fiction writer which describes the parameters within which he can speculate. The sf method is parallelistic, universal, and antideterministic. If we throw dice and see a six come up, the layman sees only a six; the writer using the sf method sees that a six *has* come up, but that any of five other possibilities *might have* come up.

I do not pretend, of course, that all sf writers consciously view the universe in this way, or even that sf stories do not exist in which this feature is minimal if it exists at all. What I do think is that it is this feature which gives sf the special qualities which make it more interesting than any other kind of fiction. I think it is what Arthur Clarke meant, for instance, when he said that he wrote sf in preference to other kinds of fiction "because most other literature isn't concerned with reality."

Science fiction makes good propaganda literature, and there have in fact been times when the freedom to think and say unorthodox sentiments was severely repressed outside of science fiction. Probably that is why Jonathan Swift chose (or innovated) the sf form for *Gulliver's Travels;* he could not compare France to England to the disadvantage of England in open terms without running risks to his livelihood, but he could say the same things without fear as long as he used the science-fiction disguises of "Blefuscu" and "Lilliput." In

---

*For the term "the science-fiction method" I am indebted to an English sf writer named John T. Phillifent, more frequently seen under his pen name of John Rackham. I am not sure that he means the same thing by it as I do, but the first use of the term I encountered was in a private communication from him.

America a decade or two ago, when Joseph McCarthy reduced journalists, academics, and even statesmen to terrified silence, sf magazines went right on talking about anything and everything as though the Senate Permanent Investigations Subcommittee had never existed.

The existence of sf-as-agitprop has obscured the to-my-mind far more important feature of sf-as-analysis. But it is the analytical powers of the sf method that make its effectiveness as propaganda great; an sf story not only makes a statement about a particular imaginary world but carries the broad general implication that an infinite number of differing worlds are possible, and that small random changes in causal factors may produce overwhelming changes in social structures, kinds of morality, and even "human nature."

For one example, consider religion. Theologians are just now beginning to catch up with science-fiction writers in thinking about the religious implications of possible non-human life on other planets. Few if any of them have yet faced the problem of wholly *alien* theologies. Nearly every human society stipulates One True God, a Heavenly Father who rewards and punishes. Clearly this is biology-related; humans have two sexes and a helplessly dependent infancy, requiring a family structure for survival. But what would be the theology of a sexless race, or one hatched from eggs laid and abandoned like the sea turtle's? Nor has any theologian that I know of approached the question raised in Brian Aldiss's *The Dark Light-Years*. Most humans, Aldiss argues, attach sacramental importance to such biological functions as sex (ritual marriage) and eating (saying grace at meals, ingestion of bread and wine at mass, etc.). But why should some other race not attach equal sacramental importance to such other biological functions as, for instance, excretion?

It is this systematic investigation of what causal factors are possible and what social consequences may follow them that makes science fiction a splendid tool for social analysis. To be sure, it need not be done exclusively within the pages of *Analog* or *Amazing Stories*, or even in the form of a story at all. Think tanks like the Rand Corporation, the Hudson Institute, the Institute for the Future in Connecticut, Bertrand de Jouvenel's "futuribles" panels in Paris, and many others do in fact use these techniques in nonliterary ways. But science fiction taught them all how, and science fiction is still the most pleasurable way of doing these things.

In essence science fiction reduces the entire continuum of human knowledge to a sort of board game, and by systematically changing the rules of the game one or a few at a time investigates the possibility of alternate societies. Is this an important thing to do? No, not just important; it is transcendental, for there can be no hope of making a change in any condition we deplore until we know what alternatives are open to us. Science fiction gives us a sort of catalog of possible worlds. From the wish-book we can pick the ones we want. Without it we can resent and deplore, but our capacity to change is very small.

One of the great personal satisfactions of living in the world of science-fiction readers and writers is observing how game-playing reduces partisan tensions. Our uptight "real" world affects science fiction, too. Some sf people are right-wingers and some are left; some are deeply religious, some not at all; some battle for women's lib or black power or the freedom of the drug scene and some are firmly for the Establishment; and yet all of them are able to join in the game.

In a real world that every day seems more partisan, more grimy, more sullen, and more violent, this is a source not only of pleasure but of hope. Perhaps The Method can spread. Perhaps the world at large can learn from sf. And perhaps then the ants won't have to replace us after all.

ABOUT THE AUTHOR

FREDERIK POHL is a double-threat science fictioneer, being the only person to have won science fiction's top award, the Hugo, both as an editor and as a writer. As a writer, he has published more than thirty novels and short story collections, including *The Space Merchants* (with C. M. Kornbluth), *The Age of the Pussyfoot*, *Day Million* and *The Gold at the Starbow's End*. His awards include four Hugos and the Edward E. Smith Award. As an editor, he published the first series of anthologies of original stories in the science fiction field, *Star Science Fiction;* was for many years the editor of two leading magazines in the field, *Galaxy* and *If;* and is currently science fiction editor of Bantam Books. His interests extend beyond science fiction to national affairs (his book, *Practical Politics*, was a handbook for party reformers in the 1972 election year); history, (he is the Encyclopedia Britannica's authority on the Roman emperor, Tiberius); and almost the entire range of human affairs. He is currently president of the Science Fiction Writers of America, and makes his home in Red Bank, New Jersey.

THE DOORS OF HIS FACE, THE LAMPS OF HIS MOUTH by ROGER ZELAZNY

A collection of fifteen stories of man in the future, ranging in time from a few decades to a few millenia into the future, in setting from the solar system to deepest space. The prize-winning title story is the highly imaginative and very be-lievable tale of a fishing expedition for an enormous sea monster under the oceans of the planet Venus; the rest of the collection maintains the high standard thus set, with tales of a rebellious preacher's son finding a different religion on Mars, of an expedition to an electrically-haunted mountain where a girl is discovered in hibernation state awaiting the discovery of a cure for her fatal disease, and of man's penchant for aggrandisement. All display the style, wit, imagination which have made Roger Zelazny one of the most highly praised writers of science fiction today.

0 552 10021 8 – 50p

LOGAN'S RUN by WILLIAM F. NOLAN and GEORGE CLAYTON JOHNSON

It was a nightmare society – a world of the 'cubs' – rebel hipsters drugged to a point of frenzy – of a vast underwater city gradually collapsing under the pressures of the sea . . . of an ice hell in polar regions where criminals were sent to survive if they could . . . of a desert inhabited by psychotic savages.

It was a world where there was little beauty and no peace . . . where man, condemned to a short lifespan, fought against his own terror and dreamed of Sanctuary . . .

0 552 10123 0 – 50p

THE SHAPE OF THINGS TO COME by H. G. WELLS

First published in 1933 it was described by Wells as 'A Short History of the Future', and spans the period from A.D. 1929 to the end of the year 2105. It is a chronicle of world events, a memorable catalogue of prediction involving war, technical revolution and the cultural changes which await mankind in the years to come . . .

0 552 09532 X – 95p

THE SHAPE OF FURTHER THINGS by BRIAN ALDISS

'Haven't you ever thought to yourself after a pleasant evening – or even a dull afternoon – that if you could have it all again, preferably in slow motion, then you could trace in it all the varied strands of your life?'

In this provocative book Brian Aldiss seeks to recapture some of the strands of his life, and in basic diary form he works alternately back into the past and forward into the future; the realities of our world alternate with the un-realities of fantasy.

The result is an autobiography spanning one month – a month in the life of a speculative writer, with topics ranging from the growth of science fiction in Britain today to new theories on the nature and importance of dreams.

0 552 09533 8 – 65p

THE SHIP WHO SANG by ANNE McCAFFREY

The brain was perfect, the tiny, crippled body useless. So technology rescued the brain and put it in an environment that conditioned it to live in a different kind of body – a spaceship. Here the human mind, more subtle, infinitely more complex than any computer ever devised, could be linked to the massive and delicate strengths, the total recall, and the incredible speeds of space. But the brain behind the ship was entirely feminine – a complex, loving, strong, weak, gentle, savage – a personality, all-woman, called Helva. . . .

0 552 10163 X – 65p

RESTOREE by ANNE McCAFFREY

There was a sudden stench of a dead sea creature. . . .

There was the horror of a huge black shape closing over her. . . .

There was nothing. . . .

Then there were pieces of memory . . . isolated fragments that were so horrible her mind refused to accept them . . . intense heat and shivering cold . . . excruciating pain . . . dismembered pieces of the human body . . . sawn bones and searing screams . . .

And when she awoke she found she was in a world that was not earth, and with a face and body that were not her face and body.

She had become a Restoree. . . .

0 552 10161 3 – 65p

A SELECTED LIST OF CORGI SCIENCE FICTION
FOR YOUR READING PLEASURE